# BOUND BY THE STARS

Suzanne Cass

S C

STORM CLOUD
PRESS

*To Chris and Andrew, thanks for all the boat stuff.*

# CHAPTER ONE

"Oh, you poor thing." Mia Winslet knelt in the wet sand next to the large Hawksbill turtle as it struggled on the shoreline. "Hold still, baby," she crooned. "I'll get you some help."

As if the large animal understood she meant no harm, it stopped floundering on the sand and turned a dark, watery eye in her direction. She ran her gaze over the damaged turtle, taking care not to touch it. A large gouge ran across the top of the mottled-green shell, and one of the front flippers dangled uselessly on the sand.

"Stupid bloody tourists," she muttered under her breath. It looked like the turtle had been run over by a fast-moving boat. Sadly, this was a common occurrence here in Maho Bay, where the turtles often came to feed in the shallow, sea-grass beds.

Mia plucked her cell phone from the little bag slung over her shoulder and found the number she was after. The Friends of Virgin Islands ran a sea turtle rescue program and would come out and collect the injured animal. They were a dedicated group of locals, mostly volunteers, who wanted to help protect these beautiful and critically endangered species.

She stood, staring down at the damaged green-and-brown shell, as she relayed the details over the phone, then waited as the man on the other end confirmed he would send someone out as soon as possible. As she put her cell away, a little boy ran over and stopped to stare at the large marine reptile. "It's hurt," he said, pointing at the cracked shell.

"Yes, she is," Mia replied, kneeling to look the child in the face. "But don't touch her, you might frighten her." She took the little boy's hand to stop him from getting too close.

"She's not going to die, is she?" The child's face crumpled, tears welling as he stared down at the injured beast.

"No, honey," Mia soothed. "Some nice people are going to come soon and take her away to a turtle hospital. They'll make her all better and then put her back in the ocean, where she belongs." At least Mia hoped that'd be the outcome. Some turtles were so badly injured they could never be released.

Soon, a small crowd gathered, and Mia had her hands full keeping people away from the turtle, stopping them from touching her. They meant well, they were just curious or upset by the injury. But the poor animal needed space and calm, not a load of humans stressing her out. The turtle seemed to have lost all her fight, however, and lay exhausted on the sand. Mia hoped the rescue party would come soon. She didn't want the beautiful sea creature to die.

Rummaging around in her bag, she pulled out the long-sleeved white shirt she'd worn to the beach over her bikini top and dipped it in the ocean. Then she came back and draped it over the turtle's shell, to try and keep her moist. She asked the little boy if he had a plastic bucket and in a few minutes he came running back, proudly waving a small red bucket and spade. Using the child's toy, she ferried water from the ocean to the sea turtle, keeping it wet and as cool as possible.

It was nearly an hour before the sound of an outboard motor reached her, and she lifted her head to see a large inflatable boat round the headland into the sheltered bay.

Most of the spectators had drifted away by that time. Bored with the unmoving animal lying defeated on the sand, they'd been enticed back down the beach by their ball games or their picnic lunches.

She waited, watching the boat skim across the azure water and waved her arms as it came closer, then drove straight up onto the beach beside her. One man jumped out of the boat even before it came to a complete stop, while a second man made sure the outboard engine was secured up and away from the sand.

"Hi, I'm Tom." The young man held out his hand and gave Mia a roguish smile. She took in his shaggy, blond hair and three-day growth. The guy looked familiar, and she wondered where she'd seen him before. "I work at UVI," he continued, almost as if reading her mind. "I'm doing a PhD with Dan Brown, on the turtle tracking project."

Comprehension must've flashed in her eyes, because he nodded his head. Of course, she'd seen him with some of the other volunteers a few times, over at the turtle hatchery. Along with Dan, the academic in charge of the University of the Virgin Islands project.

Before she had a chance to answer him, however, he stepped around her and knelt down next to the stricken turtle, not touching, but instead, raking it with his gaze. He mumbled something incomprehensible, but she got the gist of his words. She watched him studying the turtle, keeping her distance.

A voice sounded next to her left shoulder and she jumped. She hadn't heard the other man's light-footed approach over the sand.

"Sorry, didn't mean to scare you," he said, as she turned to look at him. "I'm Logan." He held out his hand in greeting. "I've seen you around at the hatchery a few times and helping out with the egg hunts. It's Mia, isn't it?"

She shook his hand. "Yes, that's right." A little taken aback that he knew her name, she frowned at him. And nearly stumbled backwards as she caught his eye. So, *this* was Logan. In the past month, when she first started volunteering her time with the turtle rescue, she'd heard his name a few times. The women especially, seemed quite taken with him. And now she could see why. He was gorgeous. Model-type gorgeous. How could she not have noticed him before now?

"Do you work with Tom and Dan, as well?" she said into the awkward silence that'd descended as she studied him.

"Yes, I'm their lab technician and field hand. A bit of a Jack-of-all-trades, really." He smiled, and she almost lost her breath. His smile was sexy and cheeky and mysterious all rolled into one. No wonder all the women were swooning over him, how could anyone resist that kind of temptation?

"Thanks for calling us." His gaze flickered towards the turtle, and Mia felt as if she'd been released from the tractor beam of his gaze, that'd been slowly pulling her in. "And thanks for keeping all the rubber-neckers away." His gaze came back to rest on her face but this time she was ready for it and quickly averted her eyes.

She shook her head and took a step back. This guy was dangerous.

"They teach us well at the turtle rescue," she said. "Do you think you can help her?"

"I think this one might need to go to the turtle hospital at Coral World, over on St. Thomas," he replied, a deep frown marring his otherwise perfect, dark eyebrows. "They have a great vet over there, Novak, have you heard of him?"

Mia nodded. Everyone involved in the turtle rescue here on St. John had heard of the legendary Novak and all the great work he did at the world-renowned marine park over on the bigger island; especially his work with endangered turtles.

Logan went to kneel quietly next to Tom, speaking in hushed tones to the other man. Mia studied his profile. Straight nose, strong sensuous lips, pulled down at the corners in concern as he looked over the injured animal. A slight designer stubble roughened his square jaw and high cheekbones. Dark hair kept short on the back and sides but allowed to curl longer over his high forehead. Indigo-blue eyes that seemed to take everything in with easy perception. He wore casual shorts and a light-gray T-shirt, with deck shoes on his feet. But instead of looking scruffy in the beach-going attire, the T-shirt seemed to hug his pecs and biceps, highlighting his athletic body. And his shorts were the perfect length, cut exactly right, so that his long, tanned legs were shown off to perfection, even as he curled them under so he could settle on the sand next to the turtle. How could anyone look so perfect? He should be striding down the catwalks in Milan and New York. And yet, he hadn't acted either pampered or vain. Merely down-to-earth and friendly.

Even though her own father was English, her mother always said no good would come from her dating a white boy. She should stick to a good Jamaican boy, instead; stick to her own kind. In the few words they'd exchanged she'd detected an accent, but she hadn't been able to quite pick it up. She remembered one of his admirers had mentioned he might be from Australia. That intrigued her. She'd heard of Australia, but never really had any desire to visit there. Until today. America had always been her goal. But that land of milk and honey remained elusive; the United States Virgin Islands were as close as she had ever come.

"I'll go and get the equipment," Logan said, suddenly standing and breaking her contemplation. "Can you give me a hand?" he asked, as he strode past her. "We need to move her as soon as possible for her best chance at survival."

"Sure," she said, hurrying to fall into step beside him,

hoping she hadn't been caught staring.

A few minutes later she made her way back from the inflatable boat, one arm full of old towels, while helping Logan carry a large, metal box by the handle with the other. She watched quietly as Tom and Logan worked together to line the bottom of the box with wet towels and drape more over the turtle's back and head. Logan was efficient and graceful in his movements and she could hardly tear her gaze away from those tanned arms and legs.

By this time, more people had drifted back to see what was going on.

"What are you going to do with it?" asked one of the teenage kids in the crowd.

Logan looked up and fired a one-hundred-watt smile at the kid. "We're going to load her as gently as we can into this box, using the towels as padding, and then keep her as cool and as comfortable as we can while we move her to the turtle hospital. She's a small one. How much do you think she weighs, Tom?"

Tom stopped what he was doing. "Hawksbills are amongst the smallest of sea turtles." He glanced quickly down, as if measuring the turtle with his eyes. "Probably weighs around a hundred pounds." Mia could see what they were doing. Any chance to educate the public to the turtle's plight was a good one. "She's an adult though, and she should be laying her eggs around now. They're endangered, you know. Every one of her eggs counts."

"Will she go back into the sea when she's healed?" A girl asked from the back of the crowd.

"Maybe, only time will tell," Logan replied.

"But she's so beautiful," the same girl replied. "I was snorkeling out in the bay and one just like this swam right past me."

"Yes, they're beautiful, and if you want to keep swimming

with the turtles, then you need to help us keep them protected. Who wants to give us a hand lifting her into the box?"

Lots of arms waved in the air, but Tom picked the two strongest-looking boys and they carefully lifted her underneath each flipper and lay her down on the towels in the box. Then the same boys took a handle each and helped to carry the box over to the boat.

Mia trailed along at the back of the crowd.

Suddenly, Logan's voice sounded loud over everyone's heads. "Mia, would you like to come with us?" The group of people parted, and Logan appeared in front of her, that tempting smile on his face. "You rescued her. Would you like to come and see how she fares?"

Mia's heart jumped in her chest. She would like to see Coral World and what they did there, had wanted to ever since she'd heard about the turtle rescue. She didn't have any other plans for this afternoon, so why not?

"Yes, I'd love to, if that's okay. And as long as you have room."

"The more the merrier," he said, his eyes twinkling as his smile got even wider.

After they settled the Hawksbill in the bottom of the boat, and while she was helping the two men push the inflatable backward off the sand, a small voice kept asking her if the turtle was the only reason she'd agreed to go.

* * *

Logan stared at the bright-blue ocean as they sped back towards Cruz Bay, the main township on the island of St. John. They were on one of the University's research boats, a thirty-foot motorboat with a small cabin, great for island hopping between St. Thomas and St. John. The boat made the twenty-minute trip with ease, and the large, flat deck was perfect for transporting injured sea creatures. After they rescued the turtle from Maho Bay, they'd carefully transferred her to the larger boat from the inflatable so they could take her over. They'd deposited the injured turtle into Novak's healing hands and then he and Tom had given Mia an intimate guided tour of Coral World and the famous turtle hospital. And now, they were on the return trip home.

He couldn't help casting a quick gaze over to the woman standing on the other side of Tom as he maneuvered the boat. He hadn't had a lot of time to talk properly to Mia while they were on St. Thomas, he'd been caught up in the job, his professional persona kicking in while they cared for the injured animal and then showed her around the facility. There had been no chance to get to know her on a more personal level and now he was running out of time, as once they reached the island, they'd all be heading their separate ways.

Mia fascinated him. She was the most beautiful woman he'd ever seen. All that cocoa skin and long, dark hair, with eyes the color of an Egyptian queen. He'd been looking for an opportunity to introduce himself for weeks, noticing her from a distance at the hatchery. Finally, here she was. And now, he found himself completely tongue-tied. Which was so out of character, no one would ever believe it if he told them. His mother often said he could talk a dog off a meat wagon. While he didn't quite agree with that, he knew he was good with people, loved chatting to them. Sweet-talking the local beauties was usually something he was good at. Really good.

He was about to lose his chance to talk to her, however. All his normal self-confidence seemed to disappear whenever she got close. While he might see her again at the hatchery, it wasn't guaranteed. He gave himself a mental kick. *Get on with it, Logan. What's wrong with you?*

"We're nearly home," he said, bending backwards to see Mia from around Tom's back, and then wanted to slap himself on the forehead for saying something so banal and obvious. Of course she could see they were nearly back at St. John. They were rounding the headland into the small, protected bay. The lights of Cruz Bay were starting to flicker on as dusk descended.

Tom cast him a sideways glance, then gave a quick wink that only Logan could see. Bastard. It was one of many such glances Tom had thrown his way since Mia had come on board. He could see Logan was going through some kind of internal torment but wasn't in the least bit sympathetic. Actually, he seemed to be enjoying Logan's obvious discomfort.

"Yes," Mia replied, also leaning backward so she could catch Logan's eye. "It's beautiful from out here, isn't it? I don't often leave the island, it's nice to see it from this perspective."

It was now or never. Logan stepped around Tom and went to lean on the gunnel, next to Mia, who was staring through the front Plexiglas panel. "Yes, I never get tired of this view," he replied. And it was true. He'd sailed into Cruz Bay nine months ago, almost to the day, and it still made his chest ache whenever he saw it. The ultramarine water, set against the back drop of verdant jungle mountains. It was truly paradise on Earth.

He moved closer to Mia, and a slight buzz flashed across his skin. An acute awareness of her presence. He was mere inches from her smooth, brown shoulder. Close enough to touch. And he did want to touch. Very much. When they'd covered the turtle with the wet towels from their boat, Mia had retrieved the damp shirt she'd been using to keep the Hawksbill moist and tied it around her waist, over the top of her tiny, white shorts. She seemed to have no problem with the fact she only wore a bikini top all afternoon, seemed to be very at home in her own skin. Not self-conscious or uncomfortable baring her body. And a very nicely toned body it was, at that. Her skin was perfect, not a blemish to be seen. Smooth and silky, like molten milk chocolate. His mouth went dry as his eyes traced the lines of her shoulder blades, then down over the undulations of her spine.

Licking his lips, he dragged his eyes away from the smooth lines of her back, and asked, "Have you lived here long?" It seemed like a safe place to start the conversation, but then he suddenly wondered if he was being too forward, asking her that kind of question. What in hell was going on with him? Normally, conversation flowed out of him with consummate ease, now it felt like he was the tongue-tied teenage nerd standing in the corner, waiting to talk to the prettiest girl in the room.

She didn't seem fazed by his question. Turning those coffee-colored eyes toward him, she said, "Only a few months. But I was on St. Thomas for nearly a year before that." She returned her gaze back to the approaching town as they slipped past the moored boats, coming into a small dock. The University was lucky to have somewhere to keep its research vessels. All other boats, including his, had to stay on a mooring out in the bay.

Tom was going to ask him to go up on the bow and tie the boat off any moment now. He had mere seconds left to come up with another topic to keep Mia talking, before she hopped off the boat and disappeared from his life forever. Why was this so hard? She probably thought he was a complete moron.

He said the first thing that came to mind. "So, that's when you started volunteering with the sea rescue?"

"Yes, I'd heard about the group on St. Thomas, of course, but it wasn't until I got here and saw how much the community is involved, how much they want to save their wildlife, that I thought I'd join in."

The Friends of Virgin Islands was a volunteer organization run by the locals, who'd set up a hatchery and sea turtle rescue program on St. John. Because of their first-hand experience and knowledge of the turtles from their work at the uni, he and Tom volunteered their time whenever they could. The uni encouraged its staff to help out when they could, but also was pleased by the fact that the community ran its own, independent group, leading the way in helping to preserve their own wonderful marine life. That must've been when Logan first started noticing her, when she joined in the groups doing nighttime, turtle egg hunts. Somehow, he'd never ended up in her group. He could've asked to be moved, but for some reason, he never did. He wasn't really sure why. Perhaps part of him wanted to admire her from afar? Which was stupid. He loved women. Loved being around women. Loved their sexy smiles and delicious curves and soft, honeyed voices. And they usually loved him back. But Mia seemed immune to his smiles. Which only made her that much more intriguing.

"Thank you for taking me with you. That was so interesting, seeing how Coral World works. It was sad to see all those poor turtles who'll never be returned to the ocean, though."

"It is," Logan agreed. "But every little bit helps. One more turtle saved means more eggs laid, more hatchlings. Who knows, maybe our work up at the uni can help save the few Hawksbills that are still out there."

"You mentioned the project you're working on up at the uni while we were touring turtle hospital. I'd love to hear more about it," she said, eyes lighting up with animation. "What do you do up there?"

Here was his chance. "Well…" He needed to get this right. "I'd love to tell you more," he said with a smile. "But I'm starving, I haven't eaten since breakfast. I was going to pop over to Sunny's for a quick bite. Would you like to join me? Then I can tell you about everything we get up to." He tried to give her a cheeky wink, one that'd normally turn a woman to putty in his hands, but it felt awkward, and he almost cursed out loud. This woman was turning everything he thought he knew about himself on its head. "As long as you like spicy food, that is," he added in a hurry.

Her dark eyes fixed him with a stare, but she didn't reply. She was going to turn him down; he knew it.

As he was about to brush the invitation aside and turn away, she surprised him by saying, "Okay. I will. I'm hungry, too. And I've heard about Sunny's. My friends tell me I should try it."

He could hardly keep the astonished look off his face. "That's great. The food is awesome, you're going to love it."

"You going to fend us off, or shall we just let the boat crash into the dock?" Tom's laconic voice broke into his thoughts and Logan started, then leapt over the gunnel and onto the small foredeck. Leaning down over the bowsprit, he was just in time to grab the fender and drag it into position before the bow hit the wooden wharf with a gentle bump. He jumped down, taking the bow rope with him and tied off the front. Looking up, he saw Tom give him a knowing glance as he strode down the dock to tie off the aft end. But he wasn't going to let Tom dampen his mood. Mia had agreed to go to dinner with him, and he no longer cared what Tom thought of his teenage antics.

He reached up to give Mia a hand to step off the boat. Her cool, slim fingers entwined with his and that buzz he'd felt earlier went up a notch as their hands met.

"I'll finish off here," Tom said, and Logan glanced guiltily up at his friend. He should really stay and help secure the boat and make sure everything was put away properly. But his guilty pang disappeared as he watched Mia pull her shirt back on and knot it around her waist. Goddamn, he didn't think it was possible, but she looked sexier with the shirt on than with only the bikini top. It accentuated her willowy waist, sitting above the low-slung, white shorts that showed off her long legs.

"Thanks, mate," Logan replied.

"No probs, mate," Tom said, emulating Logan's Aussie accent perfectly. For once, Logan ignored the jibe.

"Thank you, Tom," Mia called up, and gave him a smile that was probably supposed to be a friendly farewell, but had Logan fighting down a sudden jealous surge.

It was only a two-minute walk up North Shore Road to Sunny's. The owner was a large, West-Indian woman named Sunny, who loved to mix contemporary Caribbean food with lots of spice. Tucked in behind a large, stone building that'd been built in the eighteen-hundreds, not many tourists knew this café existed, so it was generally full of locals. Which was exactly the way Sunny liked it.

They walked in companionable silence along the busy street. It was early June and tourism was slowing because hurricane season was on the way, but there were still plenty of locals going about their daily tasks. A lot of the restaurants and small roadside eateries would close over the hurricane season, to have a well-earned holiday, but while everything was open, people made the most of it.

It'd been a little over two years since the fearsome hurricane Irma had wreaked its destruction over the Caribbean. A lot of places had re-built, and Sunny was lucky, her place was fairly-well sheltered by the stone walls of the building surrounding her courtyard. Her café was back up and running within a few months after the hurricane. But there were still signs of the ruination everywhere you looked. Houses that'd been destroyed and hadn't been re-built, leaving an empty block or a naked scar on the landscape. At least the jungle, that'd been mere black, skeletal remains in the days after the hurricane, had now recovered. Growing lush and green again, it covered the scars of human habitation left behind.

Cruz Bay was a small place, and most people knew each other, at least by sight. Logan nodded in greeting to a couple as they went past and raised a hand to wave at his mate, Paz, in the distance. Paz was getting into his taxi, probably just finished a delivery. Logan knew without having to look back that Paz would be staring after them, wondering who this new girl was. The sound of steel drums drifted to them from Franklin Powers Park, locals playing for the passengers disembarking from the ferry. It was a sound Logan had come to associate with the island, and he found himself feeling upbeat and happy.

Force of habit had him checking each face, each figure, in the distance as they walked, and for once he pulled himself up short. There was no way the Ramirez brothers would ever find him here. They would've given up the hunt ages ago. He needed to stop looking for ghosts around each corner. Needed to get on with his life and act normal. But a small voice kept reminding him it didn't hurt to be careful. He knew firsthand what they were capable of.

Which got Logan to wondering why he hadn't seen Mia around more often in this small community. She was such a stunning woman; she would surely stand out in a crowd. She must've been keeping a low profile for Logan not to have seen her around except at the hatchery.

"What brought you to St. John?" he asked as they walked side by side along the road, curiosity finally getting the better of him.

"This and that," she answered cryptically, glancing up at him and then quickly away. "My younger sister, for one."

"It's great you have family here that you're close to."

At the mention of family, Logan felt that familiar stab of guilt as images of his two sisters' faces, Sierra and Keira, flashed in his mind. He hadn't been in contact with either of them for nearly two years. It wasn't unusual for Logan to be slack with his communication, but even they would be worried about him by now. But it was safer this way. The fewer people who knew where he was, the better.

"I'm not sure you could say that," she laughed. "I live with Tianna, supposedly. But I usually only see her when she gets tired of her current boyfriend, or runs out of money." Logan liked the sound of her laugh. It was rich and deep, and sent ripples of pleasure through his chest. He was so taken by her laugh, that he almost missed her next words. "The rest of my family are back in Jamaica."

Aha, she was a Caribbean local. That answered a few of the many questions he had about her. "So, you work on the island, then?"

Something flickered across her face at this question. Something that made him suddenly wish he hadn't asked. She looked away, fixing her gaze up the street.

There was a heartbeat of uncomfortable silence before she said, "Is this the place?" She pointed across the road to an alleyway, partially hidden by a stall selling colorful local fabric and clothes.

"Yes. Follow me." He ducked down the dingy alley between two old buildings. The passage opened up into an open-air courtyard, where a large boab tree in the center was strung with little fairy lights that twinkled through the canopy in the growing dusk. The ground was bare earth, but it was swept clean, with lots of mismatched wooden tables and chairs were set up haphazardly beneath the branches.

"Oh, this is gorgeous," Mia said softly, tipping her head back to stare at the lights.

"Yes, Sunny does a good job. Come and I'll introduce you." On instinct Logan took her hand to lead her through a rickety, wooden doorway in the large stone wall. She froze, as if about to pull back, but then her fingers relaxed and she entwined her hand with his, accepting his touch. Logan's heart rate tripled, and he could barely get the words out to present Mia to Sunny, his mind was so full of the feel of her hand in his. Of the strange things her touch was doing to his breathing.

# CHAPTER TWO

Mia leaned back and patted her stomach. "Gosh, I'm so full, I could burst. That was absolutely delicious."

Logan wiped his mouth with a paper napkin and copied her, leaning back in his chair with a sigh. "Sunny has outdone herself tonight. Those conch fritters were her best ever."

"Yes, but it's the hot sauce that makes them so special," she replied. The local delicacy was offered at many street stalls and even high-end restaurants, each made with their own *secret recipe*, but these were definitely some of the finest she'd tasted so far.

Mia tipped her head back to study the fairy lights again. She'd done this many times during the night, but the dancing lights kept drawing her gaze. They were so pure, and bright, they infected her with happiness. This whole place did, actually. The wonderful, spicy meal, the soft chatter, most of the locals talking in the native creole patois was a glorious soundtrack to the night. And there was Logan, of course, as warm and tantalizing as the food. This place, and his company, was so vastly different to the bars and clubs she'd been frequenting lately; so different to the men who tried to seduce her. She suppressed a shudder at the thought.

This was the first time in four months she'd allowed

herself to feel totally at ease. Totally free with another man. That concept brought her crashing back to reality. What did she think she was doing? The minute Logan found out what she did for a living he'd either run for the hills, or at the very least, those soft, provocative glances he was directing her way would harden; turn into something more primal and lecherous. She'd seen it happen with other men. Logan would be no different.

She needed to finish this date—or whatever it was—and get home. Make sure Harry didn't see her with Logan. There would be hell to pay if he did. Logan was a sweet guy, he didn't deserve to be dragged into the seedy underworld of Harry *The Hook* Hagman.

It was time to go. Tearing her gaze away from the lights, she said, "Thank you so much for bringing me here. What you're doing up at the uni sounds so interesting and is an important project for the Hawksbills."

"Like I said, I'm only the lowly tech, Dan and Tom are the brains behind it all."

Mia liked that he was so self-deprecating, but she also wanted him to know he wasn't *just a tech*, that his work was important. She'd loved hearing about how they were studying the breeding habits of Hawksbill turtles, about how they hoped to find a way to breed them up in captivity and release them back into the wild. At the moment, they were running trials, catching wild turtles, placing tracking beacons on each animal and then plotting their movements over the weeks and months. All this data was vital, if they were to understand the ecology of the Hawksbills.

Logan's study might even help protect the turtles from a more ominous and unwelcome problem, as well. Poaching. Not only did the sea creatures have to battle the elements to survive, they were being hunted almost to extinction by dirty, greedy poachers. The word in the turtle rescue group was that poaching had increased here in the islands over the past few months. There were rumors that a highly organized gang was operating in the area. Volunteers had noticed a steep decline in the numbers of wild turtles spotted in the ocean lately.

If only she could get more involved. The turtles were truly special, she felt a wonderful affinity to them. But the little bit of volunteering she did was an aside, something she could do every now and then in her few spare moments. Harry would never let her do more. So why torture herself? She decided not to delve into the topic of poachers with Logan. Not tonight.

"Well, I think what you're doing is special. Not just Tom and Dan, but you, as well."

"Thank you," he muttered. Then he flashed her that smile again. The tractor-beam that seemed to hook into something in her chest and pull her inexorably toward him.

"You're welcome," she replied. "But I have to get home. I need my beauty sleep."

"I'm not sure that's true," he shot back. "I think you're beautiful just as you are."

Mia pushed her chair back and stood. The last thing she needed from Logan was compliments, not when she didn't intend to see him again. She should never have agreed to come with him. Certainly not the way he was looking at her now. It meant she'd have to give up her volunteering with the turtle rescue. She couldn't take the chance of running into Logan. She was stupid to have agreed to this date.

"Let me at least walk you home," he said, also standing and laying some money on the table. She shouldn't let him pay. Because that really confirmed it as a date. But she didn't want to belittle him by refusing, either.

Mia shook her head. She couldn't let him walk her home. The last thing she needed was him knowing where she lived.

"Please." He lifted one dark eyebrow, reminding her of an imploring puppy.

"How about you walk me to the ferry terminal." It was about halfway to her little studio apartment on the other side of town.

He studied her for a second. "Okay. If you're sure. Will you be safe walking the rest of the way on your own?"

If only he knew. Harry would make sure no one ever touched her. He probably had someone keeping an eye on her, even now. "I'll be fine," she replied with a smile.

Logan called out a goodbye to Sunny, who waved a fleshy arm in their direction and went back to serving another table. Then he took her hand to lead her back down the alley. And she surprised herself by letting him. What the hell. It felt nice. Normal. Safe. Like they were an everyday couple. She could dream for a few more minutes.

They strolled back down North Shore Road. It was completely dark, and the few weak streetlights did little to illuminate their way. But Mia liked the dark, it enveloped her like a cloak, made her feel almost invisible to the real world.

It occurred to her that she'd never asked Logan where he lived. But just as she opened her mouth to ask, she knew it would bring up the same question about her again. So instead, she asked, "I gather from your accent, you're Australian?" She glanced over at him, but all that was visible in the gloom was the outline of his profile against the backdrop of the twinkling lights from the boats moored out in the bay and the stars in sky. He nodded and she continued, "Tell me about it. It's always seemed a bit of a fantasy land to me. Full of extremes, and strange, imaginary animals."

He laughed. "You got it in one." The sound set off a quake somewhere deep inside her. "I was born in Adelaide. Do you know where that is?"

She shook her head, slightly ashamed by her lack of

knowledge.

"It's right down at the bottom, in South Australia, and it's very hot and dry. But they produce some of the best wines in the world in the surrounding hills," he added. She could see he was grinning, as his white teeth flashed in the starlight. Her hand was still captured by his, resting loose and warm in his palm.

They continued to walk and talk, Mia slowing her pace to a dawdle so they wouldn't reach the ferry dock too soon. She was enjoying herself too much. But eventually they came abreast of the large, chain-link gates that protected the dock, already padlocked shut for the night. Which meant it was past midnight and the last ferry to St. Thomas had already gone. It'd been late when they returned from St. Thomas, but Mia still couldn't believe the time had passed so quickly.

"This is my stop," Logan said, coming to a standstill, but not releasing her hand.

She was confused. "Sorry?"

"I live on a boat. Out there." He swung his free hand out towards the bay and pointed into the dark.

"Oh. Wow!" He lived on a boat. What an amazing thing to do. This just added to his appeal. Such freedom. What would it be like to be able to just pick up and go; sail away whenever you wanted to? She had a sudden urge to see his boat. To keep walking and talking with him. To find out more about this interesting, gorgeous man.

"It's a forty-foot catamaran. My dinghy is down there." Again, he pointed, this time to a set of steps set into a low stone wall where a row of mismatched, little boats were tied up.

"You live a very interesting life, Logan Goldstein," she said. And then she did something completely unexpected and totally out of character. She leaned in and kissed him on the lips. A light peck, really. Just enough for their lips to brush across each other.

The effect on her insides was completely unexpected. Her stomach flipped over so fast she felt like she was accelerating in a Formula One race car. Her heart rate rose so much, she could feel the blood pumping through her veins, constricting her throat and turning her limbs to jelly all at the same time.

The light brush of lips turned into something more, as his mouth claimed hers. Completely of its own accord, her hand snaked up to capture the back of his neck, pull him in even closer. She was tall, nearly five-foot eleven on the old scale. Logan wasn't a whole lot taller than her, probably just shy of six foot, but it made him the perfect height for kissing. Before she knew it, she'd pushed her body up into his, enjoying the feel of his washboard abs flat against her own stomach; the growing bulge of his erection. It hit her almost like a wild thing, a flash of hunger, a desire so hot and piercing, it scorched her veins. A wanting. Like nothing before.

What the hell…?

She pulled back as if he'd burnt her, only just resisting the urge to put her fingers to her lips, to make sure it'd all been real.

"Sorry, I… Ah…" Why was she apologizing? And why was she lost for words? The look on his face told her he was equally stunned by what'd passed between them.

"Don't apologize," he said, and opened his mouth, as if to say more, but his gaze zeroed in on something behind her, and he froze. The back of her neck prickled.

She swung around. A shadowy figure stood a few feet away. She couldn't see his face in the dark. But she could see the glint of metal reflecting the faint streetlight. She drew in a sharp breath. What in God's name was going on?

Logan's grip on her hand tightened, and he tugged her closer.

"Who are you? What do you want?" His voice came out

strong and sure. The exact opposite of how she was feeling. Her mind was reeling. This kind of thing didn't happen on St. John. People didn't get held up at gunpoint. Did he want her purse? Or Logan's wallet?

Then a light went on in her head. This must be Harry's doing. But what the hell was he up to? Why would he do this to her now? She'd made a promise, she'd pay him back all the money. She was working off her sister's debt. It made no sense to take her life out of petty spite. Not now. Then something else twigged in her mind. Of course. One of his spies had seen her out with Logan. This was his way of teaching her a lesson. She belonged to him, and no one else. And she'd better not forget it.

She went to take a step forward, but Logan jerked her back. She spoke up anyway. "Look, this is a misunderstanding. I helped this guy rescue a turtle, that's all. He's leaving now, and I'm off home. So, you can just tell Harry to knock it off."

"Shut up," the figure growled at her out of the dark.

"What are you doing?" Logan hissed out of the side of his mouth. "Don't antagonize him, you don't know what you've got yourself in to. Let me handle this."

Poor Logan was disillusioned. This guy was here because of her, not him. But if he wasn't careful, Harry's man might get nasty. She wished she knew exactly what Harry meant to happen. Was it only to scare Logan off? Or did he have something more malicious in mind? Her legs began to tremble at the thought.

"Both of you, just shut up," the man demanded, much louder this time. He waved the gun at Logan, and said, "Over there. Go and stand over there, in the light, where I can see you."

"I'll go with you quietly," Logan said, moving to stand in front of Mia. "Just leave the girl, she's of no consequence."

What was Logan talking about? It was almost as if he knew

this guy.

"Both of you, do as you're fucking told," the man growled, taking two steps forward and pointing the gun straight at Logan's head.

Mia let out a startled scream.

This was getting way too real, way too quickly.

Suddenly, Logan lunged, pushing her backward at the same time, so she stumbled and fell on her backside, nearly tumbling down the first few steps into the water.

There was a muffled sound, like a whoosh of air. Was that a bullet? Had the thug just tried to shoot Logan? Then a thump as the two men hit the pavement. Mia could hear them struggling together, wrestling like two prizefighters. Shit, she'd scraped her elbows in the fall, but she shrugged off the pain. She scrambled to her feet, just in time to see the two men break apart. Logan rolled over and stood up, just as the other man did the same. They began to circle each other, like wary lions.

That's when she saw it. Logan had the gun. And he had it pointed straight at his opponent.

"Mia, get over here," Logan demanded.

But it was as if she were frozen to the spot.

"Mia," he said loudly.

This time she moved, sidestepping away from the other man and moving toward the safety of the curbside. The other man now had his back to the ocean, ignoring the sharp drop-off behind him.

"You can't shoot him," she said under her breath to Logan. All the repercussions of what could possibly happen if he did something completely and utterly rash flashed through her head. It'd mean police involvement. And that was absolutely the last thing she needed.

"Logan, you can't shoot him," she said loudly, this time with conviction.

"I won't, if I don't have to," Logan replied. He was holding the gun steady, in both hands. Like he'd done this before. And he definitely wasn't shaking like a leaf, like she was. "Turn around and go back the way you came. I'll pretend I never saw you, and you can pretend you never saw me."

"That ain't gonna happen," the other man snarled. Then fast as a striking snake, the shadowy figure lunged toward them.

* * *

The gun went off in Logan's hand, almost before he could think. It made a muffled whooshing sound, the same as the first time. Not the ear-splitting retort he was expecting. Thank God that first bullet had missed him; gone wide as Logan lunged. It must have a silencer or something on it. Logan was by no means a weapons expert. But he had spent some time in a shooting range; knew the different types of guns, knew how to release the safety catch. And he knew how to pull the trigger. That was all that mattered at this moment in time. But it was as if the bullet hadn't registered, because he kept coming.

He fired again.

From behind him, Mia gave a muffled scream, as if she'd covered her mouth with her hand. But he couldn't turn around to check she was okay. His gaze was fixed on the enemy. This guy must've been sent by the Ramirez brothers. It was the only explanation.

This time, the other man staggered backward, his headlong rush stopped in its tracks. Then he made an odd noise. An animal sound, deep and guttural.

The man tried to speak, but it came out all wrong. He sucked in a deep breath and moaned. He finally seemed to get his tongue working, when he said, "You fucking ass—"

But as he spoke, he took one more step backward and disappeared into the blackness. A loud splash indicated he'd hit the water below.

"Oh, fuck," Mia swore from behind him. Before he could stop her, she raced over to the side of the seawall and peered into the dark. "Can you see him? Oh, Jesus, where did he go?"

Logan stood, numb and undecided for many long seconds, while Mia continued to peer over the edge, on her knees now.

"Logan, help me. We have to find him," she demanded, breaking his paralysis.

"Leave him, Mia. We need to get out of here." His mind had finally started to work, and the implications of what he'd done were crowding around him.

"No." Her voice rang out sharp and clear in the night air. "We need to know what happened to him. What if he's still alive? What if he can identify us?"

Smart lady. She was thinking better than he was. Of course, they had to make sure he was alive. Or dead. The gun still dangled from his right hand, and for a second, he wasn't sure what to do with it. Then taking his lead from the many Hollywood movies he'd watched over the years, he gingerly tucked it into the back waistband of his shorts.

Dragging his phone out of his pocket, he found the flashlight app and used it to illuminate the water below. They were standing to the left of the stone staircase, and no boats were allowed to moor here. Ironically, it was left clear for emergency vessels. Small wavelets lapped against the stone wall, the only sound to break the peaceful night. His flashlight beam reflected back at them off the black water.

"Where is he? Can you see him?" The note of hysteria in Mia's voice was beginning to affect him.

There was no sign of anyone floundering in the bay. Nothing broke the calm surface of the water.

"Oh, Jesus Christ. Mother of God. Shit, shit, shit."

He agreed with her sentiments, but at the moment, it was

as if a strange kind of numbness had descended over him, like he was in a bubble of untouchability. Then, over on the very edge of the reach of his flashlight, something moved. A shape rose to the surface. And bobbed there, lifeless.

"Oh no," Mia moaned. "He's facedown. And he's not moving."

A slight breeze blew in from the bay. The night was balmy and calm. A perfect island night.

Apart from the dead body now floating in the harbor.

A heavy silence descended as they both took in the scene before them.

"You have to go in and get him. We can't leave him in there," Mia said into the silence.

"What? No!"

"I'll go then." She began to strip off her shirt.

"What are you doing?" Logan asked, incredulous. All his instincts were screaming at him to get out of there. To move. They still had a chance to escape if they left now. He could get on his boat and sail right out of here and no one would be the wiser.

"We need to dispose of the body," she replied calmly. "It will buy us some time. Time to get off the island."

Logan stared down at Mia, who was still on her knees by the rock wall. Who was this woman? How could she possibly be thinking about hiding the body, when he couldn't even get his brain to function properly? She was making an odd kind of sense, however. But why would a woman like her want to hide a body and then get off the island? A normal law-abiding citizen would report this kind of thing to the police immediately. Which meant that she wasn't just any law-abiding citizen. She had something to hide. Just like him.

"Well?" she continued. "What are you waiting for? Quick, we need to do it before anyone sees us." She cast a nervous glance around the deserted harbor. She had her shorts halfway down her legs before his brain finally caught up.

"I've got an idea," he hissed. "Put your clothes back on. We'll go around and get my dinghy. We can pick him up in that."

Mia hesitated, her shorts down around her knees. She was hard to see in the night. But every now and then he would catch a reflection of her eyes, and her white shirt and white shorts stood out against the darkness. It was almost as if he were talking to a wraith.

"Good idea," she finally replied, shimmying her shorts back up her long legs. Even in the dim light the movement was sexy and sensual, and Logan had to pull his mind back onto their task ahead. He took her hand to lead her back down the dock to where his dinghy was tied up. Her hand trembled in his. It was the first sign that she wasn't really as fine with all this as she was making out. But outwardly she showed no other signs of her distress. He was surprised to discover he felt as calm and rational as an iceberg. He was sure that would change—probably sooner rather than later—but at the moment, it was as if he were one of those cold-blooded killers, who felt no emotion for their victims; went about it as if this was an everyday occurrence, just doing a job.

His dinghy was fairly large, as far as dinghies went. Which was good, because it meant they could easily fit both of them in it, and still leave room for a dead body. Logan got Mia to sit on the bench seat in the aft, while he rowed, as quietly as he could back to where they'd last seen the body. He wouldn't use the small, outboard motor unless he had to.

"Can you see him?" he whispered. Although why he was whispering, he wasn't sure. If anyone had witnessed what they'd done, then whispering wasn't going to save them. All he could hope was that to anyone walking past the docks, they looked like a couple of drunks who'd lost something overboard.

"No. Row over to the left a little more," she replied. All he could see of Mia was her silhouette, as she was backlit from the flashlight app on her phone. "I see him," she suddenly squeaked, her voice going high pitched in alarm.

"Turn the light off, for God's sake," he replied, stowing the oars and sliding to the back of the boat, next to Mia. The last thing they needed was to point a spotlight at the dead body for anyone on shore to see.

"Sorry," she apologized, and he felt like a bastard for almost yelling at her. This was stressful for both of them. A slight thump signaled that the body had drifted into the wooden side of the dinghy. Logan reached down and grabbed a handful of the man's jacket.

"What are we going to do with him?" Mia's voice was small and forsaken. Perhaps reality was now hitting home. What they had done. What they were about to do. Now was not the time for him to be fainthearted. He'd shot the guy. It was up to him to dispose of the evidence. If this guy had been sent by the Ramirez brothers, getting rid of the body might give him a few days' reprieve, in which to escape the island. But how was he going to find out for sure?

"Give me a hand. We'll try and drag him into the back of the dinghy." But it was harder than they thought. The man was heavier than either of them expected, weighed down by his wet clothes and the fact his limbs fell uselessly around him. After a few minutes of grunting and pulling, shoving and swearing, and once when they nearly capsized the small craft, they'd only managed to get the top half of his body hanging over the edge into the back, the rest of him dangling, like shark bait, in the black water.

"That'll have to do," he gasped. "I'll try and row, while you hang on to him."

"Where are we going?" she asked.

"We'll take him out to my boat. Decide what to do with him then."

Rowing with the man's dead weight hanging off the back like an anchor dragging along the bottom, was almost impossible. It took them much longer than normal to get to his catamaran. But Logan knew the route like the back of his hand, he'd come out here almost every night, and his eyes adjusted quickly to the dark, until he could see shadows and shapes against the black of the ocean. He navigated between the other moored boats without a sound, slipping quietly past them until he could see the little light on the back that told passersby the boat was at anchor.

Mia didn't say a word all the way out, not even when they came alongside his boat and he tied the rope off on the cleat at the back. Out of habit, Logan patted the back of his catamaran, a ritual he'd started the very first time he came aboard. It was a stupid superstition, he knew, but it felt as if his boat welcomed him home, kept him safe from harm.

Logan slid onto the bench seat beside her, and said gently, "Let go, I'll take it from here." But it was as if she was in a trance. He almost had to pry her fingers loose from the man's jacket, where she had gripped him by the collar. She gave a shudder as she let go and grimaced in distaste.

"Never in my wildest nightmares did I think..." She didn't have to finish her sentence; he knew exactly what she meant. The stranger was still limp in his hold, but the body had already begun to cool, the water lowering his temperature quickly. Logan wondered how long it took for rigor mortis to set in.

"I'm going to see if he has any kind of ID on him. Something that might give us a hint as to why he was holding us at gunpoint."

"Good idea," she said, nodding in agreement. "But I think I already know who sent him." She gave another shudder as she spoke. She'd said something similar back at the dock, and he needed to find out what she thought was going on here. Because he was sure *he* knew what was going on, and they couldn't both be right.

Logan felt in the man's jacket pockets and came up with a wallet and a mobile phone. He handed them back to Mia, while he searched under the water, through the man's pant pockets. Nothing; the guy kept it to a minimum. Unlike himself. Logan had all kinds of odds and ends in his pockets. A Swiss army knife, a ball of string, loose coins, along with all the normal stuff, like a wallet and phone.

"Now what?" Mia's voice had taken on a wooden, robotic tone. He wondered if shock was setting in.

"I'm going to tie him to my spare anchor, row farther out to sea, and send him to the bottom," Logan replied, in much the same deadpan voice.

"Dear God, help us," Mia whispered.

# CHAPTER THREE

The man's body disappeared beneath the surface. Mia felt numb, like none of this was happening to her; it was happening to someone else. Sure, her life was lived on the seedier side of normal, and the men she dealt with were often greedy and dangerous. But this? Never in a million years did she think she'd be involved in a murder. Even if it had been in self-defense, it was still murder, really. Logan had no other option; he'd had to shoot him. Hadn't he? It'd all happened so quick. She replayed the scene over and over in her head.

Logan turned the dinghy back toward shore, and she curled into herself, watching the lights get slowly brighter. They'd decided to dump the body, along with his gun, as far out to sea as they dared go in his tiny boat. Take it as far away from Logan's catamaran as possible. How he knew which boat was his in all this darkness was beyond her and so she let him guide them back, keeping her gaze fixed on the bottom of the inflatable and her mind away from what they'd just done.

"Come on, climb aboard." In the dim light she could see Logan reaching down for her hand, and on instinct she took it and let him help her up onto the catamaran until she was standing beside him on the small rear deck. It was her first time on a catamaran. Now that she was up here, she could see it looked like two smaller boats tied together—hulls, she reminded herself. They were standing on the rear of the left-hand hull. A strange sort of netting, almost like a trampoline, hung between them. Logan led her along the skinny deck, and they stepped down into a slightly lower section that opened up, spanning across both hulls. She felt much safer here.

Something brushed up against her leg and she screamed and fell against Logan's chest. His arms wrapped around her to stop her from falling.

"What was that?" she asked breathlessly.

"That's Captain, my cat. He's in charge of the boat."

"Oh." She gave a laugh, feeling silly. Then she remembered she was still in Logan's arms. Strong arms that were wrapped around her waist, holding her steady. And a hard, male chest pushed up against her breasts. She stopped breathing.

"Are you okay?" His voice was like warm milk and honey in the dark of the night.

The cat brushed her leg again, letting loose a loud meow that broke through her daze.

"Yes," she said and took a step back, breaking their embrace. "I didn't think cats liked the water."

"He doesn't." Logan laughed quietly. "Which is why he stays on the boat. He came as part of the package when I bought it from the last owner."

"Doesn't he ever go ashore?" She was intrigued, welcoming the chance to think of something else besides the man they'd just sent to the bottom of the ocean.

"Sometimes. If I can get a berth in a harbor, he will often hop off and go for a wander. And there have been the odd occasions where he will jump into the dinghy and come ashore with me. But he likes it out here. This is his domain. It's also a little ironic, and perhaps fitting, as the name of my boat is *Leopard*."

Mia laughed. "Fair enough…" What an odd cat. But then, who was she to judge? She'd done no sailing of any kind.

"Let's go inside." Logan was already moving, not bothering to take her hand this time. She grabbed the edge of the cabin canopy, used it to hold her steady as she gingerly followed him. There was a scraping sound and then a light shone at her from below. "Mind the steps," he cautioned, extending a hand to help her down.

"Oh, wow." Even in her disoriented state, she could tell she liked it. This wasn't what she'd been expecting, at all. But then, she'd never been aboard this type of boat before. Her only experience with boats was the modern, motor yachts, built for speed, meant to show off exactly how much money their owner had to splash around. The kind Harry organized, on which to hold one of his special parties for selected VIP guests.

This one was made completely of timber. Three steps led down to an open area, with padded benches and a large table in the middle.

"It's lovely."

Logan snorted. "Don't let the soft lighting fool you. I've been working on her, but she still needs a lot of TLC before she's up to scratch." He said this with a hint of pride in his voice. Now that he'd pointed it out, she could see the cushions on the benches were faded and worn, and the wooden table could do with a good coat of varnish. But it was clean and cozier and more welcoming than those horrible modern ones.

"I've redone the floorboards in the saloon," he said with a self-effacing shrug, pointing at the ground and Mia saw they did indeed look almost new; a lovely rich mahogany color. "But I haven't got around to the table or berths yet."

Mia squeezed around the side of the table and sat on the

soft cushions with a sigh.

"Can I get you a drink? I don't know about you, but I definitely need something to calm my nerves."

"God, yes. What have you got?"

"I've only got rum, I'm afraid."

"That'll do," she replied.

Logan disappeared down a hatch in the left hull and his voice drifted up to her from somewhere in the depths. "Catamarans take a bit of getting used to. The galley is on this side, but if you need to use the head, there are two, one in each hull."

As far as Mia was concerned, he'd just spoken a whole lot of gobbledygook.

"Pardon me?"

Logan's head appeared in the hatch. "Sorry, I forget when I'm not around other boaties. The galley is the kitchen, and the head is the toilet. But watch out, the toilet on this side is a little temperamental."

"Oh. Right." She gave him a faint smile, still wondering what on earth he was talking about. Mia felt the same brush of fur against her shin, but this time, she didn't freak out. Instead she leaned down and tickled the cat between his ears. Captain set up a loud purr at her touch, then jumped up onto the seat beside her. He was a large tortoiseshell, and living onboard a boat looked like it agreed with him; his fur was sleek and shiny and he was in perfect condition.

Logan brought his hand up with a triumphant flourish. "Found it." He climbed back into the saloon, two tin mugs in his other hand. "Sorry, I don't have any glasses on board." His gaze caught the cat and he lowered his eyebrows in a frown. "I hope you're not allergic. I can lock him outside if you like."

"No, don't. I love cats, but I don't often get the chance to pet one." She continued to stroke the cat's soft fur as he curled up in a ball on her lap. "And I don't really care what I drink out of right now," she said, taking one of the mugs from him and holding it out impatiently. Logan poured a slug of rum into each cup, placed the bottle on the table and came around the table to sit next to her. She'd already downed her shot before he even brought his mug to his lips. The alcohol was hot and sharp against the back of her throat and made her cough. But she held her mug out for another.

Logan downed his in one swallow, and refilled both mugs. Mia took this second one a little slower, sipping it as she looked around the saloon. The rum was good, now that she took the time to taste it, and she turned the bottle around to face her.

"It's Appleton," she exclaimed in surprise.

"Yes, it's my favorite." Logan glanced at Mia as he poured them both a third one. "You sound like you know it."

"Yes, it's my father's favorite, as well." Memories flooded in of warm nights sitting outside in the garden with her father, as he sipped the rum and talked about his most-loved topic—his church and his congregation. For a while, Mia had been taken in by her father's dedication, his fervor to serve his Lord and his parishioners with love and humanity. Until that fateful day when she turned ten and she learned a valuable lesson about certain men and their lack of humanity that changed her views forever. How a friend of her father could betray her, and then her father not believe her when she told him the truth. "My father is an Apostolic clergyman."

"Shit, really?" The surprise on Logan's face was so comical she had to laugh. "Sorry. It's just that I would never have picked you for the daughter of a preacher."

Mia felt her irritation stir. Of course, no one would pick her for that, she'd made damn sure she did everything in her power to be the exact opposite of what her father expected.

The cat moved in her lap, as if it could feel her irritation, and she went back to stroking it, the feel of his soft fur calming her. Which was a good thing, because this was not the time or place to get into that kind of argument. They had much bigger things to discuss.

Swallowing the last of the rum, she banged the mug down on the table and waited until the burn of the alcohol subsided a little before she spoke. "What are we going to do about the man we just sent to the bottom of the ocean?"

Logan's surprise quickly morphed to a frown. He pulled the man's very wet wallet and phone out of his shorts' pocket. At least they'd put the gun back in the man's jacket, so it was now at the bottom of the ocean. There was no way Logan wanted to hold onto the thing, and Mia wholeheartedly agreed with him. "Let's see if we can figure out who he was, first. That might help us understand what he was doing here in the first place."

"And who he wanted," Mia amended.

"You're still sure it was you he was after?" Logan questioned.

"Yes, I think it had something to do with Harry."

"Who's Harry?"

"It's complicated," she replied with a grimace. "I'm a dancer at one of his clubs. I'll need a couple more of these," she pointed to the rum, "before I tell you about him."

"A dancer, huh?" Logan narrowed his eyes, as if he wanted to ask more. But after pursing his lips he said, instead, "Well, I still think that thug had something to do with the Ramirez brothers."

"Who are they?"

"It's complicated," he said with a wry grin.

Mia gave an exasperated sigh. This conversation was getting them nowhere. She picked up the cell, but it was as dead as a doornail. Saltwater would have ruined it and it was utterly useless, they'd get no information from it. Then she grabbed the wallet off the table and opened it with cautious fingers.

Wads of US dollars were buried deep in the folds. "Jesus," she whispered. "This guy carried a lot of cash."

"That tells us something about him already," Logan replied. "What about ID?" He reached for the wallet, but she pulled back, snatching it out of his grasp. She was just as mired in this whole debacle as he was. She'd heard phrases such as *accessory to murder*, and all those other clichés. The last thing Mia wanted was to end up in jail. Harry wouldn't like that one little bit. And he might take his spite out on Tianna. Nope, she had to stay as far away from the cops as possible.

She pulled out his driver's license, vaguely wondering if she should be worried about leaving fingerprints behind. But surely, she was way too deep in this thing now to worry about something as insignificant as leaving fingerprints. If the police found the man's body, there was probably all sorts of evidence she'd inadvertently left on him.

"The guy's name is Renu Marquize, and he's a Cuban national." She turned the license over in her fingers. "That doesn't tell us much of anything."

"Not really," Logan conceded. "Anything else in there?" He pointed at the wallet.

Mia suddenly felt repulsed at the idea of going through a dead man's things and pushed it toward Logan. "You look," she said. While he went through all the little folds and pockets, she poured them both another drink. The rum was finally doing its job, taking the edge off the terror that'd been clawing like a wild beast at her insides ever since she saw the man with the gun. To Logan, it may have looked like she kept herself pretty much together, but she was only hanging on to reality by the merest thread. A hysterical breakdown was just around the corner, if she chose to let it in. The only thing keeping those swirling emotions at bay was the thought of Tianna. And what Harry might do to her if Mia was suddenly absent.

Mia watched as Logan thumbed through the leather folds. Became entranced by his long, agile fingers. They were quite fine, for a man, at least. It was strangely calming, watching his hands. And strangely, increasingly arousing. Mia found herself wondering what they might feel like, stroking down the length of her thigh.

"Here's a ticket stub," he said, and Mia snapped her gaze back to his face. "It's a ferry ticket, from St. Thomas. Three days ago. There's no return ticket."

"That's not unusual," Mia replied. "Most people buy them at the dock on the way out."

"Hmm. But it means he was on the island for a few days before he held us up at gunpoint. What was he doing all that time?"

Mia could think of lots of things the guy might've been doing, none of them pleasant. She yawned. Couldn't help it. A combination of the rum and the fading adrenaline, and the fact she'd had a long day rescuing a turtle. How could she be sleepy at a time like this? Nevertheless, another yawn broke free, and she had to cover her mouth. This was her only night off in a whole week. If she'd been at work tonight, none of this would've happened. How could such a lovely day, snorkeling and swimming at Maho Bay, then rescuing the injured turtle, and dinner with Logan, turn into such a sudden nightmare?

"Wait a second." Logan stilled, focused in on something caught in the wad of hundred-dollar bills. "It's a hand-written note." Gingerly, he pulled it out between thumb and forefinger. The paper was still wet and fragile, and he was careful not to pull too hard, so it didn't tear. "Shit, the writing is smudged."

"Let me see." Mia shuffled around the bench seat until she was right up close to Logan. They both peered at the tiny slip of paper. "That looks like it says *Cruz Bay*," she said, squinting through eyes that didn't want to focus. Perhaps she had overdone the rum a little. "And that definitely says *St. John*." That bit was much clearer. "Is that a dollar amount?" she asked, squinting even harder.

"That could be a dollar sign," Logan admitted.

"Does it say two-hundred-thousand dollars?" Mia almost couldn't believe what she was saying. "Did someone put a hit out on one of us?"

* * *

Logan glanced at Mia. It was her third yawn in a row, and she couldn't hide them behind her hands, even if she thought she was doing a good job of stifling them. She looked small and delicate, her slight shoulders hunched as she sat at his saloon table. There was a pale tinge to her cocoa skin, and her beautiful eyes were sunken and dark. She looked like he felt. Shocked. Stunned. Incredulous. And very, very drained by the whole episode.

It was funny, he barely even knew Mia, and yet here he was feeling protective of her. Frighteningly so. They'd both been through something utterly traumatic, something most people would never experience. It was as if a strange kind of bond had been forged between them. Even if that bond was forged in a desperate need to keep this huge secret they now owned, it was still a strong one. Logan felt he could trust Mia. He hoped she felt the same way.

"There's nothing more we can do tonight," he said. Mia startled at the sound of his voice and turned those sable eyes on him.

"What are you suggesting?"

"We're here now." Logan gestured to the boat around them. "Why don't we stay on board for the night? Try and get some sleep. And come up with a plan in the morning. Things always look brighter when the sun comes up."

"But we don't know what information that man with the gun had on us. What if there's another man with another gun waiting in the wings to come and murder us in our sleep?"

"That's true," Logan mused. Something told him the guy had been alone. That at least in the short-term they were safe. But how did he articulate that to Mia? "I hear what you're saying, but I also think we're not in any danger. If we were, we'd already be dead." It was a hard thing to say, but it was probably the truth. If the thug had a partner, he would've come after them, guns blazing.

Mia stared at him for so long he thought she was going to disagree. Then she pushed her long hair out of her face and said, "All right. I'm too tired to argue with you."

"No one will miss you if you don't come home tonight?"

"No. Tianna won't be home tonight. And Crystal and Scarlett—I sort of share with them, they're my downstairs roommates—they're dancing tonight. So, they won't know whether I'm home or not."

"So, you don't have a husband or a boyfriend waiting for you?" It was a pertinent question, he needed to know. But it was also an underhanded way of finding out if she had a man in her life. He should've asked her right at the start of dinner, but he'd chickened out. Had been enjoying her company so much, that he'd decided he didn't care. He really hoped that she wasn't the kind of girl who would agree to go on a date with another man while she had someone waiting for her at home. But sadly, he'd dated all types of women in his time, and had been stung more than once by a woman intent on cheating on her husband or boyfriend.

"God, no. Harry wouldn't allow it."

There was that name Harry again. Logan needed to get to the bottom of who this guy was and why Mia said his name with a certain amount of trepidation.

"First of all, I need to do something," Logan said, standing up and scooping the wallet, the phone and all the bits of paper and ID scattered on the table.

"What are you going to do with it?" Mia asked.

"Get rid of the evidence," he replied flatly.

"Oh." He could tell Mia hadn't really thought about it until right at that moment. It was evidence that would link them to a crime. The crime of murder. It was all too surreal. He walked to the edge of the cockpit and ditched the items as far out into the ocean as he could. He hoped they would sink quickly and lay forever at the bottom of the sea. But even if they floated and were eventually found, he hoped he and Mia would be well away from St. John by then.

When Logan reappeared in the saloon, Mia asked, "What about the anchor? Can they trace that back to you? To us?"

Logan stopped in his tracks and pursed his lips. He hadn't thought of that. All he knew was he needed something heavy to weigh the dead man down.

"I don't think so. That type of anchor is small and cheap. It was a spare that I used in the dinghy, one of three I had on board. Most boats have a spare and I'd hazard a guess at least half the boats moored in this bay have something like it stuffed down in their holds somewhere." After another second's thought, he added, "I've also heard that water erodes evidence, like fingerprints, pretty quickly. Maybe even after a few days."

Mia nodded, while he crossed his fingers behind his back, hoping he'd learned that fact correctly, and hoping the man would stay submerged for as long as possible.

"Follow me," Logan said, gallantly offering her his hand to help her around the table. She went to stand, then seemed to remember she still had Captain on her lap—that cat had taken a liking to her, as if she were some long-lost friend, which was highly unusual. She scooped him up and dropped him gently on the seat beside her. Captain gave them a baleful stare that said he wasn't pleased with being moved, then began to clean himself, effectively dismissing them both. Logan had to stifle a laugh.

"Where does Captain sleep?" Mia asked, as if suddenly concerned about the cat.

"He usually curls up on deck somewhere when it's warm like this. And if the weather is bad, he sleeps in the saloon. But he learned early on not to sleep on my bed. I move around too much." Logan grinned when she shot him an inquisitive look.

He led Mia back down the same hatch he'd gone into earlier, but this time he turned right. Flicking a switch as he led her down the narrow passageway, the small light cast a soft glow throughout the hull. All his lights were run off a battery pack, powered by two solar panels situated on the cabin rooftop. This was the very first upgrade he'd made, a few weeks after he bought the boat. Bought the panels from a dodgy boat dealer in Havana the day after he sailed into the harbor. There were so many other things he wanted to do with *Leopard*. When he had the time. He'd bought the boat in a hurry, sight unseen. At the time he needed a quick escape route out of Mexico and this had been like manna sent from heaven. The boat was a diamond in the rough, or at least that's the way he liked to think of it. A self-built, wooden boat, nearly twenty years old, it'd had a hard life. Logan doubted the boat had ever been dry-docked, or had much of any kind of maintenance done on it. But that was okay with him. Because, at the time it helped him go incognito. Let him fly under the radar. Because no one looked twice at a shabby old Wharrum Catamaran. There were plenty of others like it in the Caribbean. It was the perfect disguise.

But Logan had never counted on how attached he'd

become to the boat. All of its eccentricities and quirks. And the cat, Captain. He'd never owned an animal before. It really felt like he was home when he came aboard.

They reached the front of the hull, and he opened a little sliding door to reveal a double bed tucked into the pointed end. "This is my berth," he said, then immediately regretted it. What a stupid thing to do, bring a woman to his bedroom. She would probably think he wanted to sleep with her.

Which he did.

But that wasn't his intention when he'd led her here.

"Oh…ah…but I didn't mean… It's not like—"

"It's okay, Logan," Mia interrupted. "I just need somewhere to lay my head down for a little while. And this looks very cozy."

"Oh. Good." He let out a whoosh of relieved air. "I'll be up in the saloon, if you need me."

He turned to leave when her voice stopped him in his tracks. "Stay with me a while," she entreated. "My head is spinning with everything that's happened." He swiveled slowly to face her.

"Sure," he replied, climbing onto the bed beside her. He reached up and opened the little forward hatch, so a cool breeze fell down on them, then lay on his back, hands behind his head. The open hatch let them see straight up to the sky. He loved to lie here and look at the stars on the nights when he couldn't sleep.

Logan had always loved to stare up at the night sky; wonder what was really up there, trying to count the stars, dream and ponder the meaning of life. It wasn't until he bought *Leopard* that the stars began to have special significance to him. They helped him navigate his way through the islands. Yes, there were now GPS guidance systems, and newfangled technology which meant he didn't need to use the stars at all. But he loved the struggle involved in plotting a course using the sky. Of having to use an old-fashioned sextant to measure the distances between certain celestial bodies and the horizon.

He'd found the sextant buried underneath a pile of ropes in one of the many storage bays, a few days after he acquired the boat, along with some battered, old, equatorial star charts. And taught himself how to use it. It was a fascinating art; he would often marvel at the explorers who'd sailed these oceans so many hundreds of years before, using the stars as their only guide. Maybe it was the scientist in him, the little voice that wanted to know how everything worked. But more likely, it was the sense of calm he often felt, sitting up on deck, staring at the stars, learning all their names, learning which ones were important and which ones not so much.

Logan gave a sigh and tucked his hands beneath his head, getting more comfortable. Mia surprised him by snuggling into his side, laying her head on his shoulder.

"Sorry, I think I'm a little drunk," she admitted. "But I need you to hold me. I'm scared and I don't know what to think, or what to do."

Logan didn't have to be asked twice, he'd wanted to wrap his arms around her all day. They lay, entwined together and stared up at the night sky.

As she draped her arm over him, he heard the slight jangle of a bracelet on her wrist. He'd noticed her wearing it earlier tonight, while they were at dinner. It was a fine silver loop, with a single blue bead in the middle.

His fingers found the jewelry. "This is pretty," he said, rubbing the cool metal between his thumb and forefinger.

"Turquoise is my birthstone," she replied. "It's kind of my lucky charm," she admitted. "I bought it from some old lady back in Jamaica, before I left. I never take it off." She gave a small, self-conscious laugh. "Call me superstitious, but a small part of me thinks it's a link back to my home. To make sure I get back there one day." There was longing as well as consternation in her voice.

"It'll be okay. You'll get to go home. We'll get out of this, I promise." He wasn't sure if he'd be able to keep that pledge, perhaps his words had been rash in his need to protect her. But he was going to try damn hard, nonetheless. His words seemed to calm her, she snuggled in closer, her breathing becoming deeper and more regular.

"Your birthstone, huh?" He raised an eyebrow. "So that would make you a…Capricorn?" He took a punt, he had no idea what month had turquoise as its birthstone.

"Sagittarius," she said with a smile in her voice. "And before you ask, I'm the ripe old age of thirty."

"The perfect age," he replied. "Young enough to have fun but old enough to know better." He hoped she didn't think he was prying, but was secretly pleased she was closer to his own age than he'd first guessed.

"Exactly," she agreed. "What are you looking at up there?" she asked, her gaze following his up through the small hatch above. Not sure if her change of topic was deliberate, he went with her question anyway.

"I like to look at the stars," he replied. "But then, doesn't everyone?"

She laughed. "I guess so. I can't say I have much time to stargaze. I'm usually working to the small hours of the night. Either that or sleeping. I don't know much about them. What's that one up there?" Her finger pointed to a star, much brighter than the rest, hovering on its own on the lower edge of their field of vision.

"You don't know Venus?" he asked, then wished he hadn't sounded quite so incredulous. It wasn't her fault she knew nothing about the stars; lots of people spent their whole lives looking down, instead of up.

"Well, I've heard of Venus, of course," she replied. "But I

never knew which one it was."

"It's the brightest object up there, apart from the sun and the moon."

"Really?" she breathed, and snuggled in a little bit closer. "What about that one over there? It's in a group of five other ones."

Logan squinted as he followed the direction of her finger. "That's Cassiopeia. It's the brightest star in the constellation, also called Cassiopeia. The name comes from a queen in Greek mythology who thought she was the ultimate beauty."

"Wow, you do know a lot."

"There's not a lot to do on a boat at night." That was partly the truth. The other part was it had become a bit of a fascination for him.

"Tell me more. What's that one over there? It kind of has a red glow." She sounded like a happy child, eager to learn.

"That's Antares, part of the Scorpio constellation. It's known as the heart of the scorpion." Logan didn't say it out loud, but Antares was one of the reasons he'd chosen to come to St. John. On the night he was sitting in Cap-Haitien wondering where he should go to next, he'd looked up at the stars, and there was Antares, burning bright, calling to him. When he looked at it on his star chart, it was hovering directly above the island of St. John on that particular night. He decided it was as good a place to go as any. Perhaps it'd been leading him to Mia all along.

They spent many more contented minutes talking about the different stars, until Logan decided it was time to change the topic. He needed to hear Mia's side of the story.

"Tell me about this Harry guy," he said. "It might help us figure out what's going on, if I know more."

"Okay, as long as you promise to tell me yours afterwards."

"Will do."

Mia took a deep breath. "You may well have heard of him, just by a different name. Have you heard of Harry *The Hook*?"

Logan searched his memory banks. Something twigged at the name. There were rumors, passed on by his mate Paz, about someone by that name. He was into something disreputable. But Logan couldn't remember exactly what. "Not really," he replied.

"He runs a…shall we call it a gentleman's club here on the island. And another one on St. Thomas."

Logan was surprised. "I've never heard of anything like that. I thought St. John was a sleepy little island where nothing much happened."

Mia gave a languid laugh. "Most of the time, you'd be right. Only certain people even know of the club's existence. It has a very high-class VIP clientele. Harry brings in bigwigs from all over the world and entertains them with gambling and dancing girls."

Logan's skin began to prickle as realization dawned. "So, when you said you're a dancer…"

"I think exotic dancer is probably more of a correct term," she replied.

# CHAPTER FOUR

Early-morning rays of sunshine played over Mia's eyelids, until she eventually turned over and gave a leisurely stretch. She'd just had one of the best night's sleep in almost forever. Which was absolutely preposterous, after what she'd seen and done yesterday evening. She'd thought she wouldn't be able to sleep a wink. Maybe it was the very gentle rocking of the boat on the waves. Maybe it was the way she felt somehow cocooned and safe, floating out here on the ocean. Or maybe it was the fact that Logan was asleep next to her.

Mia turned slowly, so as not to wake him, and stared at his face. Last night had been crazy, wild, unbelievable. At the very least, she was an accessory to murder, could perhaps even be put in jail. At worst, her own life, and her sister's life might be in danger.

But as she stared at Logan, none of that seemed to matter. She was more worried as to how he'd received the news she was an exotic dancer. Most guys gave her one of two reactions. There were the ones whose eyes widened with delight, and then quickly narrowed with licentiousness. They were the ones who thought she was an easy target, that her body was for sale. Because she danced for them, she was available to be bought by them, as well. Which wasn't the case at all. Mia never slept with any of her customers. Ever.

Then there were the ones who took a step back from her, as if she had some kind of disease. As if she were dirty, to be looked down upon and pitied.

Which was why she didn't mention it to most people. It was easier that way. Because no one understood what it was that she did, and why she did it.

Dancing was her life. Ever since she was a young girl, all she'd wanted to do was move her body to music. But her family hadn't been able to afford the expensive dance lessons Mia craved. They were for rich, white-people. Not for the clergyman's half-caste kids. There was one dance studio Mia liked to visit on her way home from school, where she could stare in through a crack in the doorway and watch the beautiful girls, all dressed in dreamy pastels, with their little tutus on as they learned to plié and glide around the room. She dreamed of one day becoming one of those graceful ballerinas behind the door.

Her father frowned on her compulsion to dance. He was forever telling her to sit still and stop fidgeting. That good girls learned how to cook with their mother, and how to find ways to better serve their community. With her father it was all about helping others, but never about helping those he was closest to—his family. So, she had danced in secret, in the tiny backyard when no one was looking, on the way from walking home from school in the little alley way next to the dance studio. When she was sixteen, she volunteered to mop the floors at another contemporary dance studio, just so she could stay and watch the classes. Then she would practice what she'd seen the teacher train her students to do in secret.

The day she'd turned eighteen, she'd left home and gone to Kingston, Jamaica's capital city. And straightaway, she'd landed a job waitressing at one of the big hotels. The guy who hired her had leered and couldn't keep his hands away from her ass. But she didn't care if he'd hired her for her looks, because she now had a job at one of the most prestigious hotels in town. And the best part had been the cabaret show they put on every night for the guests in the beautiful outdoor garden. Mia had been entranced by their garish costumes and by their total lack of inhibition when it came to moving their bodies. One of the dancers, Leticia, had taken pity on her one night and began teaching her some of the moves. Mia auditioned a few months later for another cabaret troupe and had never looked back.

Until things began to spiral out of control when Tianna became involved with Harry *The Hook*.

But Logan had reacted differently to most men. Yes, she'd definitely seen surprise in his eyes, but the first words out of his mouth had been, "I bet you're a beautiful dancer." It wasn't the words so much, as the way he said it, with reverence and pure admiration. "I'd love to see you dance, one day."

She'd laughed at that and said, "I'm not sure your idea of what I do and the reality of what I do are the same thing." Which was true. Nowadays her dancing was less about expressing herself to music than about being as sensual and sexy as possible for Harry's guests. It was about enticing them by using her body—but not letting them into her soul, they'd never see through to her truest self. But she would love to get back to real dancing. One day she'd do it. She was determined to start her own dance troupe and tour around the islands. Take bookings from the local bars and hotels, perhaps even start up her own dance club. Be the master of her own destiny.

"Well, I totally respect you, anyway. A woman as beautiful as you should be allowed to dance any way she wants to," Logan had said.

Then his dark brows had lowered in a frown. Mia had

never seen such perfect eyebrows on a man before. It was almost as if they were sculpted, defined and dark with a little winged arch at the ends that gave him a come-hither look she couldn't ignore. Even when he frowned, he was appealing.

"So, what does this Harry dude have to do with anything?" Logan had asked.

"Like I said, it's complicated," Mia had sighed. An image of Harry came to her, standing at the back of the club, small, piggy eyes taking in everything, glaring at the girls, making sure they were all doing their jobs. His dark beard was kept fashionably trimmed to hide his pockmarked skin, and the stylish, tailor-made suit he thought made him look professional and imposing stretched at the seams over his growing belly. But the external dressing did nothing to hide his unsavory persona, which Mia could see shining through in the sour turn of his mouth and the arrogant tilt of his chin.

"I'm not going anywhere." And as if to highlight his words, Logan pulled her in a bit tighter.

"Harry is not a nice man," Mia had stated. "And he's not a man to be messed with, either." This was said as a warning to Logan, just in case he had notions of confronting him. "He has friends in high places. And also, friends in low places."

"Like the guy with the gun from last night?" Logan asked.

"Exactly," Mia replied. "He has connections, and he likes to guard his property and his business jealously."

"Okay. You've cautioned me on how bad a dude this Harry is, but you still haven't told me how you're connected to him."

Mia drew in a deep breath. "It actually started with my little sister. You see, Tianna was always my little shadow when we were growing up. I guess you could say she idolized me. And that was good, because it meant I could keep an eye on her, protect her."

Mia stopped as a memory seeped in. A dark memory, of a

man they thought they could trust, and exactly what lengths Mia had to go to, to protect Tianna from him. She had stepped in to stop the man's sick advances toward Tianna, and had instead ended up as his target. She shuddered at the thought. It was their secret, only Tianna and Mia—and the man, of course—knew what'd transpired that day. Another clergyman, a colleague of their father, had taken advantage of his friendship. Pretended to be looking after the girls' spiritual convictions, and had instead been only looking to pleasure himself. Had threatened to tell their father about their behavior, twisted the disgusting things he was doing all around to make the girls think they were in the wrong. Thankfully, the man had only been staying with their family for a short time. But their father hadn't believed them when they finally worked up the courage to tell him, and so they decided to keep the story a secret; because if their father didn't believe them, who else would?

Mia had taken up her story again. "Anyway, when I left Spanish Town, where I grew up, Tianna fell in with a bad crowd, without me there to guide her." Again, Mia was wracked with images. Guilty images of how Tianna must've coped without her big sister to help her. But Mia had to get out, to escape. Otherwise she may well have drowned under the weight of their poverty and her father's expectations. "I have two older sisters, Kalise and Sabryna. And an older brother, Devan. But they were a lot older, and at that stage Devan and Sabryna had already left to get married and start families of their own."

"Wow, how many brothers and sisters do you have?"

"I'm one of six," Mia had confided. "Which is not unusual for Jamaican families. Especially families of a clergyman," she added darkly.

Logan only nodded, obviously keen for her to continue her story.

"Anyway, about a year ago, I was dancing in a cabaret show at the Emerald Beach Resort in Charlotte Amalie. You know, the capital of St. Thomas?" Logan only nodded his answer. "I began to hear rumors, through my older brother back in Jamaica, that Tianna had supposedly come to find me. She had this dream of becoming a dancer, as well." Mia shuddered at the memory of that phone call with her brother. The things he told her about Tianna, and what she'd been up to before she left Jamaica. It seemed she'd become dependent on drugs; cocaine, to be exact. And owed some people a lot of money. Which was one reason she'd left Spanish Town.

"It took me a few days to track her down. She was working for Harry *The Hook*, at his gentleman's club. But she wasn't just dancing for him." Mia gulped and swallowed the lump that'd formed in her throat. It hurt to admit this part. "Some of the girls in the dance club will also have sex with the men. But they get to say who and when and how much, because really, they're supposed to be there to dance. I guess you could say they are high-class hookers. Tianna was one of these girls. But she wasn't doing it out of choice. Harry was forcing her to do it, because she owed him money for drugs. Lots of money." Mia shook her head. She still couldn't get over how stupid Tianna had been. But she was still her baby sister. And she needed protection. Mia was older and wiser and could take care of herself. And a small part of her felt guilty at leaving Tianna behind in the first place. Like she owed her something.

"I offered to dance for Harry for a year, to work off her debt. As long as he let her go."

"Jesus, Mia." Logan's eyes had softened, and his hand snaked up to brush her cheek.

"But I'm not like those other girls. I never sleep with any of the men," she'd blurted out quickly. It was suddenly vitally important that Logan not think she did that, too. "I'm not a prostitute. I would never stoop that low." Even though the money was excellent, and Harry was constantly pressuring her. Even though one man had offered her an obscene amount of money for one night. She stood her ground. But she knew it was a slippery slope. Harry was constantly threatening that if she didn't do what he wanted, then Tianna would become fair game again. At the moment, he was leaving her sister alone. Mia had managed to get her clean and drug free—for now—and away from the gentlemen's club. And had pleaded with Tianna to leave the island; to go home. But when Tianna had refused, she made her promise to at least not go near Harry. She was worried he might try and hook Tianna on cocaine again, and then there would be no escape. For either of them.

Mia's fingers had found the familiar feel of her silver bracelet. She rubbed the blue bead softly. Logan had said the bracelet was pretty. But she wasn't sure he understood the significance it had for her. It reminded her of home. Reminded her of her brothers and sisters. It was her promise that she would return home soon, and bring Tianna with her.

"So why do you think that guy with the gun last night was connected to Harry?" Logan had asked.

"Because he keeps a close eye on me. On all of his girls, really. None of us are allowed to have boyfriends, or God forbid, be married, as a man might distract us, or give us the wrong ideas." Mia mimicked Harry's deep baritone. "But it's really all about control. Harry truly believes we're his possessions. And as such, he has a right to control who we see and what we do." Mia rolled over and stared up at the stars through the small hatch. "I'm certain he has me followed, just to make sure I'm sticking to the rules. And so, when the guy with the gun appeared, I knew he'd been sent to scare you off. And to send me a warning. Not to mess around. Not to break the rules. Maybe he thought we were on a date, and he was nipping things in the bud, so to speak."

Logan propped himself up onto one elbow, so he could look at her. "Why don't you just leave? Take Tianna and the both of you go. Why are you so scared of this guy?" Mia stared up at his face, hovering above her. If only things were that simple. Did he not think she had thought of every scenario, every way to get out of this predicament? He didn't understand Harry like she did.

"Because, I've heard things. There are rumors, stories, amongst the other girls. A few years ago, one of his dancers was found floating in the harbor. She'd been missing for a few weeks, everyone figured she left the island. This girl had made no secret of the fact she wanted to go home, that Harry's tactics were uncivilized and plainly corrupt. She also said she was going to send the police to the *gentleman's club* as soon as she got free. I'm not sure if it's true or not. Maybe Harry started the rumor to keep us all in line. But would you be prepared to test it? Because I'm not." There had been other rumors as well, all along similar lines, of how Harry treated the girls who displeased him, or who didn't toe the line.

Logan had shaken his head slowly. "He sounds like one sick dude. But I'm sure there's a way we can get you out of there. I'm not scared of him." Logan had fixed his gaze on Mia as he said those last words and she could see he meant it. But he should be afraid. They both should.

They had talked into the wee hours of the night. She hadn't been able to convince Logan the man with the gun was indeed connected to Harry. But it'd been cathartic to finally reveal to someone the ordeals she'd been going through for the past few months. She'd wanted to hear about his story, about why he thought the armed man was after him, and not her. But her eyelids had drooped, and sleep eventually claimed her, even as she desperately tried to fight it. Instead of continuing their conversation, Logan had taken her in his arms once more, and stroked her hair. It was wonderful. He was a calming influence on her churning mind. And he was the perfect gentleman all night. He cuddled her, but it was companionable and warm. Not sexual at all.

Maybe that was why she had slept so well last night.

But today was a new day, and decisions needed to be made.

As if he could hear her thoughts, Logan stirred and opened his eyes. Jesus, he was gorgeous, even first thing in the morning. Hair all sleep rumpled, eyes all brown and peaceful. Sometime during the night, Logan had removed his T-shirt, probably to stay cool. And now Mia was confronted with a whole lot of ripped male stomach muscles, and a broad chest. She'd never really thought white guys could ever look as good as a gorgeous black man in his prime. But with Logan, she might have to revise that idea.

His arms and legs had that deep tan only hours spent in the sun every day can achieve. The rest of the top half of his body was lighter, but he still had a golden hue about him, as if he removed his shirt often to soak up the sun's rays.

He gave her that cheeky smile and said, "Morning. How did you sleep?"

"Really well, surprisingly."

"Me too," he admitted.

"I've got a few eggs in the refrigerator. Can I cook you an omelet?"

Mia's stomach growled at the thought of food. Even after that wonderful meal they'd had at Sunny's last night. Had that only been last night? It seemed like eons ago.

"Yes, please." She sat up and pushed her hair away from her face. It was a tangled mess, but that was the least of her worries. "Then I need to get home. If I'm not back soon, Crystal and Scarlett will begin to wonder."

"Right, we need to come up with a plan," Logan agreed.

"And you need to tell me who you think this man with the gun is, so we can decide what our best options are."

"My head is telling me that we need to get out of here, as quickly as we can," Logan admitted, pushing himself to the end of the bed and then levering himself up.

She watched as he dragged his rumpled T-shirt over his well-defined pecs. There was something so sweetly sexy about a man in the morning, and just looking at Logan was making Mia's heart rate rise.

"We could pull up anchor and be out of here within an hour, if you wanted to," Logan said, glancing back at her as he walked down the narrow passageway towards the kitchen —galley, she mentally corrected.

The idea had a lot of merit. Mia could see herself sailing away with Logan, to a new life. A new beginning.

"I can't leave Tianna," she said with a dispirited smile. Much as she'd like to teach Tianna a lesson and just up and leave, she'd never do it for real. She was stuck here, whether she liked it or not. At least, until she found Tianna and then they could both escape together.

"Hmm, that does put a wrench in the works," Logan agreed. "You go up to the saloon," he said with a tilt of his chin. Then he hunched down in front of a small refrigerator and began rummaging through the contents. Mia climbed the ladder slowly and sat at the table, her mind churning with thoughts and ideas. A welcoming meow greeted her from the hatchway, then Captain jumped down into the saloon, and stretched and leaped lightly up onto the seat beside her for a pat. He really was very endearing. Mia had never thought about a cat living on board a boat before. But he obviously coped very well.

"If I could convince Tianna, would you let her come on the boat with us?" she called down through the hatch. She could see part of Logan's back as she stood at the small gas stove and cracked eggs into a frying pan.

He popped his head around the corner. "Of course. You know I would. Why, what are you thinking?"

"I'm liking your idea of getting the hell out of here as soon as we can," she replied. If she left with Logan, they could get lost amongst the islands of the Caribbean. They could island hop, go under false names. Run away from Harry and his cronies. As long as Logan let her stay on board, that was. But even if that idea was a stupid fantasy, Logan could drop them off in Cuba, where she and Tianna could easily get lost in Havana. Or even down to South America. Venezuela or Columbia. There were lots of options.

# CHAPTER FIVE

Logan stuffed another forkful of eggs in his mouth, and watched Mia do the same. He was starving. Perhaps killing a man made you hungry.

That thought brought Logan up short, his fork stalled halfway to his mouth. Holy shit, he'd actually killed a man. Shot him dead. Logan would need to process that concept. He hadn't allowed it to take hold last night, there was too much else to think about. A frantic dash out to the boat and a body to dispose of.

And Mia to protect.

What did Mia think about all this? She'd been shocked and dazed last night, but she'd never once said she blamed him for their current predicament. He'd half-expected her to run away from him right there on the dock, yelling and screaming for the police. Turn him in and point the finger directly at him. Because she really had nothing to do with the killing, she was an innocent bystander. Then, when they got to the catamaran, she would've been well within her rights to accuse him of landing her in this situation. To be angry and panicked and take her emotions out on him.

But she'd done none of that. Instead, she'd remained rational and fairly calm. Scared—and who wouldn't be—but not hysterical. He liked that in a woman; a strong sense of self-control and an ability to think things through logically. He guessed that in her job as an exotic dancer she'd probably seen it all—the more sordid side of humanity, at least. And had had to deal with all kinds of men, learned who she could trust and who she couldn't. This had made her tough, streetwise, and mentally strong.

Should they have gone to the police? He still didn't know the answer. One thing he did know, was the police might not have seen his side of the story, might've indeed called it murder, rather than self-defense. And then he would become an easy target for the Ramirez brothers, like a sitting duck, if he was locked up in jail.

"You all right?" Mia asked.

Logan realized his forkful of eggs was still hanging in the air.

"Yeah." He flashed her a smile that he hoped made it seem like he wasn't thinking about a dead man weighed down on the seabed by his anchor right now.

"I know you said your story was long and complicated," Mia said. "But have you got an abbreviated version you can tell me while we finish breakfast? Because I really need to get home." As she spoke, she took a small piece of egg and fed it to Captain, who took her offering and then licked his whiskers, obviously looking for more. But even the cat's antics couldn't distract Logan this morning.

"Right. Sure thing." Logan had almost forgotten he needed to let Mia in on his secret. But how did he give her an abbreviated version, when it was so complicated and wrought with emotions that even he couldn't untangle fact from fiction? Suddenly the rest of the eggs and toast looked less appetizing, and he lay his fork gently down on his plate.

"I was in love with a woman called Sofia," he said at last.

"Okay," Mia replied, but the quizzical lift of one dark

eyebrow showed her confusion. *What did falling in love have to do with a man with a gun?* her gaze seemed to say.

"I met Sofia in a little town called San Cristobal del las Cassas, in Chiapas state, down in the south of Mexico. It was about four years ago."

Mia nodded, nibbling on her toast.

"I was working on a conservation project down there, helping to catch and tag Tequila Bats, to try and set up a breeding program for them." He'd loved that job. Was there for over two years. Loved the area, loved the food, loved the people, and thought he would stay there for the rest of his life. Sofia was the epitome of the South-American queen. A doe-eyed beauty, who'd seduced him right from the start.

"Sofia and I were engaged to be married."

That seemed to bring Mia up short as she turned to stare at him.

By the time he and Sofia had become engaged, he was practically living with her, in the family home. He thought he got on well with her mother, Juana and father, Mateo. The family was tight-knit, with her two brothers, Leonardo and Diego, living in a second house just down the street with their wives and children. The large, rambling family home had always been full of people and laughter, with Mateo lording it over the whole scene like some long-lost Aztec noble. They seemed to accept Logan into the family. Sofia was the spoiled only daughter, allowed pretty much anything she wanted. Mateo was rich. Sofia said he was into politics, a leader, aligned with the government military. She was a bit vague on the details, said he made his money helping to build the new airport near the capital of Chiapas. And Logan never questioned her. Something, some little internal warning bell, had told him not to trust Mateo Ramirez completely. But he'd been blinded by love and ignored that little voice. Until it was almost too late.

"A few days before the wedding…" Logan swallowed reflexively. He'd never said these words out loud before. Who knew it was going to be this hard? "I found out her father was involved in something illegal, and downright morally corrupt."

"Oh, no." Mia's hand landed on Logan's arm, a gesture of support, which helped him to continue.

"He was a dirty people smuggler," Logan said with a grimace. "I remember the day I found out. It was like I suddenly couldn't breathe, like there wasn't enough air left in the whole world to keep me alive."

The day was indelibly inked onto his mind. Logan had stopped in one of the long, cool corridors of the Ramirez's large house to check his phone. A message from Sofia had come in—she was out shopping. As he texted a reply, he overheard voices in an office down the hall. It was Mateo and Diego, discussing work. Or so Logan thought, at first. But the more he listened, the more dumbfounded he became. It sounded like they were talking about moving African refugees up the coast, into American waters. Logan stood and listened for a few more minutes, until it became startlingly obvious he was right. A righteous rage had swept over him, and he'd stormed into the room demanding answers. At first the men had been surprised, and Diego had become angry and quarrelsome, getting right up in Logan's face, threatening him with all kinds of violence. But Mateo soon admitted that if Logan was going to join the family, then he had a right to know where the money came from. So, he went on to explain.

Logan already knew a lot about the refugee crisis gripping Mexico and America. Such as the African refugees, fleeing war-torn countries like Cameroon. They would somehow fly or travel by sea and arrive in South America, then make the long trek towards the Mexican border at Chiapas. The migrants who were camped out at the border often staged protests, demanding the Mexican government let them through. Conditions were dire, and it was no wonder the refugees were desperate. Mateo and his sons—who were the ones who did all the dirty work, Mateo merely directed them from the safety of his mansion—would organize boats to take the refugees father up the Mexican coastline and into American waters, where they would land on deserted beaches, usually in California.

Diego proudly told him they could get anywhere from three-thousand dollars to ten-thousand dollars per refugee. Logan was astounded. But not in good way. Diego went on to say it wasn't only the Africans they made their money from. There were plenty of South American refugees who wanted to go to the US for a better life, as well. They even had a boat organized to bring desperate Haitians over to Mexico, so they could join the growing throng of displaced persons.

But Mateo made one vital error that day. He assumed because Logan was marrying Sofia that he would remain, if not compliant, then at least quiet about their illegal dealings. Which would leave him and Sofia free to continue to make the most of his riches and enjoy the lifestyle they'd become accustomed to. But Logan's moral compass wouldn't allow him to continue the charade.

"I couldn't live with myself if I'd married Sofia, and had to keep my mouth shut about the disgusting way they made their money. So, I escaped. Fled the city that night on my motorbike. Then I dumped the bike and bought a boat, sight-unseen from a guy in Cancun. I wanted to tell Sofia I was leaving but I knew she'd try and stop me. Or get her brothers to stop me. I left her a note. A stupid note explaining why I couldn't be with her. I wish I'd done more. I *should've* done more." He banged his hand down on the table.

And to this day, the guilt still sat heavy in his gut. What

must she have thought of him? He could guess how she would've screamed and cried; that fiery Latino temper of hers would've been a sight to see. He had thought about asking her to come with him. Two young people in love could conquer everything, overcome all obstacles. Couldn't they? But something told him if he forced her to choose between him and her family, she would stay. And he wouldn't have blamed her. Family meant everything to her. It tore his heart in two to have to leave her. He had truly been in love with her.

She'd sent him a text the morning after he fled. It started off pleading with him to come back and ended up demanding to know why he didn't love her enough to stay. He'd never answered her message, because he didn't know what to say. There was no way he could ever make it up to her for what he'd done. Time and distance might've cooled his ardor, but not the guilt.

"That's terrible, Logan. And so sad for you." Mia's hand was still on Logan's arm, and she gave it a gentle squeeze. A sudden lump formed in his throat. It'd been a while since he thought of Sofia. Telling someone made it all the more real.

"Yes, well, the brothers, Leonardo and Diego didn't take too kindly to me leaving their sister *at the altar*, as they liked to put it. Before I ditched my cell in the ocean, they sent me some very interesting texts. They vowed to hunt me down and bring me back to Mexico, so I could face the wrath of their father and apologize to their sister. Then they were going to kill me. I'd been let into the inner sanctum of the family, and I'd betrayed them. I knew too much. I was liability, as well as a defector."

"Oh, God." Mia's hand flew to her mouth. "Now I see why you thought the guy with the gun might be working for them."

Logan had read the menacing texts from Diego and knew

the brothers would carry out their threats. Which was when he knew he'd underestimated the extent of their wrath. And why he'd fled to Cancun and bought the first boat he could—for cash, under a false name—and sailed out of there on the very next tide. Logan had done a little sailing in his life, mainly when he was younger back in Adelaide. In much smaller boats. And never on his own. It was a steep learning curve, and he made many mistakes as he limped the boat first towards Jamaica, and then onto Haiti.

"I know you said Harry *The Hook* knows some unsavory people. But I can guarantee, the Ramirez brothers are worse." He ran a hand through his hair, pushing his plate with the now cold eggs on it away. "They have the money and the power and the contacts to make my life a living hell. They nearly caught up with me in Barbados about a year ago. I heard a rumor some guy was looking for me from the harbor master at the dock where I was tied up. He gave a pretty good description of someone who sounded a lot like Leonardo. So, I hightailed it out of there. I've sailed all the way through most of the Caribbean islands." Logan sucked in a deep breath and pursed his lips. "Perhaps I was getting too nonchalant, after not hearing a thing for nearly a year," he admitted. "I hoped that maybe the Ramirez brothers had finally given up and left me alone." Logan snorted. What a vain hope that'd been. He should've guessed they would never stop hunting for him, not as long as they thought he was alive.

"Did you ever think of changing your name? To try and get them off your tail?"

It was a fair question, and yes, he had thought about it, and even acted on it, sometimes.

"I have used different names, off and on. Or else I worked for cash when I could, then you don't really need a name at all. It's also one of the reasons I live on my boat, to help keep everything low-key, try and fly under the radar. Make as small a footprint as possible. I stay off all social media, and only use a cheap flip phone. I don't have too many friends. Not close ones, anyway. This job with the UVI is the first real job I've had in two years. My money was running out, I spent most of my spare cash when I bought the boat, and eventually, I needed something more to live off."

It sounded sad and pathetic, the way he lived his life, now that he said it out loud. So, he left out the bit about how, after a single phone call from Cancun right before he left Mexico, he'd not contacted his family for the past two years and how the self-reproach sat like a heavy weight on his shoulders.

"Wow." Mia pursed her lips and stared at him. "Now I can see why you're worried. And you think this guy with the gun is what…like a bounty hunter, or something…or a scout, for the Ramirez brothers?"

"Exactly," he said.

"But we don't have a lot of info on him to help us decide," she continued, running a finger thoughtfully under her chin. The move was sexy as hell and caught Logan's attention. "All we know is this guy is a Cuban national, came over to Cruz Bay three days ago and may have been offered a large sum of money to do a job. But we don't know what that job is. Was," she corrected herself.

"There were other things that might help. Small details, like he had a lot of cash on him. A good way to pay for things, if you don't want to be tracked. And he was extremely well dressed. He took pride in his appearance, and dressed like a professional." A professional what, Logan was loath to say out loud. "He handled that gun with ease, wasn't afraid to approach us in a public area. Even if it was dark and there was no one in sight, it still took a certain degree of balls, nerves of steel, to try and abduct two people from the main dock of Cruz Bay."

Mia gave him a thoughtful look. "You think all these things point toward him being sent by the Ramirez brothers, rather than Harry?"

"I think so. Wouldn't Harry be more likely to use a local?"

Mia still didn't look convinced. "Harry has a lot of men around him, and they change all the time. I think Harry has his fingers in more than one pot of honey. I don't think his clubs are his only source of income. He's always meeting with strangers in the back of his club. He might think us girls don't notice, but we do. Sometimes, one of his special VIP guests might even bring their own security guards. It could've been one of those." Mia raised her slim shoulders in a shrug.

Logan couldn't disagree with Mia's logic, even though his gut was telling him the man had been after him, and not Mia. Instead, he said, "We need more evidence to really pin it down. But in the long run, if we're going to up and flee, does it really matter who hired that guy?"

Mia shook her head. "I guess not." She looked down at the table, and her long hair fell over her face. Logan pulled a lock of it aside, so he could see her expression. Her face was a picture of misery and fear, and his heart contracted.

"I made a promise to you last night. That I would get you out of here. And I mean to keep it. We'll be okay." He scooted over on the bench seat and pulled her in towards his chest, enfolding her in a hug.

"I'm trying my hardest to believe you," she said, her voice muffled against his T-shirt. "But I'm way out of my depth here."

*So am I.* He kept the words to himself. She didn't need to know his heart was racing at a hundred miles a minute and he was wound up tighter than one of his father's antique clocks. That every small sound from outside the boat made him flinch and listen for more tell-tale sounds of someone climbing aboard. That his mind was racing with so many scenarios, he could hardly form coherent speech. And the look on the man's face, the second after Logan shot him, kept re-appearing, uninvited, in his mind's eye. He needed to stay strong, to calm down. For both their sakes.

Mia stiffened beneath his hands and wiped at her eyes. "I need to go home. Pretend like everything is normal, like you said. Not let on that anything happened last night." She ran her hands through her hair and tugged on the knotted shirt to straighten it. "Then I'm going to find Tianna. And we're going to get out of here. All we have to do is make it through today, then we can meet back here and be safely off the island before anyone knows where we've gone. Right?" Her dark gaze speared into him, and he knew the logical, feisty Mia was back in control.

"Right," he replied.

"What did you have planned today?" she asked.

"Normally, I'd skipper a boat for Cruz Around Sailing Charters. But because it's low tourist season, they've got no bookings this weekend. Saturdays are also my day for stocking up on supplies, buying fresh fruit and veg from the markets. I might drop by the hatchery, to see how many eggs and hatchlings we've got." Logan didn't want to admit it, but one of the things he'd miss the most about leaving St. John was the wonderful volunteers and the feeling he was actually doing something good with his time, helping out with the turtle rescue. It also bugged him that there was a brazen gang of poachers out there, defying the Coast Guards and rescue volunteers alike, taking more turtles from the wild and selling them on the black market. He and Tom had made a pact that they would start an investigation of their own, start talking to locals to see if they could glean any rumors or gossip from the streets that might help the Coast Guard's investigation. That was never going to happen now. Logan sighed.

"Why don't you do both of those things, then?" Mia said. "Go about your normal Saturday routine. But keep your eyes peeled. And your ears open. See if anyone heard anything last night. Or saw anything. Cruz Bay is a small place. If anyone did see anything, it might already be doing the rounds in the rumor mill."

Mia was right. Logan could go also and talk to his mate, Paz. Being a delivery man, Paz heard all kinds of things from all kinds of people. He was usually one of the best sources of gossip on the island. Feeling more invigorated, he stood and gathered the plates up.

"What about you? Are you working tonight?" he asked, throwing her a searching look over his shoulder, before taking the ladder down into the galley.

"Unfortunately, yes. But fortunately, it's not at Harry's club tonight. It's on a yacht he's chartered for one of his bigwigs. Which is good, because it means we finish earlier than we would at the club. I should be back by midnight, at the latest."

"Good." Logan didn't let the surprise show on his face as he came back into the saloon. Midnight sounded late to him, but then again, his clubbing days were behind him. Being a boatie, he often went to bed early because he had to get up with the sun.

"Come on, I'll take you back to shore." He hadn't changed out of the clothes he'd been wearing yesterday, but it was too late now, and he didn't think anybody would notice.

Logan helped Mia into the dinghy, and they started back towards shore, leaving Captain sitting on top of the forward hatch staring after them.

"Mind the boat, buddy," he yelled back, and Mia giggled softly. The first real happy sound she'd made all day.

"Give me your cell," Mia demanded a few seconds later,

and he watched her punch her number into his phone. Then she did the same for hers, so now they had each other's phone numbers.

"Great idea," he said. "Keep me updated. And text me when you find Tianna."

"I will," she agreed.

"So, the plan is, as long as nothing changes, we'll meet by my dinghy at one a.m."

"It's a deal," she said with a smile, showing off those gorgeous, white teeth. "And I'll bring Tianna with me," she added fervently.

He hoped she wasn't deceiving herself, thinking she could talk her sister into joining them on the run. Tianna sounded like the kind of girl who didn't like to play by the rules; who thought she was capable of solving her own problems, when clearly, she wasn't. Logan hadn't met Tianna, but he wasn't sure he was going to like her. She sounded like a handful. Headstrong and rebellious. A recovered drug addict. And Logan knew recovered drug addicts had a high chance of relapsing. Not a good combination, if he was to take both girls on board a boat and flee for their lives.

"What if someone sees us? Together?" Mia asked, suddenly looking nervous as they got nearer to the little dock where Logan tied up his dinghy.

Logan cast his gaze over the area. It was still early, Cruz Bay only just waking up. Things would get busy once the first ferry of the day arrived. And if there was a cruise ship anchored out past the bay, they would start to bring in the tourists around nine. But until then, the place was almost deserted. A few people could be seen walking down North Shore Road, mainly locals out running early errands.

"I guess we don't have a choice," he said. They were both recognizable people, especially Mia with her cocoa skin and long, dark hair. They'd have to take a chance. Mia hung her head and pulled her hair down to cover her face. But Logan knew it'd do no good; if someone was looking for her, she was immediately identifiable.

He held his breath as he eased the dinghy into his normal spot, then moved past Mia to tie it off the front. No one was nearby. There were two people walking up The Strand in the distance, but neither of them turned their heads to look in their direction.

"Quick, take my hand. Up you go," he urged. "No one's looking."

"You be careful," Mia warned. "See you tonight."

"You too," he replied.

And then she was gone, walking quickly and deliberately around the corner of the nearest building. He watched her, allowing himself one final glance at those, long coffee-brown legs. They were spectacular. He could well imagine her kicking those legs up high in the air, taut and muscular, twirling them around as she danced for Harry's guests tonight. Boy, he'd like to be there, to experience it firsthand. It was like an aching need. He wanted to see that side of her. To make sure she really was as good as he imagined. Soon, he promised himself. Soon, he would watch her dance.

She'd had those legs curled around him last night, and it'd taken all his willpower to ignore the heat building in his stomach, then moving down to his groin.

Logan had to readjust his shorts, as they suddenly became uncomfortably tight. Daydreaming about Mia, and how she would look dancing for him wasn't going to get him anywhere. He had things to do. Information to dig up.

He was going to start with a visit to the hatchery, to check out the rescued eggs. That would take an hour or so, and then he was going to head over and knock on Tom's door. Tom should be up by then. Sometimes, Dan would have them work on a Saturday, usually to take the boat out and record and tag turtles. But Dan had said no work this weekend. He was heading off to Jost Van Dyke, an island in the British Virgin Islands, for a friend's wedding. Logan wanted to quiz Tom, see if anyone had been asking about him. Try and find out how the Ramirez brothers might have found him. If it was, indeed, the Ramirez brothers causing the trouble.

# CHAPTER SIX

Mia hustled through the back door and slammed it behind her. She was still puffing from her fast walk up the steep hill. Normally, she took it at a leisurely stroll, enjoying the sights and sounds of the nearby restaurant, renowned for its barbecue ribs, or calling out to the old West Indian couple, who lived two doors down and were always sitting on their rickety front porch.

"Is that you, Mia?" a woman's voice called out from the kitchen. A second later, Crystal poked her head around the doorway. "Where have you been, girl? We've been worried about you." Crystal was only a few years older than Mia, but she always acted like the mother hen of the house. It probably had a lot to do with the fact Crystal was actually a mother, with three young children all living with their dad back in Haiti, while she danced and made money to send back to them every week. A fact Harry did not know, and they all planned on keeping it that way.

"Have you been out all night?" Crystal narrowed her eyes at Mia, taking in yesterday's rumpled clothes. "You know what Harry thinks about that kind of thing."

Damn, she was hoping she hadn't been missed. And yes, she knew how Harry would view it. But he was never going to find out.

"What are you doing up so early?" she asked, deflecting Crystal's questions. Neither Crystal or Scarlett were ever normally up before ten or eleven in the morning, especially if they'd worked the night before, which they had. It was now only a few minutes before seven.

"Your harebrained sister. That's why we're up so early." Crystal put her hands on her hips. Uh-oh. This didn't sound good. Neither of Mia's flat-mates liked Tianna much. They thought she was lazy and selfish and relied on the kindness of her older sister way too much. But then, they didn't know the whole story. No one else did. Except Logan.

"She came banging and crashing in here at exactly five-thirty-nine a.m. And do you know why I know exactly what time it was she came home?"

Mia gave a rueful smile. She could guess what was coming next.

"Because that damn girl woke me up with all her noise. Scarlett too. But Scarlett managed to go back to sleep. Me, however..." She didn't need to finish the sentence.

"I'm sorry, Crystal. I promise it won't happen again." Mia couldn't remember how many times she'd made this promise. But funnily enough, if things went according to plan tonight, and they got out of Cruz Bay, then she might actually mean it this time.

Crystal and Scarlett were also dancers in Harry's club. Harry had brought them all over together from St. Thomas when he started up the club on St. John. The two women shared the flat in the downstairs section, they had two beds crammed into the single bedroom, while Mia slept upstairs in a separate little studio, with its own tiny kitchenette and bathroom. Accommodation was at a premium in Cruz Bay, and rent was high, especially after Hurricane Irma destroyed so many houses and buildings. That meant this was all they could afford. When Tianna stayed over, Mia shared her double bed with her. But she didn't mind, because if her sister was sleeping in her bed, at least she knew she was safe.

"I know it isn't your fault, honey." Crystal came and wrapped an arm around her shoulder. She was nearly as tall as Mia, and just as stunning, with slightly more luscious curves, and dark, almost ebony skin. Which the men all went wild for. But Crystal kept to dancing, like Mia, and politely but firmly rebuffed all offers for anything more. She loved her husband and her kids, and was only doing this because she had to. She kept telling Mia that she only needed a few more months and then she would go back to Haiti forever.

"She is your family. And we got to look after our family. But that girl could do with a good smacking, if you ask me."

Mia smiled, then gave the other woman a hug. "Thanks Crystal. I owe you. I owe you both." She itched to tell Crystal her secret. Tell her she might well be leaving the island and never coming back. But she and Logan had agreed to tell no one, so she kept her words to herself.

"Is Tianna upstairs, then?" Mia was already headed towards the cramped stairway leading up to her room.

"No. She banged around upstairs for about ten minutes, then she left again."

Mia's heart sank. "Oh, no."

"And before you ask," Crystal held up a hand, "I asked her where she was going as she hightailed it out of the door, but she didn't answer."

"Thanks," Mia said, her shoulders sagging. Then she went upstairs to her room. Crystal mumbled something as she went back into the small kitchen, and even though Mia couldn't hear the words, she got the sentiment.

It was so like Tianna to come charging in here, not caring if she woke anyone else up, not caring that Crystal and Scarlett had probably only been in bed for a couple of hours. What the hell had her sister been up to?

But as Mia got to the top step, she suddenly knew. The room was a mess. Piles of clothes lay on the floor, pulled out of the tiny closet at the end of the bed and all the kitchenette drawers were left open. It was hard to keep such a small place tidy, but Mia did try, and everything usually had its place. Except now everything was topsy-turvy; even the bedclothes had been pulled back. But Mia guessed this was more than just Tianna being messy. She'd been looking for something.

Her hand flew to her mouth. No, she couldn't have. Mia hurried to the corner cupboard in the kitchenette, got down on her hands and knees and peered in. All the plates and cups looked like they'd been pushed around and were all in a jumbled mess. Mia put her head right inside the cupboard and tipped her chin up. Reaching deep into the cabinet, she felt around in the upper part of the cupboard, then breathed a sigh of relief when her fingers found the tin box. There was a hidden shelf in the top of the cupboard. Mia had only discovered it after she'd got down to give the cupboard a good scrub when she'd first moved in. You could only see it if you put your head right inside. And Tianna hadn't been smart enough to take a really good look. Either that, or she was in too much of a hurry. Mia's fingers shook as she opened the box. Then she let out an audible sigh. The money was still there. It wasn't a lot, a little over two-thousand dollars of Mia's hard-earned tips. But it was enough for Tianna to get into quite a bit of trouble if she found it.

Mia had never outwardly told Tianna about the money, but Tianna was canny, she might've picked up on hints Mia may have dropped inadvertently. What would Tianna buy with that money? A million different scenarios flittered through Mia's head, and not many of them were good. She closed the tin with a bang. Tianna had better watch out. When Mia found her, she was going to… Well, she wasn't sure yet what she was going to do to her younger sister, but she had a lot of explaining to do. If only Mia could find her.

Mia dialed Tianna's number. It went straight to voicemail, and Mia swore under her breath, before leaving a short, sharp message. "Tianna, call me as soon as you get this, it's really important." Then she took a quick shower and changed into a fresh pair of white shorts and a T-shirt. She pulled her hair back into a ponytail, and was headed back downstairs inside ten minutes of first coming home. The mess would have to wait, she could clean it up later. She'd swapped her small shoulder bag for a backpack, which she slung over one arm. The tin with the money was safely nestled at the bottom. She wasn't letting that money out of her sight; it was going to help her escape from this island.

"I'm going to look for Tianna," Mia said, poking her head into the kitchen. Crystal sat at the small table, sipping a coffee and smoking. They weren't allowed to smoke inside, but Mia didn't comment. "If she comes back, will you make sure she stays here? Sit on her if you have to, and then give me a call. It's really important I talk to her."

"Sure thing, honey girl." Crystal waved her cigarette in Mia's direction. "I won't have no problem sitting on that little sister of yours if she comes back." Then the Haitian woman gave her a broad smile, showing off her white teeth, and Mia felt a surge of affection. She was going to miss these two women, they'd been like family to her over the past year. On impulse, she went and hugged Crystal.

"Thank you," Mia said.

"No problems," Crystal patted her arm. "Are you coming to work tonight?" There was a hint of concern in the other woman's voice, and Mia knew she needed to alleviate her fears. The last thing she wanted was anyone thinking she wasn't acting normally.

"Of course I am," she stated.

"Good, because me and Scarlett were worried when you didn't come home last night." The woman pursed her lips at Mia. "You're not up to something, are you?"

Mia feigned surprise. "What do you mean?"

"Well, we wondered if you'd met a man, or something, and that's why you didn't come home. It's not like you," Crystal cautioned.

"Crystal, you know I value my job too highly to break any of Harry's stupid rules." Mia waved a hand in the air, pretending nonchalance. The two friends didn't know why Mia was tied to Harry, didn't know that she was doing it for Tianna's sake. But they did know she was reliable and dependable, and did nothing to incur Harry's wrath.

But she needed to come up with an excuse to keep Crystal off the scent, and an idea flashed into her mind. "I volunteered to stay at the hatchery last night." The hatchery was a small, makeshift building over in the isolated little beach at Salmon Bay, where the turtle eggs were kept, safe from poachers and stored at just the right temperature so they would hatch. Turtle rescue volunteers would often go on egg hunts at night, to find and dig up any recent nests, then bring the eggs back to the hatchery. They did this to save the eggs from poachers. They had four or five different species of turtle eggs in there. Every night, a volunteer would stay at the hatchery, to make sure it wasn't raided by poachers, or even locals, who saw the eggs as a delicacy. Local poachers were usually after the eggs, or the meat of the turtle to feed their families or sell in local restaurants. But some of the meat ended up in Asian markets, and all the volunteers had been told about a massive seizure of products made from turtle shell in China a few months ago. Some Chinese people believed turtle products, such as bracelets, pens or even glasses brought them good luck. The haul had been valued at over a million dollars. Mia had also heard the story only last week of a young Hawksbill turtle head found floating near Trunk Bay by some snorkelers. It'd made her sick to her stomach that there were humans around who would exploit these beautiful creatures for money. Rumor had it, that the turtle products from the recent haul had come from the USVI area. That there was a large, well organized gang of poachers taking the turtles from the ocean right under their noses.

Mia had truthfully yet to volunteer at the hatchery, as she only had one night a week free, and that was precious to her. She often talked to Crystal and Scarlett about the rescue group, even trying to recruit them, but they always smiled warily and said *maybe later*.

"Oh, right. Are you sure that's safe?"

"I was really there to watch and see if any eggs hatch. It's more of a deterrent to the poachers." Most of the poachers were probably locals themselves, so the last thing they'd want is an eyewitness telling everyone their identity.

Images of what Mia had actually been doing last night rushed into her mind, and her next question blurted out before she really had time to think. "You girls didn't hear about anything...unusual going on last night?" What she really wanted to ask was had they heard any rumors about gunshots in the night, or a ruckus at the docks or a stranger lying facedown in the water. Harry's club was a goldmine for gossip and rumor. And she needed to know if anyone had seen anything.

"What kind of unusual things you talking about?"

"I'm worried about what Tianna got up to," Mia said hurriedly, as Crystal's shrewd eyes narrowed at her. "Just making sure she didn't cause any undue trouble, that's all."

"Nope. If your sister got up to anything untoward, then we didn't hear about it."

"That's good," Mia let her breath out in a whoosh. Just

because the dancing girls knew nothing, didn't mean she and Logan were totally in the clear. But it was a good start. "All right, I'm off to Todd's house. Like I said, call me if you see any sign of my wayward sister."

Crystal gave a mock salute as Mia turned to leave. "Will do. Good luck," she called after her.

Mia turned out the front door and looked up the hill. Todd's place was a ten-minute walk up the winding road. Todd was Tianna's no-good, on-again-off-again boyfriend. Mia hoped they were on again and that was where she'd scurried off to so early this morning. Normally, she didn't mind the walk, but she was in a hurry. The three girls shared a scooter, which was locked in the tiny shed at the end of the driveway, but they hardly ever used it. Only if one of them needed to go further afield than the outskirts of Cruz Bay, like over to Coral Bay on the other side of the island. More often than not, they would use the island's colorful, open-air taxis instead. Today called for a faster method of transport, so Mia turned and unlocked the shed. If Tianna wasn't at Todd's, there were a few other places Mia knew to look, and the scooter would make her trip faster. When she found Tianna, her sister would damn well sit on the back and behave herself, so Mia could take her home. Then they would organize tonight's escape plan.

* * *

Logan banged on the door, louder this time. A guilty flash of heat sliced through his stomach, but he ignored it. If Tom was still asleep, then it was time he got up. This was important.

Logan let his gaze drift out over the view, while he waited for Tom to answer the door. Rooftops of houses below led down to the azure water of Cruz Bay, which unfolded below. The boats moored in the bay were indistinct white splotches. Logan could just make out his catamaran, it's twin hulls standing out amongst the smaller boats. The bigger island of

St. Thomas lay on the horizon. It really was an amazing view from up here. He fanned himself with his hat, the day was already hot.

This villa up on Lind Point Road had to cost a bomb to rent. Even though Logan had never asked, it was obvious Tom came from money. His parents had to be loaded for Tom to afford this place. But Tom never once bragged, or lorded it over Logan or any of the students. He was one of the most down-to-earth, likable men Logan had ever met. He often held cookouts at his place, and invited all the project team members over. He was generous with his time, and was friends with almost everyone he met.

Tom had chosen to live on St. John, rather than on the bigger island of St. Thomas, where the main university campus was situated, with all the student dorms and other facilities. St. John had a small academic hub and research center in Market Place in Cruz Bay. Dan Brown, along with the other academics, all lived on the much larger island of St. Thomas, and used one of the research vessels to come over every morning.

Finally, the sound of footsteps echoed in the house and Logan turned back to face the door. It opened and Tom's sleepy face appeared in the darkened interior.

Tom's shaggy blond hair stuck up at all angles and he rubbed his eyes as he said, "Logan. Hi, man. This is a surprise."

"Hello, Tom. Sorry to wake you. Do you mind if I come in?"

"Sure." Tom opened the door wider, and beckoned for Logan to precede him down the long, cool corridor. This place had air conditioning. Proper air-con was a luxury on the island, where most of the locals relied on the sea breeze to cool their houses. His boat was like a coffin some nights, when it got airless and humid; on those nights he opted to sleep out on deck. But this villa was modern, with white tiles on the floor, and large picture widows to make the most of the view.

"I need a coffee. Can I make you one?"

"I'd kill for a coffee, thanks." Logan planted himself at the kitchen table and watched Tom shuffle around—still only half-awake—finding the coffee beans.

Logan wondered how to begin this conversation, but he was saved from finding the right words when Tom said, "So, what are you up to? You're up early for a Saturday."

Which wasn't technically true, because Logan was up early every day, but on the weekends, if he wasn't needed on the project, he would often laze around on his boat and not come to shore until mid-morning. If only Tom knew exactly what Logan *had* been up to last night.

"How did your date with Mia go?" Tom waggled an eyebrow at Logan.

Shit, he'd been so preoccupied with the man with the gun, he'd forgotten Tom knew he and Mia had been out.

"Yeah, it went well. She's lovely. Then she went home, and I went back to my boat. I don't think I'll ask her out again," Logan said briskly. He needed to change the subject, and get to the real reason he was here. "But I was actually up at the hatchery this morning. Just wanted to see if any more eggs came in last night." There had been no scheduled egg hunts, but sometimes a well-meaning local—one who didn't condone the practice of eating turtle eggs—would bring in a haul if they happened to see a turtle come up to lay.

But that wasn't what Logan wanted to talk to Tom about. He continued. "And while I was there, you know Patrice, the French Master's student?" When Tom nodded, Logan proceeded. "Well, he mentioned something about a great photo of me he'd seen on the UVI Facebook page." Logan tried to keep the accusation out of his voice but failed miserably. Tom had his back to Logan, still fiddling with the coffee machine, but his spine suddenly stiffened.

"You wouldn't have posted a photo of me, by any chance? After I specifically asked you not to?" There was a really good reason Logan was no longer on Facebook. He'd shut his account down the day he left Mexico. It was one less way the Ramirezes could track him. But without that connection, it was like he was flying blind. He never knew if anyone else had posted something about him.

Tom turned around, remorse written all over his handsome face. "Yeah, I did. Sorry, man. But it got so many likes and comments, that—"

Logan cut him off. "And you listed my name in the post?" he demanded.

Tom raised his hands in the air in a show of humility. "I wasn't thinking, you know. But it was such a great photo, of you with that Leatherback turtle right up on the sand…" The rest of Tom's words were lost in a haze of numbness that descended over Logan.

He interrupted Tom's apology to ask sharply, "How long ago? When did you post this photo?"

"Well, when did we tag that Leatherback? Was it a little over a week ago? Something like that."

Which would've made the timing about right. If the Ramirez brothers were searching for him, it would've only taken a day or so for them to find the post, and then track down where in the Caribbean he was. The guy with the gun had been on St. John for three days. Probably scoping out the place, tracking Logan's movements, deciding on the best time to strike. But Logan had put a dent in the guy's plan, by showing up with Mia by his side. Had the guy reported back to Leonardo and Diego? Told them he was bringing Logan in, to expect him soon? How had he planned on getting Logan off the island? He couldn't very well have hoped to smuggle him on the ferry, not at gunpoint, it would've been too obvious.

There were too many questions and not enough answers.

"I really wish you hadn't," Logan said wearily, then stood.

"You never said why you didn't want your photo up there. I hope I didn't get you in any sort of trouble?" Tom's face was lit up with worry. Of course, Tom couldn't have realized exactly how much trouble he'd landed Logan in. It wasn't his fault. Not really. Logan should never have taken the job in the first place. Never have put himself in a situation where he needed to use his real name. But Dan had been so keen for Logan to work with them. And the work visa required a name and a passport.

Logan loved his job. It made him feel legitimate again, that he was worth something, and he was doing it to make a difference in the world—at least, to the Hawksbill Turtle. It'd been stupid and vain of him. He'd put his misgivings on the backburner, telling himself that Leonardo and Diego would have given up looking for him. And now he was paying the price.

"Thanks, Tom," Logan said, dispirited. "I have to get going." He made his way toward the front door.

"But you haven't even had a coffee, yet." Tom followed behind, desperation in his voice.

"It's okay, I'll grab one back in town." He walked toward the door.

"Look, man. I'm really sorry." Tom's hand landed on his shoulder.

Logan turned around slowly. The guy meant well. He hadn't known, and Logan didn't blame him.

"No probs, Tom. I might see you at the Gekko later on tonight, huh?" The bar was Logan's local haunt; he and Paz, and Paz's mate Azacca could often be found there, enjoying a Leatherback Beer, brewed locally. He wouldn't be there, though, and this might be the last time he saw Tom. He reached out a hand. Tom shook it, a dazed look in his eyes. Poor guy, it was probably all too much for him this early in the morning.

"See you soon," Logan said, and turned on his heel to stride back down the driveway. He was more determined than ever that they got out of here tonight. It was too dangerous to stay any longer.

Logan strode down Lind Point Road, the sun beating hot and heavy on his back. He took his trusty sailing hat out of his pocket and slapped it on his head. It wasn't the most flattering hat, but it kept the sun off, and the low brim protected his eyes from the glare. It was warm already, the humidity high, and sweat formed on his brow in seconds. He let his gaze take in the view below, but he wasn't really in the mood to appreciate it. Cruz bay was idyllic, with the crystalline-blue ocean, perfect beaches and amazing wildlife, it was no wonder the tourists flocked here. It'd taken a while to recover from the destruction of the hurricanes nearly two years ago, but a lot of the infrastructure had been rebuilt or replaced, and the vegetation was now back, lush and verdant as ever.

It was one of those rare occasions when Logan wished he had a car. Normally, he could get around the island either by walking, catching one of the brightly painted, open-air taxis, or hitching a lift with a friendly local. But today, he wanted to get back to town and finish running his errands.

The walk back down the road from Tom's place only took a few minutes, and soon he could see the break in the jungle that heralded Centerline Road dead ahead. A bus ran on the hour between Coral Bay on the other side of the island and Cruz Bay and there was a bus stop a hundred meters from the corner. If he hurried, he should get there before the next bus was due, otherwise he would have to walk the fifteen minutes or so it would take to get back to town.

At first, he was so busy looking up the winding road, to see if the bus was on its way, he didn't notice the black SUV parked off the road, right on the corner. Then, a guy standing next to the passenger door said something to him.

"Sorry," Logan apologized. "What did you say?"

"Is this Lind Point Road?" the guy asked, pointing back up the way Logan had just come. "This damn island has no damn signposts." The man was big, broad across the shoulders, with thick dark hair and a heavy brow. And ugly. A large scar ran across his chin, dragging one corner of his mouth down. But that wasn't all. His face was lumpy and square reminding Logan of a bulldog. The guy must be sweltering in this heat, in his long black pants and sports jacket over his T-shirt.

"Yeah, yeah, it is," Logan replied with a wary smile, waving his hand in the general direction. Something about this guy didn't feel right. Were they tourists who'd got lost on their way up the mountain? "The Hibiscus Villas are up on the right about three hundred meters. Are you booked to stay with them?"

"We're not here for a holiday," the man said, with a sneer of contempt, which made the hairs on the back of Logan's neck stand up. The man got back in the car and slammed the door.

Definitely not tourists, then. Logan tried to get a look at the guy behind the wheel as he wound his window up and pulled the large car back onto the road. He only caught a brief glimpse, but it tugged at something in the back of his mind. The sound of the bus grinding its gears as it negotiated a sharp turn in the road above caught Logan's attention and he dropped the thought as he sprinted down the hill, arriving at the bus stop just in time.

It wasn't until he settled himself in a seat on the bus, and was staring at the jungle flashing past the window he finally worked out what had been bothering him about the man behind the wheel of the SUV. He was dressed identically to the man in the passenger seat. Had the same heavy-jawed appearance, the same dark set to his features. What were two men who looked more like night-club bouncers than tourists doing out on Lind Point Road? He pondered the question all the way back to town.

# CHAPTER SEVEN

Mia turned off the scooter and sat astride it in the shade of a turpentine tree, letting the cool sea breeze tickle her face. She glanced up and read the sign across the doorway of the restaurant on the opposite side of the road. Tony's Café and Bar. One look told her this place was a dive. But this was her last chance of finding Tianna. If her sister wasn't here, then Mia had run out of places to look.

It was now late afternoon and she needed to go home to get ready for work soon. She was hot, hungry, and thirsty after a fruitless day's searching for her wayward sister and her temper was building with each minute Tianna remained out of touch. Mia couldn't remember the number of times she'd phoned that girl, but the little pain in the ass had obviously been avoiding her calls. Either that, or she'd run out of minutes.

Her mind wandered back to the start of her unproductive search, to the boyfriend's house. Mia snorted at the thought of Todd. He was a white boy, had lived on the island for the past five years, and was a no-hoper from way back. Why did her sister insist on hooking up with the worst bad-boy she could find?

Todd was passed out on his couch when she knocked on

the door—probably from smoking too much weed. When no one answered the door, she went in anyway and found the place in a complete shambles. It'd turned her stomach just to look at the mess. It took her a good couple of minutes to wake him up, finally shaking him so hard she heard his teeth rattle. It was already evident Tianna wasn't there, but she wanted to ask him if he knew where she was.

At first, he hadn't wanted to talk, was belligerent and downright rude. Until she reminded him of the fact she worked for Harry, then he reluctantly told her Tianna had spent the night with him. But very early this morning, she'd asked him for money. Said she was going to the local markets to buy some fresh fruit and veg, because his place was bare. And that she'd be back to make him lunch. Mia didn't add that she doubted very much Tianna would be back. She wasn't the cooking type, and had never offered to buy food when she was living with Mia.

But Mia went to the market anyway, searching the rickety road-side stalls high and low, on the off-chance Tianna had actually done what she said she would. But none of the stallholders had seen her.

Mia sat on her scooter in the dirt road outside the markets, wondering what her next move would be. Tianna had a girlfriend over in Coral Bay she visited regularly. The only problem was, Coral Bay was on the other side of the island. Tianna usually caught one of the open-air taxis over. Mia clenched her teeth and started the scooter, but the ride over the twisting, mountainous Central Bay Road had put Mia on edge. She'd been hot and bothered when she arrived, and it hadn't helped her mood when Paulette told her she hadn't seen Tianna in days.

Mia had been about to stomp away in a fit of temper, thinking it'd all been a wasted trip, when Paulette called her back. She said Tianna had been boasting, was excited to be starting a new job. At Tony's Café and Bar.

So back to Cruz Bay Mia trundled on her scooter.

Mia had to stop the urge to cross her fingers, in the vain hope Tianna was actually inside this place. There was only one way to find out, so Mia got off the scooter and crossed the busy road. Evening was draping her cool fingers around the township of Cruz Bay, taking the heat of the day away. Mia drew in the familiar smell of salty air, mixed with the fumes of the taxis that puttered up and down the street. A group of West-Indian women walked down the road towards her, their brightly patterned dresses clashing with the equally bright colors in the shop windows. Goods such as, hibiscus-flowered fabrics, turtle canvas painting, mixed with spices and handwoven baskets overflowed in the small shops huddled tougher. It was a bustling street, a few tourists returning from their shopping spree or out on the hunt for somewhere to eat, as well as locals stopping for a chat at the street corner, or hurrying home to their families. Bicycles and scooters mingled with SUVs and taxis, all jockeying for a place on the road.

She stopped in the open doorway of the café, to allow her eyes to adjust to the dim interior. Surprisingly, the restaurant was over half full. It had to be the beginning of the Saturday evening rush.

And there was Tianna, flitting around as if she didn't have a care in the world. She was wearing some outrageous red-and-white-checked uniform that made her look like a waitress straight out of some vintage diner on a New York street corner. Which is probably what the owner was going for, now that Mia got a look around the place. It was full of tacky American souvenirs. As Mia watched the unaffected way her sister bounced around, so full of energy and lighthearted banter, her anger began to rise. She was outwardly flirting with a couple of the customers as she breezed past them. How dare her sister lead her on a merry chase all around the island—Mia had been worried sick about her—to then be here, safe and sound and completely unworried. To her credit, Tianna knew nothing about Mia's anguish, or her terrifying night, but Mia's rising anger was helping her overlook that fact.

Mia stood in the middle of the restaurant like a black thundercloud until Tianna finally noticed her.

"Hi, sis." Tianna waved a plate in Mia's face on her way to the service door at the back of the room. "Back in a sec." Much to Mia's disgust, Tianna actually disappeared through the double doors, leaving her standing there while some of the other patrons stared openly at her.

She glared at the doors for a few seconds more, before making her decision. Tianna needed to take her seriously. She wasn't here for the sake of her own health. Mia dived through the doors and into the kitchen area.

"Hey, no customers allowed," a loud voice bellowed at her. But Mia ignored the red-faced cook yelling at her from behind a large burner. She searched for her sister, finally catching sight of a flash of red out the back. Tianna was depositing her pile of plates on a large shelf.

"Tianna, I need to talk to you. Now." Mia gave her sister *the look*. The one that said she wasn't going to take no for an answer.

"What are you doing back here?" Tianna hissed at her. "Do you want me to lose my job?"

Mia stood her ground and stared at her younger sister, until she finally said, "Fine, come out the back door." She dragged Tianna by the shirt out into an alleyway.

Mia didn't wait for Tianna to speak. "Get your things, we're leaving."

"What?" Tianna's face was a picture of confusion. But Mia didn't have time to explain things in vivid detail to her little sister. For once, she just wanted her to do what she was told.

"We need to get off the island. Now! We're both in danger if we don't. I'll explain everything to you later."

"What the hell are you talking about? I'm not leaving my new job. And I'm certainly not leaving this island. I like it here. I have a life here. A boyfriend." Tianna's face had gone from confusion to growing rage.

And Mia's rage grew in the face of her sister's pique. "Don't argue with me, Tianna. You're coming with me. End of story. Now go and get your things." Even as she said these words, Mia knew she'd probably stepped over the boundary of good sisterly behavior. But she didn't have time to stand here and argue with her sister. They had to leave, go home and pack, then Mia had to get to work.

Tianna stood back, hands on hips and stared Mia down. "I'm not going. And you can't make me." Tianna was yelling now. A tirade of words spilled out of her mouth as she shouted, more and more hurtful things. Mia took a step back, shocked by her sister's vehemence. She cast a quick glance around to make sure no one else could hear them, wondering if Tianna's yelling would bring an unwanted audience.

Then the back door swung open, and an obese man wearing chefs' whites poked his head out. "What the fuck's going on out here? I've got customers up to my eyeballs, and you're out here, taking a break? Tianna, get your ass back inside right now. Otherwise, you can stay out here and not bother ever coming back." Just as suddenly as he appeared, the fat man withdrew back into the kitchen.

"See what I mean?" Tianna shrieked. "God, I hope you and your bullshit haven't just cost me the first good job I've had in years." With that, Tianna turned her back on Mia and vanished inside, leaving her staring in disbelief at what'd just happened.

What was she going to do now? Her hands were shaking,

and she had to go and sit down on an upturned barrel before her legs gave way. Never in her wildest dreams had she imagined her conversation with Tianna would go that badly awry. And she hadn't even mentioned the mess in the apartment, a sign that Tianna had been searching for the tin of money. Mia carefully held that accusation back, not wanting to add to the tension. But Jesus, she was so mad she could spit. How dare her sister act so high and mighty. Anger got the better of her and she stood up and kicked the barrel. She could storm back in there and cause a scene. Even get Tianna sacked, then at least she would have to leave. But there was no way Tianna would listen to her now, especially if she did that.

No, she'd lost Tianna. At least for tonight. She'd have to find another way to reason with her. But that wouldn't happen until tomorrow, now. And they needed to leave tonight. And she needed to turn up to work, otherwise Harry would be on her case. She needed to keep Harry onside, now more than ever, especially if she couldn't leave the island straight away.

Out of habit, she jangled the silver bracelet gently on her wrist. The feel of it calmed her a little. Everything would be okay. Tianna would come around. The bracelet was her reminder, her promise she would take her sister home again.

Mia wandered down the grungy alleyway, hoping it would lead her out to the road, not daring to go back through the restaurant. Her mind was lost in other thoughts as she emerged out of the alley and onto the dim street—dusk had descended while she was arguing with Tianna. She swung her gaze up and down the street, trying to get her bearings. Yes, there was her little red scooter, parked across the road underneath the big turpentine tree. A taxi blared its horn as she went to cross the street and she stepped back in shock. *Get your head back in the game.* She drew in a deep breath and pushed everything that'd just happened to the back of her mind.

There was a gap in the traffic and Mia dashed across, arriving at her scooter a little out of breath. She swung a leg through the footwell and settled her butt on the seat.

Out of the corner of her eye, she saw a man step forward, coming from the shadow of the tree. He must've been leaning against the large trunk, just outside of the glow cast by the streetlight. Her gut clenched. She snapped her head around, to get a better look at him, but the guy kept back, out of the glare, still in the shadows.

"I've got a message for you."

Mia's fingers gripped the handlebars so tightly her knuckles hurt. Oh, God! Who was this man? Did he have a gun? Like the one from last night? Was he going to abduct her from the street, in front of all these people? Her heart was beating a thousand miles a minute. Should she start the scooter? Would she be able to outrun him on a stupid little bike?

But a part of her wanted to hear what he had to say. It might be vitally important. He took another step toward her and she tensed, still undecided. She remembered hearing that you needed to act unafraid, stare a mugger down so he didn't think you were an easy target.

"What is it?" she asked, feigning nonchalance. She even managed to put a smirk on her face. But it was the wrong thing to do, because, quick as a snake, the man had her by the throat. His hand was so tight she couldn't even scream.

"Don't fuck with me, little lady," he snarled in her face. "The message is, you need to stay away from that turtle-rescue guy. The good-looking one. Got it?"

She was too petrified to even answer. But just as quickly as he'd grabbed her, he let go again. Then he was gone, walking away as if nothing had happened.

Her own hands flew to her throat as she dragged in a few ragged breaths. It'd all happened so quickly. No one else in the street seemed to have noticed. It took a second for the man's menacing words to sink in. He was warning her to stay away from Logan. But why? Mia chanced another glance back, to see if she could identify the guy. Was he familiar? It was hard to tell in the dim light. Then the man turned around and strode off down the street, his back to her. Was it one of Harry's guys? Had he seen her out with him last night? Did Harry know she was involved in a murder? Her head swirled with so many questions she felt giddy.

Then she remembered where she was, and quickly started the scooter, taking off down the road. Back to her home. But not necessarily back to safety. Because now she didn't know where it was safe anymore.

* * *

It was Captain that first alerted Logan to someone outside the boat. Logan was in the galley, storing all the supplies he'd bought in town that afternoon. There were some fresh fruit and vegetables from the Starfish Market, but they wouldn't last long. It was mainly tins of food; beans, soup, some tinned meat, and cat food. Captain lived most of the time off his dry kibble, but every now and then Logan gave him a little taste of luxury. As if the cat knew what was in the tins, he lay at the top of the ladder looking down, paws folded neatly underneath, watching with that half-bored, half-interested expression only cats can perfect, while Logan stacked the tins in one of the small cupboards. If he and Mia—and possibly Tianna—were going to take to the seas to outrun the Ramirez brothers, they'd need food for at least a few weeks, so they wouldn't have to take the risk of going into a harbor. Logan would take the catamaran into the dock soon and refill his water tanks. The boat was fitted with a small desalinization plant, which would see him through many days out at sea. It used reverse osmosis to produce clean drinking water, and it had been another surprise discovery when he'd bought the boat. The previous owner must've used this catamaran for some serious cruising to have bought one of these. But it was always better to fill up when he could.

Logan's mind had been spinning while he worked over everything he still needed to do this afternoon. To ready the boat for what might be a long-term sail, before he went back in to pick Mia up tonight. He should really have been paying more attention, but he'd talked himself into thinking that the man they'd killed might be the only one who really knew where they were. If the man had indeed been a bounty hunter, then perhaps he hadn't had time to relay his find to his boss, whoever that was. His mind also kept replaying the incident with the two men and the SUV. Why they were niggling him, he couldn't be sure. Were they connected to the man that now lay at the bottom of the ocean? It all added up to the fact they needed to get out of town tonight.

Captain suddenly sat up, his ears twitching. Then he shot off like the devil had his tail, straight out through the saloon and into the cockpit. Logan froze and strained his ears to listen. A voice drifted to him through the wooden sides of the hull.

Oh, shit. Someone was outside. Logan cursed his own lack of vigilance. He looked around for something he could use as a weapon. Anything. At last he grabbed a short-bladed kitchen knife and held it behind his back, climbing the ladder into the saloon. He peered out of the side windows, but could see nothing. The sun was low on the horizon, turning the calm waters to burnished gold. *Leopard's* mooring was on the outer reaches of the bay, so he was one of the last boats before the bay opened up to the ocean. Moorings were at a premium here in Cruz Bay, and he was lucky to have got this one. The closest moored boat to his was a couple hundred meters away, and he could see it bobbing lightly on the waves. The people who owned it generally only sailed on weekends, but there was no one aboard today. His gaze slid to the other boats nearby, but they were all equally quiet and uninhabited.

Logan heard the voice again; it was unmistakably female. The sound was coming from the back of his boat, which meant they must be in a small dinghy. He stepped up to the cabin doorway and looked aft. All he could see from this vantage point was a series of heads bobbing just below the edge of the stern. There was more than one person. Who the hell were they? And why were they trying to get onto his boat?

Was it Mia and her sister, come early? But then Mia would've texted to let him know things had changed. Not many people knew he lived out here on his boat. Perhaps it was Tom, coming to apologize for this morning. But Tom didn't own a dinghy, so unless he'd borrowed one, it was unlikely to be him.

There was only one thing to do. He couldn't let them come aboard. If they meant him harm, then he needed to meet them head on. He stood a better chance if they stayed in a small dinghy.

What if they had a weapon? A gun?

He looked at the small knife in his hand. Fat lot of good that would do. But he kept it tucked behind his back anyway.

"Who's there?" he said loudly. He leaped nimbly over the step into the cockpit, using the back stays to steady himself, and he strode out onto the left-hand hull where he could see the tops of their heads; he could count four in total now he was closer.

"Stay where you are. You don't have my permission to come aboard." Logan hoped his voice sounded loud and authoritative enough to keep the strangers where they were.

"Logan? Is that you?"

Logan stopped in his tracks. He recognized that voice. Suddenly a face popped up over the edge, as the person stood up in the dinghy.

"Sierra?" Was it really her? Was it really his sister? His mind couldn't put all the pieces together. It'd been four years since he'd last seen her. But it was definitely her, there was no doubt.

A loud, male voice said, "Sit down, Sierra, or you'll tip us all into the sea."

But she didn't do as she was bid, instead, she kept staring at him. "You come and help us on board, right now," she commanded. "What the hell do you mean by, *you don't have permission to come aboard*? I'll give you permission. Do you know what we've been through to get here? To find you. You bloody well get down here and give me your hand."

Yep, it was Sierra, all right. His body reacted as if on autopilot, doing as his sister commanded, while his mind whirled with possibilities. What in blazes was his sister doing here? And who did she have with her? Much as he was happy to see her, this was one complication he really didn't need in his life at the moment.

As he stared down into the tiny dinghy clinging alongside, he got his second shock of the day. "Keira? Is that you?" Her hair was shorter than he remembered, but it was definitely her. Both his sisters were here? To see him?

An involuntary groan left his lips.

Logan's gaze settled on the two other people crammed into the small boat. Two large, muscular-looking men. Who were both staring back at him; weighing him up, just like he was assessing them.

Sierra's hand landed in his and he was momentarily distracted from the other men as he helped her up onto his boat. As soon as her feet hit the deck, she enfolded him in an unexpected bear hug. Sierra wasn't normally one for grand shows of affection. She was usually reserved and cool. People might see her as a bit aloof, but Logan knew better. She was just a deep thinker and liked to consider her actions first.

"Thank God we found you," she said into his ear, not letting him go, even when he tried to pull back. "We were so worried."

Those small flashes of self-reproach he'd felt every time he thought about his family over the past two years, and how he hadn't contacted them, paled into insignificance with the huge surge of guilt that threatened to knock him over at her words.

"I'm sorry." The words seemed woefully inadequate.

"As you should be," she said, finally letting him go and holding him at arm's length so she could study him. "At least you look okay. Actually, you look bloody fantastic. This Caribbean lifestyle seems to suit you. Look at your tan," she said admiringly. Then her eyes caught on the knife in his other hand and she raised her eyebrows. But thankfully, she said nothing. Sierra hadn't changed, either. She was still tall and athletic, slim, with her long hair pulled back into a ponytail. She was wearing uncharacteristic shorts and a tank top, showing off her pale, but tanned, arms and legs. Normally she lived in leggings and overly large sweaters, the cooler weather on Kangaroo Island much better for those kinds of clothing.

Sierra was interrupted by Keira before she could say any more. "Hello? Are you just going to leave the rest of us sitting down here like pumpkins, or can we come up too?"

Logan pointed Sierra toward the cockpit, and then leaned down to give Keira his hand.

Keira was a lot more like Logan in personality. She always wore her heart on her sleeve, and she squealed in delight as Logan pulled her up, also enfolding him in a big bear-hug, but with lots more wild enthusiasm. Keira had the same dark hair as Sierra and similar facial features—you could tell they were sisters—but she was curvier and Logan enjoyed her softer, warmer hug.

"It's so good to see you again," she squealed into his ear. "We've missed you." A sudden flicker of something darker flashed across her expressive face as she pulled back from him. "And I'm sorry." Her lips pursed in a moue of despair. "I've been really bad at staying in touch, too. So, don't you let Sierra say it's all your fault."

What was she talking about?

He didn't have time to wonder, however, because one of the men in the boat said, "Where can I tie up?" Logan had almost forgotten about the other two, he'd been so lost in wonder that his two sisters were here. On his boat. In the Caribbean.

"Sorry." He pointed Keira towards where Sierra was standing in the cockpit and leaned down to take the rope from the guy. The man stood up and the boat rocked dangerously, while the other guy hung on for dear life.

"Holy crap, Dalton. Will you just get off, before we both end up in the drink?"

The man he'd called Dalton obviously wasn't good with boats, but he managed to grab hold of the small ladder off the end of the catamaran and haul himself up onto the deck.

"Hi. I'm Dalton. Glad to finally meet you." The guy held out his hand, and Logan shook it. He had an air of resolve about him. He didn't miss the knife in Logan's hand, either, but also opted not to mention it, for which Logan was grateful. Logan detected a clear American twang in this man's speech. Squared shoulders and clean-cut. This man could well be dangerous if he had a mind to be. He wanted to ask who the hell he thought he was, intruding on his boat, bringing his two sisters out here? But it would have to wait, as the other man was now also clambering up the ladder.

"Hello. I'm Reed." The second man reached out and shook his hand. Logan wasn't short, just shy of six foot, but he'd had to look up to meet both of these men's eyes. This guy had a New Zealand accent, if he wasn't mistaken, and also had a bearing about him that reminded Logan of a solider. Or a cop. His gaze was intense, even as he shook Logan's hand with a smile, and Logan felt like he was being silently probed. With a sudden flash, the image of the dead man's face appeared behind his eyes, and guilt stabbed through his gut. This guy couldn't possibly know what he'd done. So why did he feel like this man was seeing straight through to his guilty secrets?

"Come over to the cockpit." He beckoned Reed to follow him. "Can I get you guys a drink? A beer perhaps?" Logan could definitely do with a beer. Actually, he longed to pull out that bottle of rum from last night, but knew it wouldn't look good.

"Yes, please," Sierra and Reed both said simultaneously. Then they smiled at each other and Logan knew. They were a couple. Oh, wow. His sister had found herself a man. Which was great news, especially because of what happened to her. Of how long she'd spent on her own since the accident. But what was going on with Keira and Dalton? Last he'd heard, Keira was married to a man called John. So, where was he? Had they divorced? Because it seemed like they were probably a couple, too. He had lots of questions.

"Four beers coming up," he said. It was lucky he'd thought to buy a carton of Leatherback Beer just this afternoon, while he was stocking up on supplies, otherwise he would've only been able to offer them water. Once down in the galley, he quickly put the knife away, hoping they thought he'd been in the middle of cutting something up and not decided he'd been carrying it as a weapon.

When Logan re-emerged, he found Keira on her knees,

stroking Captain's head. The cat was loving the attention.

"Who's this?" she asked.

"That's Captain. He came with the boat when I bought it."

"I can't believe it. You own a boat and a cat?" Sierra couldn't keep the disbelief off her face. Logan leaned in the doorway, watching them warily. There was just enough room for them all to sit in the cockpit, along the bench seats at the back.

Dalton was the taller of the other two, but only by a touch. His shoulder-length hair was held back in a ponytail, and his angular face suggested he may have Chinese heritage. Reed also had olive skin, but his dark hair was kept shorter. Both men wore chino shorts and runners, and both men's biceps bulged beneath their T-shirts.

Logan's mind was spinning. What did he tell them? How was he going to explain everything? He still needed to go and pick Mia up at the dock; what was he going to tell her? This was going to throw their plans into chaos, unless he could somehow quickly get rid of them. Which Logan knew wasn't going to happen. His sisters weren't that easily fobbed off. And he was also feeling slightly intimidated. The two men with his sisters were obviously strong, determined, and not to be messed with. And Logan had a secret to hide.

He didn't want his sisters involved. All he wanted was to get out of here, and forget it'd all happened. Start a new life over again, with Mia.

"So, tell us, little brother, what have you been up to lately?"

Logan sucked in a fortifying breath. Here came the interrogation.

"Last time we spoke to you, you were in Mexico, getting all hot and heavy with a woman called Sofia. I thought she was the love of your life. That you were going to marry her."

Four pairs of eyes turned toward him. What in hell was he

going to say?

# CHAPTER EIGHT

"Is that you?" the voice said out of the darkness.

Mia startled, and then moved forward with relief at the whispered question. She'd heard the slight swish of oars in the water, but it was so dark, she wasn't sure it was Logan until he called out. She was beginning to worry; he was ten minutes late, and fear had crept its cold fingers up her spine when he hadn't showed. Images of men with guns storming his boat invaded her mind. But he was here now, and Mia was so grateful she almost wanted to sob with relief. Logan let the dinghy bump gently against the dock, using one hand to steady it. With the other he reached up for her. "Where's Tianna?" he asked, as she took the two steps down the ladder and hopped into the small boat.

The lump Mia had been trying to force down her throat all night threatened to block her windpipe completely.

"She said she won't come with us." It hurt her to say the words, and even though Mia couldn't see Logan's facial expression well in the dim light of the docks, she could hear his sharp intake of breath. He was as shocked as she'd been when Tianna refused.

"Come out to the boat with me. We can talk," Logan said, laying a steadying hand on her arm.

"I'm not leaving without her," Mia's tone became belligerent as she moved back. There was no way she was letting him talk her into that. She wouldn't leave her little sister. Not to Harry's tender mercies.

"That's not what I meant," he soothed. "I won't leave without her, either. But we need to figure out what this all means. I've got food on the boat. Come and have something to eat, and a beer."

That sounded good. She was starving. Her whole day had been a whirlwind, dashing from one place to the next, looking for her sister. She'd hardly had time to think, let alone eat. And when she wasn't able to convince Tianna to leave, it'd been almost like a physical blow. Added to that shock was the sense of foreboding the man hiding behind the tree had left her with. The one who'd warned her to stay away from Logan. But she hadn't had time to dwell on it, because she'd rushed home to change, and worked from eight till eleven without a break. She was exhausted. Both physically and emotionally. She had no idea what to do next.

"Okay." Her voice sounded small, even to her own ears, as she placed her bottom on the front seat, dropping her small backpack on the floor in front of her.

Logan said, "I've got some interesting news for you, as well." Then he started to row, and Mia knew he was keeping a low profile and not using the outboard until he got farther out.

Mia turned to look at him but couldn't raise much curiosity at his words. She was too lost in her own world of pain. They didn't speak on the short journey out to the catamaran, and she sat, shoulders hunched, facing the front. She felt dispirited and hopeless. Not at all like the eager, hopeful woman she'd been this morning. After she got home from dancing, it'd been all she could do to throw a couple of pieces of clothing in her backpack—making sure the money tin was still safely resting at the bottom. She slipped on the same white shorts she'd worn all day, with a light, linen button-up shirt, which she knotted at the waist.

Logan helped her up on deck and led her into the saloon. Captain was waiting for them, and gave her a welcoming meow. She leaned down to give the tortoiseshell a pat, then squeezed around the bench seat behind the table. He leapt straight into her lap and began purring. His warm weight was a comfort for Mia, and she let him stay.

"I made nachos," Logan said. "Extra spicy. Do you want a beer?"

"God, yes," Mia replied.

Two plates landed on the table, and a second later, two beers. Logan squeezed in beside her, giving her a sheepish grin. "I already ate, but a midnight snack never hurt anyone." He picked up his beer and clinked it against hers.

"I'm not sure what we have to celebrate," Mia said with a frown.

"How about still being alive?" He gave her that same cheeky smile she'd loved so much on the beach with the turtle yesterday...was it only yesterday that'd all happened?

After a second, she said, "Why not? It's about the only thing we can celebrate in all this mess."

They clinked bottles again and Mia tucked into her nachos. They were delicious and still warm. Logan must've kept the bean mixture heating in the tiny oven while he came to pick her up.

"So, tell me about Tianna," he asked gently, his dark eyes searching her face.

Maybe it was the food and the beer, but Mia was finally coming back to herself, and her distress at Tianna's words was turning to anger at her little sister. Tianna was being selfish and inconsiderate, and Mia was beginning to agree with Crystal, perhaps she needed a good smack on the bottom to bring her back to her senses. After all, she was behaving like a child, so perhaps she should treat her like a child.

Mia stuffed one more corn chip in her mouth and took a swig of beer, before she turned to face Logan. "It took me most of the day to track that girl down. I went to Todd's first —that's her on-again, off-again boyfriend." Logan didn't need to hear the finer details of what she thought about that man. "Anyway, long story short, she wasn't there. He gave me a tip that she was over at the local food markets. But of course, she wasn't there, either." Mia stopped her monologue to pop some more food in her mouth.

"Then I drove over to Coral Bay—Tianna has a good friend over there, but she said she hadn't been at her house for days."

"Right," Logan said. "It sounds like you had quite a day." It was a subtle hint to get to the point, so Mia collected her thoughts. She didn't want Logan to form an even lower opinion of her sister than he probably already had, but she didn't know how to word this next bit.

"The friend heard Tianna was starting a new job at a restaurant back in Cruz Bay. Which is where I eventually found her, waiting on tables, dashing around as if she didn't have a care in the world." Mia waved her hand in the air, to punctuate just how bouncy Tianna had been. Captain lifted his head at the rude jiggling that threatened to interrupt his snooze.

"Sorry," she apologized and put a hand on the cat's head. But she was getting angrier by the second at Tianna's reaction to her news.

"I told her we needed to get off the island. Tonight. I told her we were both in mortal danger. And do you know what she did? The pigheaded little... Well, she laughed in my face. Said she didn't believe me. I was making it up just to get her away from the island. That I was jealous because she'd finally found a *proper* job." Mia used her fingers to paint quote marks in the air. "She didn't say it, but she was insinuating that at least she wasn't dancing. Like I'm selling my soul or something." Thinking back on it, perhaps Mia hadn't handled the situation as well as she could have. After all, she'd demanded Tianna leave her job and come with her straight away. Tianna was stubborn and proud and would've taken that demand like a bull to a red rag. But the tirade that'd come out of Tianna's mouth had set Mia back on her heels. It'd shocked her, and she was left wondering if Tianna might actually hate her. When all she wanted to do was protect her. Everything she did was for the good of Tianna. God, was this how a parent felt, when their children suddenly threw all their well-meaning suggestions and advice back in their face? Mia suddenly had a little sympathy for both her parents, even though neither of them was perfect, it was a harder job than she anticipated.

"I'm sorry, Mia." Logan's face was a picture of empathy. "But it is kind of all a bit far-fetched. Maybe she needed a little more time to digest the news. I'm sure she'll believe you next time."

It sounded a little like Logan was taking her sister's side. Which made her inexplicably even more irate. Tianna was her sister; she was allowed to be mad at her if she wanted. But no one else got to tell her how she should or shouldn't feel about her own sister.

"She yelled in my face. Told me to go away and leave her alone." Mia could hardly control her outrage.

Logan's hand landed on top of hers. The contact surprised her, at first. "Don't worry. We'll sort it out. I promise, we won't leave without her." Right at this particular moment, Mia would have been quite happy to leave her sister here to rot. But she knew the feeling would pass. Even as she had the thought, her anger died, blew away, replaced by contrition and sadness, caused by the empathy she felt in Logan's touch.

"Come here," he said, and for the second time in two nights, he pulled her in to his chest for a hug.

The contact helped ease the last of her anger, and she sagged into him.

But there was more to her story. Should she tell him? What if it was nothing? He would worry. But they were both in this together now, and he deserved to know.

"There's something else I need to tell you."

His fingers tightened their grip on her shoulders, ever so slightly.

"I was hopping on my scooter to go home and this man came up to me."

Logan went rigid beside her, and she lifted her head to stare into his eyes.

"And?" he prompted.

"He told me to stay away from you."

"What do you mean? What were his exact words?" A muscle in Logan's jaw jumped, and his lips were drawn into a thin line.

"He said to stay away from the good-looking turtle rescue guy." Mia couldn't keep the anguish out of her voice.

"Shit," he whispered. "And then what did he do? After he warned you away from me? Did you recognize him?"

"He turned around and walked away. That's it. He didn't look familiar, but like I said, Harry has all kinds of henchmen. If he was one of Harry's guys, then someone must've seen me with you after all."

"Hmm." Logan didn't elaborate, but his brows were drawn down, almost meeting in the middle as he stared at her. She imagined the same questions she'd asked herself were now circling through his head. If the guy was sent by Harry, how much did he know? Had they been spotted at Sunny's, was that all? Did they think she was on a sneaky date with him? Because while Harry wouldn't like that, not one little bit, it was better than the alternative. That someone had seen something down on the dock later that night.

And if the guy hadn't been sent by Harry, what did that mean? Was he connected to Logan's Ramirez brothers? And if he was, why was he warning her away from him? Unless it was to protect her somehow. Unless they meant to get to Logan but didn't want any witnesses. Any collateral damage.

"I do think Harry is getting suspicious," Mia added after a long moment's thought. He tried to get me to stay on board with his guests, to drink and chat after we docked. Which is unusual. He knows I don't fraternize with the guests, so he lets me go home. But tonight, he seemed clingy. Kept asking me what I was doing, why I was in such a hurry to get home."

"You know him better than I do. What will he do if he finds out you're with me? Do you think he had you followed tonight?" Logan asked. His gaze suddenly flew to the darkened windows of the saloon. If anyone was out there, they'd never be able to see them coming.

"I don't know." She gave a heavy sigh. "It's so hard to tell with Harry. He's got a suspicious personality anyway, he's always paranoid about everything. But I was really careful tonight. I mean, really careful. I'm sure I wasn't followed. Perhaps Harry thinks that giving me one warning will be enough for me to fall back into line. Apart from being supremely paranoid, he also has an ego the size of Jamaica. His arrogance would probably have him believing I wouldn't dare go against him."

Logan's gaze was still fixed out the window. "I'm wondering if it's even too dangerous to stay one more night?" he said softly.

"What other choice do we have? They may not even know you live on a boat. The stranger only referred to you as the turtle-rescue boy, which means they don't know your name."

"That's true," he mused. "I still have to tell you what happened to me this afternoon. It might change your mind."

That's right, he'd mentioned something as she got into the dinghy, but she'd been in such a mood, she'd forgotten all about it. She snuggled a little deeper into the crook of his shoulder. It felt good. His touch warmed her from the inside out. And for once, she wasn't going to question it, she was just going for it. His arms tightened around her, strong biceps curled around her shoulders. A shiver of heat spiked through her belly. It not only felt right. It felt damn good. She'd been interested in him even at the beach yesterday, had felt that prickle of attraction. Had even admitted to herself over dinner he was one delicious man, and she'd been tempted. Very tempted. But then everything had been buried in a deep pile of shit when the man with the gun appeared. It was buried, but it wasn't forgotten. And now that she was nestled in close, so close she could hear his heartbeat beneath her ear, that attraction was rearing its head again.

"Tell me what happened," she whispered, her lips against the fabric of his T-shirt.

"Well, it sort-of complicates things almost as much as the fact Tianna is refusing to come with us."

"How so?" She wasn't really concentrating, not anymore.

"My two sisters showed up this afternoon at my boat. With their two big, burly boyfriends."

"What?" Mia's head snapped up, her mind no longer taken up with wondering if she could run her fingers over his pecs, and whether they would be as firm as she imagined. "I thought your sisters were in Australia." Logan had mentioned his family, but only in passing. The fact that he had two older sisters, and he hadn't seen them in a while.

That was all. No mention that they were about to pay an unannounced visit. Logan also hadn't mentioned two big, burly guys before, either.

"Yes. Well, you're half right. Sierra, the middle sister, lives on Kangaroo Island in South Australia. But Keira, the oldest, is living in Hawaii at the moment."

"So why have they turned up out of the blue?" Mia was confused. They didn't need any more complications. And they didn't need any more people attracting attention to them. Which four strangers arriving on St. John were bound to do. Yes, they would be seen as tourists by some, but the people that mattered, the ones like Harry who might be keeping an eye on them, would want to know who these people were, and what they meant.

Logan pulled back a little, so he could look Mia square in the eye. "Because I've been out of contact with them for over two years. And they were worried about me."

"You what?" Mia could hardly believe what she was hearing.

"Remember everything I told you about Sofia, and her brothers?"

"Yes."

"My whole plan for avoiding them has been to fly under the radar. Make myself as invisible as possible."

She nodded her head. Yes, she got that bit. "And?"

"And, I made a conscious effort to stay away from my family. I thought the less they knew, the less information they had, the less chance Leo or Diego would contact them. Or try and use them as bait."

"Oh." Mia made an O with her mouth, unable to say anything else. She was stunned. She surely had problems with her own family. But family was still your flesh and blood. They were a part of you. There was no way she could ever cut herself off from them like Logan seemed to have done.

"You mean, you haven't talked to any of your family, not even your mom, for two years? They didn't even know if you were alive or dead?"

"I guess you could put it like that," he said, screwing his nose up and pulling away. He obviously hadn't liked her blunt words. "Actually, you sound exactly like Sierra." He winced and she had to laugh. She hadn't met the woman, but already she thought she might like her. She seemed to speak her mind, and it was a trait Mia admired.

Mia sobered. "So, what have you told them? What do they know about our…predicament?"

"Nothing," Logan admitted. "I told them what I've been up to the last few years. They know I didn't marry Sofia. I said it was because I couldn't put up with the controlling father, which is pretty much true. And I said I've been living the simple life, traveling around the Caribbean on my boat. I told them the reason was because when I left Sofia, Leo and Diego weren't happy with me. So, I was staying out of sight, just in case. Which is also true. I haven't lied to them. I just haven't told them everything."

"Which is a lie by omission," she said.

"Jesus, you're beginning to sound more and more like Sierra. It's scary." Logan winced, and Mia hid a smile. "But it's also another reason we couldn't have left tonight, even if you had managed to talk Tianna around."

"What do you mean? Where are they now?" she asked, her suspicion rising.

"They've rented an Airbnb villa up on Serendip Road. They weren't sure how long they were going to be here, or even if they were going to find me. But they want to see me again, first thing tomorrow morning." Logan's handsome face curled into a grimace. "I'm also worried because they've been poking around, asking after me. They've even been to the local police station. One of the boyfriends, Reed, is a cop back in Australia, and he was hoping they might do him a professional courtesy and give him info on me. Which is how they found my boat. The cops pointed them over here. If they can find me, then other people can, too."

"Oh, no. That's not good," Mia murmured. "Not good at all."

"And there's more," he said. There was a subtle downturn of his lips, if she hadn't been sitting so close, she would've missed it. He was more than unhappy about whatever he was going to say. He was also scared.

"I had a run-in with a stranger today as well. And now after your encounter, I'm worried this is all adding up to something much more sinister."

# CHAPTER NINE

Logan had spent a fitful night and felt like he'd hardly slept a wink. He kept dreaming about a body floating on the surface of the ocean, facedown, gently bumping against the hull of his boat, as if trying to get in. Logan had woken up more than once, drenched in sweat.

It was his subconscious worrying about the man he'd killed, he knew that. Because it was only a matter of time before that body broke free of the anchor. Even though he wrapped enough rope around his legs and torso so that he looked more like an Egyptian mummy than a man, Logan knew eventually, through decomposition, or attacks by the many fish and other sea creatures that thrived on the coral on the sea bed, the body would resurface. And he didn't want to be anywhere in the vicinity when that happened.

Logan wished he could've slept as well as he had the night before. But the magic Mia's presence had woven that night didn't seem to carry over. So even though she spent most of the night entwined in his arms, sleep had been elusive. He lay still, listening to the early-morning sounds of his boat, and to Mia's deep breathing. Enjoying the simple pleasure of holding her against him, her skin melding to his. The lap of waves on the wooden hull was soothing. It was going to be another perfect day here in paradise.

They were both fully clothed, had fallen into bed exhausted after last night's revelations. She was still wearing the white shorts and baby-pink button-up from last night. He could also make out a hint of her white bra beneath the opaque linen shirt. The shorts were brief and showed off her slim legs and pert bottom to great advantage. The white color of the shorts accentuated the brown of her skin. If she hadn't been so distressed last night, and he hadn't been more anxious about what his sisters were going to say or do next, he would've been happy to stare surreptitiously at her legs all night.

But now, the feel of Mia's legs lying alongside his, her cocoa skin so soft and silky, was awakening those thoughts again. She stirred beside him, made a little sound deep in the back of her throat. Her hand snaked over his stomach and pulled him closer. Was she awake? Or was she dreaming?

He lifted his head off the pillow a little, trying to see into her face. Her eyes were closed, long, dark eyelashes lying against smooth cheekbones. Her rose-colored lips were full and soft. And looked incredibly luscious and kissable. His mind skittered back to the night of their date, when she'd leaned in and kissed him at the docks. He remembered the sharp, surprising spike of heat that'd speared through his belly at her touch. How their kiss had turned from light and casual to hot and heavy within an instant. And he remembered how she'd looked at him afterwards, eyes wide, almost as shocked as he was.

Logan hadn't kissed her again since then. Even though he wanted to, it'd never been the right time, or the right place. But now…

Her body was wrapped around his, they'd spent the night in an intimate embrace, like two lovers. Just looking at her made his cock harden. Part of him knew it was because she felt safe with him, was seeking security in his presence. But part of him wondered if it was because she felt this connection too.

Perhaps it was time to find out.

Mia stirred again, her fingers running up his side, coming to rest on his upper body. Then her eyelids fluttered on her cheeks. His left arm was curled under her neck; she was using him like a pillow, and he brought his hand up to gently stroke the side of her shoulder. She twitched lightly beneath his touch and he felt goose bumps raise up on her skin where his fingers had been.

"Morning," she mumbled.

"Morning, sleepyhead," he replied. He drew his foot up and caressed it along the length of her calf.

Using her palm, she began to draw small circles on his chest, smoothing the fabric of his T-shirt against his pecs. Slowly her hand traced down the ridges of his stomach, until she came to the junction where his shirt met the waistband of his shorts. She stopped there, waiting. God, he so wanted to feel that hand on his skin, the anticipation was killing him. Finally, her fingers delved beneath the shirt and she slid her palm up to his chest again, tangling her fingers in the light sprinkling of hair. He almost let out a groan at the exquisiteness of her touch. His whole body seemed to become aware of every single place her skin touched his. It was like she was lighting him on fire, spark by tiny spark.

With his right hand, he reached up and tilted her chin towards him, so he could stare into her eyes. She blinked at him, slow and sleepy. But as he ran his finger down to caress her throat, then stroke along her collarbone, her eyes darkened, became sultry and inviting. His hand came back up and he captured her chin between his thumb and forefinger. He lifted his head, so his lips hovered over hers. Waiting.

Waiting for her to come the last little way to him.

And she did.

She watched him as she closed the distance, her lips meeting his. He liked the fact she kept her eyes open, wanting to see his reaction. His emotions. Because he wanted to see hers.

He groaned deep in his throat. His lips pressed harder, wanting more. She flicked out her tongue. An invitation for him to come deeper.

This was different to their first kiss. More slow and sensual, but equally intense. His heart felt like it was flaming in his chest.

Her fingers came up and tangled in the short hair at the back of his neck, dragging his mouth down toward her. Their legs were knotted together, bodies pressed so hard against each other. He wanted to get closer, even though they were almost as close as two people could physically get.

Mia suddenly levered her legs out from beneath his, and before he knew it, she was lying on top of him, straddling him. Breasts thrust into his chest. Stomach pressed into his belly. Long legs on top of his thighs. She must be able to feel his erection as it pushed into her lower abdomen. He was so hard. And she was so hot.

She broke their kiss so she could look down at him. Her lips were red and swollen. Running his hands up her back, under her shirt, he traced the bumps of her spine. She shivered at his touch and he wanted to rip that little pink shirt right off her, watching each button pop as it opened to reveal more and more.

"Logan...?" There was a question on her lips. Dark eyes wide with desire, she stared down at him. Were they really going to do this? He wanted to. Had wanted to from the second he'd set eyes on her at Maho Bay. But was it the right thing to do? With so much else going on. And it was fast. He really liked Mia. Wanted to take his time with her. Didn't want this to be just a one-time thing.

He opened his mouth to answer.

"Ahoy there. Is anyone aboard?"

A boat bumped against the side of the catamaran.

Mia sat up with a start.

Holy fuck. It was his sister. Logan took a quick look at his watch, to check he hadn't misjudged the time. It was only half-past six. She was a whole hour and a half earlier than she'd agreed.

"They're early," he growled. "Way too early."

But Mia was already clambering off him, her feet landing on the floor as she straightened her clothes.

Logan didn't want to get off the bed. Didn't want to admit their moment had been ruined. Whatever had been about to happen, wasn't going to happen now. And it was killing him. Had they been about to sleep together? He was never going to know. Which made him mad as hell.

"I'm going to kill them," he muttered under his breath as he levered himself off the bed. Mia didn't say anything, but ran her fingers through her hair, keeping her head down. She'd gone from a purring sex kitten, to quiet and withdrawn in the blink of an eye. At least the sound of Sierra's voice had caused his libido to sink like a stone.

"I'm going to use the head," Mia said, and quickly disappeared down the passage. It left him wondering if she was actually hiding from his family. Which he didn't really blame her for. She was probably more than a little anxious about meeting his sisters. And now he was left to greet them on his own. When all he wanted to do was growl at them and tell them to turn their bloody boat around and leave them alone.

"Is anyone there?" Sierra's voiced floated through the hull again.

"Yeah, yeah, I'm bloody coming," Logan yelled and stamped down the passage in bare feet. By the time he got up the ladder and out into the cockpit, Sierra was already standing on the deck, reaching down to give Keira a hand. Logan could see the tops of the two men's heads as they bobbed up and down in the small dinghy below. They were all here, and all looking bright and eager, ready to go.

"You're early," he said, by way of greeting. Grudgingly he extended a hand and helped both his sisters over into the cockpit.

"We couldn't sleep," Keira replied, giving him a quick hug as she passed by. Logan grunted. He knew that probably meant Sierra had woken them all up, because she was the one who couldn't sleep. Logan wondered how Reed ever put up with his middle sister sometimes. He must have the patience of a saint.

Reed was the next to climb up onto the catamaran, and he tied the dinghy off as Dalton waited to disembark. They were both capable and confident, and didn't need his help. At least Dalton was better for Keira than that deadbeat husband she'd been married to. She hadn't said much more about John, other than to say he was dead and to confirm she and Dalton were indeed together. Which had shocked him greatly. But neither of them would be drawn into a conversation last night about how John had died, saying it was complicated and better left for another time. They were here to see him. So, Logan had reluctantly dropped the subject, but secretly he was glad Keira was with Dalton.

"I need coffee," he said, trying not to sound sullen, but failing spectacularly. "Do you all want coffee?" He didn't wait for an answer before heading for the galley.

"Why are you so grumpy? Got out of the wrong side of bed this morning?" Sierra called after him, and when he glanced back, her knowing gaze locked onto him, taking in his rumpled hair and slept-in clothes, like she knew what he'd been up to. Which made him all the more irritated.

"No, I just don't like being taken by surprise. You're way too early," he grunted in reply, repeating his earlier words.

Both Dalton and Reed wisely kept their opinions to themselves, wordlessly taking their places at the saloon table. But he also saw the knowing look that passed between them when they thought he wasn't watching.

Goddammit, he wished he'd never mentioned Mia to them last night. He wanted to tell them all to mind their own bloody business, but knew it was useless. Sierra would give him that level stare, like she was right and why was he even quarreling, and Keira would laugh and give him that innocent look, as if butter wouldn't melt in her mouth.

Logan put the kettle on the stove and pulled out as many mugs as he could find. There was a total of five, all mismatched, and one with a large chip out of the side. He and Mia would have to share.

He yelled up through the hatch, "I've only got instant."

There was silence from above and Logan took a deep breath. He knew he was behaving like a bear with a sore head. His sisters didn't really deserve his wrath, especially seeing as how it was only the second time he'd seen them in four years.

Which got him wondering exactly when Mia was going to emerge from the head? She'd been in there a while. He lined the mugs up on the small countertop, put a spoonful of coffee in each, and squeezed a dollop of condensed milk into each one. Logan had forgotten to buy milk yesterday, but his tiny refrigerator was stuffed full of fruit and vegetables for the trip, so it wouldn't have fitted anyway.

Just as he was pouring hot water into each mug, Mia emerged in the passage.

"Are you okay?" he asked softly, as she came up to stand

next to his shoulder.

"Yes, all good." But he could tell by the tight lines around her mouth, she was worried.

"They're nice," he said, trying to placate her. "They're going to love you." He had to pull himself up short. It sounded like she was his date, meeting his family for the first time. Which she wasn't. They'd been forced together by circumstance. Even though Logan liked Mia, was attracted to her something fierce, he knew she was only with him right now because she needed him. And he needed her. It sounded crude and mercenary, but although a part of him was in this because he wanted to protect Mia. A part of him was doing this to protect himself, as well.

But his family knew none of that. So, they were playing an elaborate game right now. Logan was a little worried they might not pull it off. They had to be convincing. A couple in the early throes of a new relationship, but a couple, nonetheless. They had to make his sisters, and their boyfriends believe they were a couple. That'd been the plan they'd made last night. If they could convince the foursome that everything was fine and dandy, then Sierra and Keira might be happy enough with that. They would leave the island—sooner rather than later, he hoped—and he and Mia could get out of Cruz Bay. With Tianna, of course. He couldn't forget about her.

"Come on." He encouraged her with a quick hug. "Bring those two mugs, will you, please?" He grabbed the other three and led her up through the hatchway.

"Everyone," he called in a loud voice. The quiet conversation died as four pairs of eyes turned towards him. "This is Mia, the woman I told you about last night."

"Hi." Mia stepped forward, all signs of her earlier nervousness gone. Logan was surprised, but then he probably shouldn't have been. Mia was an entertainer. She knew how to put on a good face, a good show. She came across as bubbly and likable. Which was exactly how she was in reality, in most normal situations. But meeting four of his family was a challenge for most people, and his respect for her skyrocketed.

Mia put the coffees on the table, and shook Keira's hand first, then Sierra's. Both women smiled back and took her outstretched hand.

"Nice to meet you," Sierra said.

"Yes, we've heard a lot about you." Keira shot Logan a look as she said it, and he cringed. He had talked a lot about Mia last night, but it was mainly to try and throw them off the scent, to keep them away from dangerous topics.

Then Dalton and Reed stood up and offered their hands, smiling and murmuring their greetings.

Logan watched them all take Mia in. She had the face of an angel; they'd all appreciate that. But she also had a core of steel, she'd proved that to him over the past few days. And he wondered if any of them would see past her outer beauty to what lay beneath. A tough, streetwise woman, who could get just about anything she wanted.

Everyone settled back into their respective seats and Logan leaned against the doorway to the cockpit, coffee in one hand. Keira scooted farther around the bench seat, making room for Mia to sit next to her. After a second's hesitation, Mia sat. Logan passed her their shared mug of coffee.

Sierra took a sip from hers and grimaced, placing it carefully back on the table as an uncomfortable silence settled over the group.

"How did you find me?" Logan decided to break the tension with a question that'd been hovering at the back of his mind from the very moment Sierra had stepped aboard. It had a lot of significance, because if Sierra could find him, then so could the Ramirez brothers. Obviously, he hadn't been trying hard enough to stay hidden. "I mean, I know you asked your cop mate here in Cruz Bay, and he told you about *Leopard*. But I mean before that. How did you know I was in the USVIs?"

"I'm an investigative journalist." Sierra gave him that level stare, as if to say wasn't it obvious?

"Yes, I know," he replied, reining in his impatience. "But like I told you last night, I was being careful. After I left Sofia, her brothers were pretty mad. I thought it was better if I laid low for a while. I didn't want to be found."

"Oh, I know, you certainly didn't make it easy." Sierra gave a little laugh. "But when I set my mind to something…"

"Yeah, yeah, I know," Logan replied. She was certainly renowned for her determination, at least that much hadn't changed about her.

"In your last phone call, when you rang mum—the last contact any of us had from you—" She directed that cool, level stare at him. The one that made him want to squirm uncomfortably, as if he were nine years old again and Sierra had just caught him climbing up on the kitchen counter to get to the chocolate hidden in the top cupboard. But he was a grown man, he reminded himself, and straightened his shoulders and stared right back at her. "—you said you were bored of Mexico, had bought a boat, and were off to explore the Caribbean islands. And not to worry if we didn't hear from you for a while. Did I get that right?"

"Yes." He schooled his features into calm, trying to match her sensible stare. But he couldn't stop the internal churning of his guts as he thought back to how indifferently he'd treated his mum that day over the phone. He'd made the quick call from a public phone booth on the docks of Cancun, while desperate to get back to the boat to sail out with the tide. Little had he known back then it'd be another two years before he spoke to any of his family again.

"So, I knew the possibility of you still being in the Caribbean somewhere was quite high. At least I had a starting point, but at that stage I didn't realize just how many islands there are and how many different countries make up this chain of archipelagos. It was a very steep learning curve for me," she admitted.

"Yes, most nights I had to drag her away from her computer, and sometimes it was well after one or two a.m.," Reed spoke up for the first time that morning, other than to utter greetings, to attest to Sierra's research skills.

"I tried everything. I searched death notices, marriage notices, news articles, I even had Reed put a trace on you, to see if you'd gotten any fines or arrest warrants. Which I'm pleased to say came back clean, no criminal activity. At least you've been staying away from the wrong side of the law. I also sent out photos of you to all my contacts in the Caribbean. And I asked all my friends, colleagues, fellow journalists and everyone else I knew to pass it on. In the vain hope someone might have seen you. Someone like you, with looks like yours, doesn't go unnoticed, Logan."

"I did grow a beard," Logan protested. "For a while, anyway. Then it got too damn itchy in this heat."

Sierra ignored him and plowed on. "Anyway, I finally used a special favor with an editor friend of mine, who has a close relative who works in the Australian Embassy in Adelaide. I asked if he could tell me if your passport had been used to cross any borders recently. Normally this information is highly confidential, but because I'm your sister, and because I thought you might credibly be dead by this stage—" Again, there was that frown that made him squirm. "—he conceded and gave me a hint that you had entered the US Virgin Islands about nine months ago."

Logan nodded. It sounded highly unethical, the way Sierra

finally tracked him down, but at least he was fairly confident Leo or Diego couldn't do the same thing.

"I asked a journalist friend if he knew anyone in the USVIs and he came up with a name of a lady who writes for *The Virgin Island Daily News*. Have you heard of it?"

Logan nodded, then realization dawned. "Susie Morven," he said.

"Exactly." Sierra nodded approvingly.

"She interviewed Tom and Dan for the turtle tagging project. She took photos of them, and put an article in the news a few months ago. But I made sure I wasn't in any of the photos, and that she didn't know my name." He'd been very emphatic with both Dan and Tom on that point. He was only there to help out, not to appear in the article at all.

"She might not have known your name, but she sure as hell remembered your face," Sierra said, and Mia gave a loud snort. Logan raised an eyebrow in her direction.

"All the women at the turtle rescue are crazy over you, Logan," Mia said. "Like Sierra said, you have a memorable face, even though you seem not to notice most of the time."

"As soon as she positively identified you, Reed and I got on a flight. We met Keira and Dalton at the St. Thomas airport. Then we hopped on the ferry straight over here."

Well, at least Logan was now fairly certain the Ramirez brothers wouldn't have been able to conduct that same kind of level of investigation to find him. And they certainly wouldn't be approaching the local police to ask if they'd seen Logan, that wasn't their typical *modus operandi*. The only way the Ramirez's might've found him was that photo Tom posted on Facebook, which was still a credible threat. The faces of the two guys in the dark SUV hovered in his mind's eye. The brothers could still be a danger and the idea was making him edgy and nervous. All he really wanted to do was to convince his sisters and their entourage he was fine, so they would move on and he could proceed with the plan to get as far away from this island as possible. Besides, his sisters might now also be in peril. But how he was going to get Sierra and Keira to leave his boat—to leave the island—was beyond him right now.

"And here you all are," Logan said in a low voice, trying to sound happy about it.

"Yes, here we all are. And now you have some explaining to do. Because we've heard a few unsettling things since we've been on this island."

The little hairs on Logan's arms rose up at her comment. The tone of her voice was hard, penetrating. He knew he was in trouble. They must have a million and one questions. He glanced at Mia, but she raised her shoulders in a shrug. She was of no help.

"What do you mean?"

Instead of answering, Sierra glanced at Reed.

He cleared his throat. "Police Captain Porter, the one I talked to yesterday morning, called us up after we got back to the villa yesterday evening." Reed lowered his chin and looked directly at Logan. "He said he didn't have anything new to tell me, not anything concrete, that is." Reed paused for a second, and Logan found himself holding his breath. He glanced at Sierra, but she was glaring at him like she wanted to come over there and smack him. He had an inclination to reach for Mia's hand, but she was too far away, sitting at the table. He stayed where he was and took another sip of his coffee, trying to look nonchalant.

Reed continued. "But he did say they'd heard some disturbing rumors. Of two men who arrived on the island yesterday. Asking questions of the locals, especially the lowest-denominator type of people, if you get my drift."

"They wanted to know if these two men were related to us in any way," Sierra growled. "And we told them in no uncertain terms they weren't."

"Anyway," Reed took up the conversation again. "It seems they were showing a photo that seemed to vaguely match your description, except in the photo the guy had a hat and sunnies on, so it was hard to make out his face properly." Reed held up a hand as Logan was about to speak, cutting him off. "And they'd also had a report that a student from UVI, someone called Tom, had been assaulted. But the student refused to say who assaulted him, or why. The attending officer overheard him discussing the attack with a friend when she first arrived on scene, and it seems your name came up."

Logan's blood froze in his veins. Tom. Someone had hurt Tom? Because of him? Why would someone hurt Tom?

The answers came at him like a blinding flash of light. Because they wanted answers. They knew Tom was connected to Logan. Mia shot him a look, her eyes dark with fear and doubt.

The two men in the SUV. The image came back to him in Technicolor glory. Of course, that's why it hadn't felt right. Jesus, why hadn't he stopped them? Given them the wrong information? As it was, he'd practically sent the men to Tom's door. His insides began to tremble. Tom was hurt because of him. In more ways than one. And even scarier, those men had been looking for Logan. Why they hadn't recognized him was anybody's guess, but he thanked his lucky stars, nonetheless. If they had been sent by the Ramirez brothers, and if what Reed said was right and they were showing a photo of him around, how would they not see it was him? Perhaps it was the floppy hat he'd been wearing yesterday. Or maybe it was because in the Facebook photo—which seemed likely was the one they were using—he had on cap turned backwards and sunglasses, with a large turtle obscuring most of his body, which wouldn't give them much to go on.

The big question now was, what did Tom tell them? He couldn't have given up the location of Logan's boat, otherwise he and Mia would probably be sitting at the bottom of the ocean right now. He needed to find out what Tom had told these two thugs. And if he had any inkling of where they came from. Who they were working for?

Sierra was staring directly at him. She must've seen the multitude of emotions flitting across his face. "So," she said. "Do you want to tell us what's really going on?"

# CHAPTER TEN

Mia's heart sank. Logan's sisters knew there was something going on. She wondered what it meant for Logan. What it meant for the both of them.

Logan was still glancing between the big guy who'd introduced himself as Reed, and the sister called Sierra—was she the middle one? Logan was trying to come up with some excuse, some explanation that wouldn't give them away. His handsome features were contorted by a deep frown. But Mia decided it'd do no good. The look on Reed's face—he was the cop back in Australia, she knew that even without Logan telling her last night—said he wasn't going to believe anything but the truth.

"You need to tell them," she said quietly. She got up from the table and went over to take Logan's hands in hers.

"Tell them what," he replied, loud and brash, making it sound like he didn't know what in hell she was talking about.

"Tell them everything." She looked him square in the eye.

He stopped fidgeting, his hands going still in her grasp. For a split second it was just the two of them, him and her standing on the boat. His dark-blue eyes bored into hers. She remembered the feel of his lips on hers. How his big hands had felt on her skin. How much she'd wanted him to rip off her shirt this morning.

Then her mind tumbled back to reality. Where would that have left them? What if the others had arrived when they were supposed to? Would she have let Logan make love to her?

"We don't have a choice anymore, Logan. If it's true, and there are actually men on the island looking for you, we need to get out now." She didn't say it, but she hoped he knew anyway. They needed to get Tianna and drag her off this island, kicking and screaming, if they had to. Logan's sisters deserved to know what was going on. They might be in danger themselves, if they got caught up in this. And they also might be of some use. Reed was a police officer. He might know tactics on how to avoid these people. Might even be able to use his contacts to help them evade the island cops long enough so she and Logan didn't become the next most-wanted people on the island. As long as he didn't try and throw them in jail himself. But that was a risk they were going to have to take.

She put a palm against his cheek, feeling the rough stubble on her skin. He leaned gently into her hand, a trusting movement, but his eyes held a hint of panic.

"Do you want to tell them, or should I?"

"I will." Logan's shoulders slumped. "Move over," he said to Keira. "I need to sit down." He took two, large, fortifying gulps of coffee, while Mia sat back down and then they all shuffled around to make room for him.

To their credit, the other four had remained silent during this quick conversation, but Mia could see the impatience written all over Sierra's face. She was going to get the story out of them one way or another. Both Reed and Dalton sat forward, elbows on the table. It was a little uncanny, how much alike, but yet different, the two men were. One thing they did have in common was their piercing stare, that seemed to see right through to her very heart, into her soul.

"Two nights ago, I killed a man," Logan said, without preamble.

Keira sucked in a sharp breath, but everyone else remained calm and quiet. Waiting for him to continue. Mia was impressed with their evident restraint.

"He attacked Mia and me down at the docks. Came at us with a gun. I didn't really have a choice." Logan lifted his eyes from the table and sought out first Keira and then Sierra's gazes. Looking for their reactions. Mia guessed he was searching for a sign in both their faces. Of either condemnation or absolution. It wasn't every day a man admitted murder to his closest family.

"That wasn't what I was expecting," Reed finally answered for them all, breaking the silent plea in Logan's eyes. "We all knew something was up, but this is worse than any of us imagined," he admitted.

"Oh, I don't know." Keira spoke up from her spot next to Logan. "After what we've all been through over the past few months, I'm actually not as surprised as you might think."

Logan raised an eyebrow at his sister's words, and Mia wondered what on earth Keira could be talking about.

Sierra let out a gust of air. "What the hell is the matter with this family?" she muttered. "Can't any of us lead a normal life?"

Mia caught Logan's eye. Had his siblings gone a little mad? What were they talking about?

"It sounds like we all have a bit of explaining to do," Logan said into the following silence.

"Before we start on our stories," Reed interrupted. "Can you tell me where this guy you killed is right now? Is there a body? Are you one-hundred-percent sure he's dead?"

"Oh, yes," Mia replied, icy tentacles slinging up her spine of the memory of dumping his body. "He's definitely dead.

He's currently floating somewhere on the ocean floor, right now."

"Jesus Christ!" Sierra put her head in her hands. Reed laid a steadying hand on her shoulder.

"Not the best place to hide a body," he conceded. "But I'm guessing no one is any the wiser? At least not yet? Do the police know anything?"

"We really hope not," Mia replied again, as it seemed as if Logan had been struck dumb by Sierra's outburst. "Otherwise, we're in deep shit."

"So, you must have theories on who this man was? What he wanted?" Dalton spoke up for the first time. His oval face looked to be carved from stone, he sat so still, up until now just taking it all in.

Mia glanced at Logan, but he still wasn't talking. "We have," Mia admitted. "But we have conflicting ideas as to who is actually directing the gunman. And we aren't really sure what he wanted with us. He didn't get the chance to tell us his plans, it all happened so quick." Mia tensed her shoulders to stop the sudden tremble running through her body. Part of her still didn't want to admit she'd been part of a murder. She couldn't seem to wrap her head around it.

Mia went on to tell them her theory, about the man being linked to her boss, letting them know about his nightclub business, as well as the many dubious side hustles. She stumbled over the words when it came to telling them she was an exotic dancer. It'd been different telling Logan, part of her knew he wouldn't give her that insidious sideways glance. But she need not have worried. None of them even blinked an eyelid at her news. And Keira—Mia was starting to see what a caring soul she was already—leaned over and whispered in her ear, "I picked you as a dancer right from the start." She gave her a bright smile and then leaned in even closer. "And don't be intimidated by any of these guys, we've all done things we're not proud of. You'll fit right in with this crew."

Mia was so taken aback, she wasn't sure what to say. But Keira gave her a wink, and patted her shoulder. The others had already begun discussing Harry and how he might be involved, as well as the best way to handle him.

Then Logan told them the true story about Sofia, and what her father did to make his dirty money. And how the two brothers had sworn they'd find him and make him pay.

Reed went very quiet as Logan described Leo and Diego, and the lengths he thought they might go to find him. Then when Logan had finished, Reed told them that in his experience, while Harry was dangerous, he was probably small fry compared to the Ramirez bothers. They seemed to have more connections, perhaps even be linked to the big drug smuggling cartels. He named a few in the area, like the Sianola Cartel, and the Chadee Gang. Which all meant nothing to Mia. But being a cop, Mia assumed he knew more than she did on the topic. And she also knew the cocaine smugglers made big money, and let no one stand in their way.

Logan got up and made more cups of coffee, and rustled up some toast, as no one had had breakfast yet. Mia noticed he kept glancing out the windows and her eyes followed his gaze. There were a couple of other yachts moored nearby, around a hundred meters or so away. A small inflatable dinghy was buzzing towards the dock, leaving a wake behind it and there were two more dinghies full of people being ferried to and from other boats in the bay. Two larger, runabout motor boats, with their canopies down so the people could enjoy the sun, were making their way out towards the ocean, probably on a fishing trip or on their way over to St. Thomas. Mia's eyes swept farther and found a large cruise ship anchored about a half a mile out. They were too big to come into the bay, but they would ferry their passengers in on smaller craft over the course of the day. It was a typical Sunday morning in Cruz Bay, busy, but laid back at the same time. Nothing looked out of place or menacing. But Logan was probably right to keep alert, especially after what they'd heard about Tom. She put her hand up and touched the spot where the man had held her by the throat. He must've known his business, because although he held her tight enough to frighten her, he hadn't left a mark. She shuddered. The sooner they got off this island, the better. She thought about the money tin, still sitting at the bottom of her backpack, now nestled inside a hatch in Logan's bedroom. What to do with the money had been a question buzzing around in the background of her brain all morning. Was it safer to leave it on the boat for now? Or should she take it with her wherever she went?

Captain suddenly landed in her lap, leaping from beneath the table where he'd been sitting unnoticed. He'd obviously decided it was high time someone did take notice of him. She patted his head as he curled up and Mia drew her gaze back to the catamaran, sitting back and watching this group instead, as they talked and argued and tossed around ideas. They were sharp, witty, intelligent, the women on an equal footing to the men. The three men, Reed, Dalton, and Logan all listened when either Sierra or Keira talked. They were a team. A powerful team, one to be reckoned with. Logan seemed to fit right in. But Mia wondered where that left her? Would she be accepted into the group? They were treating her like one of their peers at the moment. None of them balked at the color of her skin or at her chosen profession. The two sisters were white, like Logan, but both men had obvious cultural differences. Dalton was Chinese-Hawaiian, if she remembered correctly. And Reed had Maori blood running though his veins. They were an interesting mix. It gave her a glimpse into a life so different from hers. A life worth striving for, perhaps. Where she could live as a strong, confident woman, amongst equally strong, yet respectful men. And finally not be afraid.

* * *

"Keira referred to it a little earlier," Dalton said. "We've all been through some trials and tribulations of our own. It's probably time we filled you in on all of that."

Logan sat back and drew in a deep breath, glad that his part of the storytelling was over. It'd been traumatic, and more than a little humiliating, revealing all of the things he'd done wrong over the last two years. None of the other four seemed to be judging him, and yet he still worried. How Sierra and Keira in particular, were going to view him afterward. His place in the family tree, at only thirty-one and the youngest of the siblings, had always made him feel like he was playing a game of catch-up with his intelligent and insightful older sisters. They'd never said anything directly to make him feel like that, it was more of a self-imposed kind of inequality. Whatever they all had to tell him could never be as bad as what he'd just revealed. Could it?

But after a few minutes of listening to Sierra—who seemed to be their self-proclaimed speaker—Logan began to think differently.

She told the tale of how she and Reed met, on the ferry over to Kangaroo Island on his very first day on the job as the new cop on the beat, over six months ago now. Which all seemed fairly regular, until her story took on a more sinister turn as she revealed that she'd had a stalker, someone who'd been subtly threatening her for at least ten years, back even before she'd had the accident that'd claimed her baby's life and caused her marriage to split.

Logan tried to interrupt at this stage, to ask why she never told anyone, but Sierra held up her hand and assured him that twenty-twenty hindsight was a great thing, and to keep his questions to the end, because there was a lot more to come.

From there her story took on a menacing twist as she revealed the abduction of a five-year-old girl on the island and how she and Reed were dragged into the story when they joined in the search. In the end she and Reed found the girl, but the pedophile had caught them, and they had to fight for their lives to escape. Logan was shocked and Mia held her hand over her mouth as Sierra recounted the villain hunting her through the thick scrub with a gun, while all she had to defend herself was a large stick and her wits. Sierra had ended up with a broken ankle, which was pretty much healed now, and the bad guy was going to rot in jail for the rest of his life.

Logan could now see where the obviously strong bond between Reed and Sierra came from. They'd been through hell together and survived. Logan's respect for this man went up even more after he heard their story. Sierra came with a lot of baggage from her life before she met Reed, but he seemed to have the mental strength to help her deal with that. They had shared psychological scars. He also had the physical energy to match her active lifestyle. Sierra was one of these people who was always on the move, so determined and vital. But Reed had a quiet reserve, he watched her with such gentle amusement. As if he was the anchor that kept her tied to reality.

"Why didn't you tell me about any of this?" Logan blurted the words out before he had time to think. And then immediately regretted them when Sierra gave him one of those level stares that made him feel like an insect pinned to a board.

"Because you weren't answering any of my calls, or emails or letters," she said.

Damn, now he felt doubly guilty. Not only had he been

avoiding his family, but they'd been going through immense trauma and he hadn't even known about it. He'd possibly even added to his sister's stress because she'd been worried about him, as well.

His own problems seemed to pale into insignificance next to Sierra's story.

But then Keira started speaking and Logan couldn't help it, his mouth dropped open in shock.

Keira's tale was of a volcano eruption that buried her house in molten lava, and of a cheating husband, who'd become ensnared in a money laundering scheme with the Yakuza. Logan had to ask her to repeat that bit, to make sure he hadn't misheard. Surely the Yakuza only existed in movies and on TV cop shows. But his normally bright and bubbly sister's face had taken on a hard edge, and he was sorry he'd even asked. Because why would she make up something like that? It was so far-fetched, it had to be true. At least he now knew how John died, and the reason Keira hadn't wanted to talk about it before now.

Dalton, who was sitting, squashed up next to Keira on the bench laid a protective hand over both of hers, which were fidgeting with a ring one finger. He never said a word, but his support and love were more than evident.

Keira opened her mouth to keep speaking, then blanched and glanced at Dalton. He nodded, and his grip tightened. Whatever she was about to say was painful for her. Instinctively, he reached for Mia's hand under the table. Whether it was to reassure her, or to give himself a small ounce of comfort, he wasn't sure. Her bracelet with the blue birthstone clinked against his wrist as she tightened her grip. He remembered what she'd told him the other night, that it was her lucky charm from Jamaica.

Keira kept her eyes downcast as she related the next part of her account. The story she told, about a husband who wasn't all he seemed on the surface, who took command of her life, who began to control her emotionally, and then finally used her as his own special prostitute to keep his VIP clientele happy, had Logan wanting to stand up and smash the man's face in. If he hadn't already been dead, Logan would've happily killed him with his bare hands.

But when Logan thought it couldn't get any worse, Keira told them about the Yakuza hunting her down, hoping she could get the money back that her husband had embezzled from them. That's where Dalton came into the picture, he rescued her from the deadly leader of the gang and took her into hiding in his hut up in the mountains. Then Sierra chipped in her addition to the story, telling Logan she and Reed had flown over to have a holiday in Hawaii, only to find Keira's face plastered all over the news.

From there, his sister's story sounded like one of those sensationalized news articles, when the Yakuza kidnapped Dalton's son and held him hostage so he would hand Keira over. Finally, there was a shootout in the face of a deadly lava flow. Dalton was shot—obviously not fatally, as the man looked in extremely good health—and Keira was able to clear her name and hand the mob boss over to the police. She and Sierra and Reed were all unharmed, but it was a shocking story.

Now he understood Sierra's comment. This family seemed to have a knack for finding trouble.

And here he was, causing even more angst amongst them.

There was that acid bite of guilt in his belly again. Because he'd been off trying to save his own ass, leaving his two sisters to deal with their traumas without him.

"I'm so sorry." It sounded woefully inadequate for the turmoil of emotions rolling through him. "I'm sorry you both had to go through that."

"Yes, well, so are we," Sierra said, in her matter-of-fact

voice. "But we all lived to tell the tale. And now you're the one in need of help."

"But before we work out our next plan of action," Reed interrupted Sierra as she was about to speak. "We have one more little thing we need to tell you."

Sierra shut her mouth with a snap. And then she did the most surprising thing Logan had seen her do all day. She blushed, the rosy red climbing up her neck and infusing her cheeks. Then she glanced at Reed almost shyly, and he took her hand and held it to his lips. The look she gave him was one of overflowing love. The show of emotion shocked Logan. It was so intimate. Full of such devotion and trust.

"Oh, no." Keira's hand flew to her mouth. "Are you going to say what I think you're going to say?"

Sierra nodded and blushed even deeper. What was going on here? Logan was lost. He already knew the couple were planning on getting married in a few months. Was it something to do with the wedding?

Then Dalton reached over and shook Reed's other hand. "Congratulations, mate," he said. "You guys deserve this happiness."

"What…?" Logan felt like he'd missed something really important.

Mia nudged him in the shoulder. "Don't you get it?" she whispered.

"No," he said out loud. "What's going on here? It's like you're all talking in some kind of secret code."

Sierra smiled at him. "I'm pregnant."

Those two simple words floored him. It was the last thing he was expecting. But before he could fully process the idea, Mia pushed him out of the way, so she could scoot out of the bench seat. Keira followed her out and then she was hugging Sierra, long and hard. "I'm so pleased for you both," she squeaked in excitement. Reed and Dalton got out and Dalton slapped the other man on the back. A little belatedly, Logan went over and shook Reed's hand as well. He hardly knew the man, but from what he'd seen he'd make a great father. There were a lot of questions hovering at the back of Logan's mind. Like, wasn't Sierra getting a little old to have another baby? She was seven years older than him, which put her at thirty-eight. And he also remembered how adamant she'd been after Grace's death she'd never have any more children. But maybe having the right guy in her life had changed all that.

Logan looked at Mia, who was hugging Sierra, holding her close and obviously so happy for Sierra. Children huh? He'd parked the idea he was ever going to have kids when he left Sofia. It wasn't something that consumed him, he was quite happy with his life the way it was.

Did Mia want kids? If he and Mia had children, what would they look like?

Whoa, where had that thought come from?

He'd only met the woman two days ago. Yes, he was incredibly attracted to her. And yes, they got on like a house on fire. Had so many things in common. But he hardly knew anything about her.

He suddenly felt all hot and flustered.

"Hey, bro, isn't it time you gave us the guided tour of your boat?" Keira broke away from the congratulatory crowd. "I mean, this is the second time we've been on board, and I've only seen the cockpit and the saloon so far."

It was true. And Logan loved showing off his boat to people. Even if it was a work in progress, he could see the potential, and he hoped everyone else could, too. Plus, it would give him an excuse to get away from this uncomfortable topic of children and undying love.

"Sure, I'd love to." He gave his sister a quick hug and then pointed towards the doorway and ladder down into the starboard hull. "After you."

She grabbed Dalton by the elbow and tugged him towards the hatch.

"Wait for us," Sierra said, hustling toward the ladder. Logan waved Reed in front of him as well.

"Are you coming?" he asked Mia.

She gave a shrug that said she may as well. Logan took one last look through the windows. He'd been keeping vigilant this morning—even though he didn't really know exactly what he was looking for, because surely no one would attack them in broad daylight, not with this many people as potential witnesses on board—he kept his eyes peeled for anything that might be out of the ordinary. But it was all normal as far as he could tell. Small boats zipped to and fro between the bigger yachts. A couple of larger charters had gone out earlier, probably fishing or sightseeing. Nothing that looked alarming.

He followed them down the ladder. It was crowded below, they were all milling around in the small sitting area at the bottom of the ladder, but he pushed his way through and began pointing out the two bedrooms—or berths, as he told them was the correct jargon—one with twin bunks and one at the front with a double bed. There were a shower and head on this side of the catamaran and a smaller head on the other. Dalton was interested in the actual workings of the boat, and so Logan lifted the floor hatch to show him the bilge area and explained that the dodgy bilge pump didn't always work properly and that's why there was water lying in the bottom. Dirty, grey water with a scum of oil over the top. He really should get onto fixing that. The girls oohed and ahhed over everything, saying the right things.

Then he took them over to the port side hull and showed them the galley, how it had lots of bespoke little cupboards and nooks specially made for storage, and how he managed to cook in such a small space, because everything had its place.

Keira needed to use the head, so he showed her how to pump it out afterward and the rest of them filed through to look at the main berth, his bedroom, and the rope lockers and other storage compartments. Reed asked if he could lie down on the bed, to see if he fitted, and they all laughed when his feet hung over the end. He decided boating life wasn't for him.

All of a sudden, Captain streaked past them, a tortoiseshell fur ball, landed on the bed next to Reed and then leaped up through the small forward hatch and out into the topside deck.

"What the hell has gotten into that cat?" Reed joked.

That's when Logan smelled smoke. What the hell?

"Stay here," he commanded as he pushed past Mia, Dalton and Sierra, back down the passage toward the saloon. He was in the galley in three more strides and had his head half-way out the hatch when a wall of black smoke rolled over him.

Shit. Was the boat on fire?

For a second, the smoke drove him backward, but when he battled to get back to the hatch, the heat hit him. A spike of icy fear grabbed at his guts.

His boat was on fire.

It was no use; he couldn't get out of the hatch to see what was going on. Which meant the saloon and probably the whole back of the catamaran was engulfed in flames. Which could only mean one thing. No normal fire started that quickly. If there'd been a spark from a loose wire or something, they would've had plenty of warning. This fire had been started on purpose. Someone had used an accelerant. It was raging far too hot and quick to be anything else.

"Everyone get out," he boomed, racing back down the

passage way. "Keira, get out now." He pounded on the door to the head, until Keira's shocked face finally appeared in the door.

"Tell us what to do." Reed's voice was calm and controlled. He wasn't arguing or asking what was going on. He understood from the tone in Logan's voice that this was now life and death.

"We need to get out through the forward hatch." Logan pointed to the small hole the cat had disappeared through.

"Right. Women first." He grabbed Sierra by the upper arm and pushed her bodily toward the bed. "No arguing," he warned icily as Sierra opened her mouth. She shut it again quickly and let Reed boost her up and they all watched her feet dangle in the air for a few seconds before they disappeared.

Mia was next. She was lithe and quick, maneuvering her body through the hatch with ease. Then went Keira. The smoke was now so thick it was becoming hard to see and Dalton began to cough. Which set Logan off. He held the hem of his T-shirt up to his mouth.

"Dalton, you're next," Reed said. This was going to be interesting. Dalton wasn't much taller than Reed, but he was definitely broader in the shoulders. He should fit through the hatch, but it was going to be a tight fit. Logan tried to rein in his impatience as he and Reed waited their turn.

"You need to get everyone off the boat," Logan said to Reed as they waited. "I'm not sure how this started, or even where. But there's a large fuel tank that drives the outboard motor in the floor of the cockpit. If that goes up..." Logan didn't need to finish his sentence; the look in Reed's eyes said he understood.

"You tell them," Reed said. "You go next."

Logan shook his head. Not going to happen. "My boat. My rules. I'm the last one off."

Reed was too much of a professional to argue. He knew the risks as well as Logan.  And Logan could see in the other man's eyes that he wanted to get Sierra away to safety.

As soon as Dalton's feet disappeared, Reed was hauling himself up. Logan could hear his muffled voice shouting instructions. Fear rolled in his belly.

Logan couldn't see, the smoke was so thick. All he could make out was the bright halo of sunshine through the hatch around Reed's darker figure. He was coughing so hard now, he almost couldn't breathe. And he could feel heat radiating up the passageway. The fire was coming.

He stood on the bed and grabbed Reed's feet, helping to push him up and out.

Then finally, it was his turn. Two hands reached down and hauled him up by the armpits. He wanted to yell at Reed to go, get off the boat. But he could hardly find the air to keep pulling himself up into the daylight. His arms trembled and he felt weak and light-headed.

Reed dragged him the rest of the way up, and then he was standing on the foredeck. He glanced backward and saw the whole back of his boat alight, flames licking greedily into the sky. Keira, Dalton and Mia were already in the water, swimming away from the boat. But Sierra was still standing near the railing. Waiting for Reed.

"Go. Go," he screamed at her. Then he saw Captain, crouched at the very tip of the front of the boat. His eyes were large and round, and he was hissing at the flames with all his might. He couldn't leave the cat. Logan lunged across the netting between the two hulls, his fingers brushing Captain's fur.

A huge explosion split the air, the sound deafening, throwing him into the air like a rag doll.

# CHAPTER ELEVEN

Mia moved around on her plastic chair, trying to get comfortable. Her clothes were still damp and salty and stuck to her skin. The white shorts were now more of a grey color, and her pink shirt had a rip in one sleeve. The odor of disinfectant drifted past her nostrils, and she wanted to cover her nose. She hated the smell of hospitals. While this wasn't technically a hospital, it was the closest they got here on St. John.

They were in the Myrah Keating Smith Interim Health Centre, brought here by the well-meaning locals who'd fished them out of the ocean. This new facility had been built right next to the old one, which'd been destroyed by Hurricane Irma. She was alone in the long, white corridor, and the urge to get up and run was getting stronger by the second.

Logan's boat had exploded. Been set alight. On purpose. Someone had tried to kill them. This was like living in a waking nightmare. How had she got mixed up in all of this?

And the worst part was, her money had been on that boat. All her life savings had gone up in a ball of fire. What was she going to do now? That money was going to be her fresh start.

There was movement off to her left.

"How's Sierra?" she asked, standing up as Logan came out

of one of the private exam rooms, his face drawn and haggard.

"Better now." He came up and enfolded her in his arms. At first, she thought it was to reassure her, but then she realized he was drawing as much comfort from her as she was from their contact.

"That's good." She sagged into him with relief. Sierra had nearly drowned. When the boat exploded, she and Reed were still standing on the foredeck. In the pandemonium that followed, it'd taken a while for them all to realize Sierra hadn't resurfaced with the rest of them. She must've been knocked unconscious by flying debris.

Reed had surfaced, coughing and spluttering, dazed and barely coherent. But it'd been Dalton who dived down to try and find Sierra. It'd taken him two goes before he found her and dragged her, not breathing, to the surface.

Luckily a nearby launch that'd been heading out on a fishing charter appeared next to them and Dalton had practically thrown Sierra on board, then leaped aboard himself and started CPR. By that stage Reed had figured out what was going on and was also hauling himself onto the boat, roaring like an enraged bull. One of the men on board the charter had to physically hold him back so Dalton could work on Sierra. Keira was helped on board by one of the other men, as Mia watched the whole thing unfold from the water.

After what seemed like hours—but was in reality probably only seconds—the passengers gave a cheer of triumph and Dalton stood up to let Reed bend down next to Sierra. She was breathing again.

A wave of nausea had swept over Mia. She wasn't sure if it was relief or pure terror at the idea Sierra may have died.

Logan had swum over to Mia, to make sure she was okay. But all she could do was nod her head to his questions fired at her like bullets. He was distracted by Captain the cat, who was trying to claw his way up onto his shoulders. Mia found out that day cats are actually very good swimmers. They just don't like to swim, but they can if they need to. Logan finally threw the bedraggled and very frightened cat on board the rescue boat, and came back to get her.

More boats pulled up next to them, and Mia and Logan were heaved up onto a smaller yacht, finally arriving, dripping and shaking on the deck.

Now Sierra was being examined by one of the doctors on call. There was some fear for her unborn baby, as there could be internal injuries, and the doctors were taking all precautions. Sierra also suffered some burns to her back and shoulders, when the boat exploded behind them.

Reed also had second-and-third-degree burns on his back and legs, but he wasn't leaving Sierra's side, and wouldn't allow the doctors to treat him until he knew for certain that Sierra—and his unborn baby—were going to be fine. Keira and Dalton both appeared to be unharmed, as was Mia, because they'd already been in the water when the boat blew up. Keira was in the room trying to calm Reed down, and Dalton was standing in the corner, offering his silent moral support, but also refusing to leave. It was close to bedlam in there, and Mia thought it better to stay out of their way.

The skipper of the boat that rescued them told Logan not to worry about the cat, he'd look after him. Logan asked the guy to find Rosie, one of the head volunteers at the turtle rescue. She was well-known on the island, had a real soft spot for all animals, and she would look after Captain for him for a few days, till he figured out what to do.

"They're going to transfer Sierra and Reed to St. Thomas."

Mia nodded. There was an ambulance boat for just that type of thing, always on standby, ready to take patients over to the main hospital.

"Are you going with them?" she asked.

"I doubt I'll be allowed," he replied. Then he lifted his head. "Besides, I think we're going to be tied up for at least the next few hours."

She followed his gaze and saw two island police officers making their way through the main door. They stopped at the reception desk, but the female officer looked directly at them.

Mia panicked. "What do we tell them?" she whispered. She looked up and could see the same uncertainty reflected in his eyes.

"Stick to the facts. We don't really know what happened on board," he said. "But I think we should keep the guy with the gun at the bottom of the ocean under wraps for now, don't you?"

Mia really wasn't sure anymore. The whole thing was one giant mess. But she nodded her agreement anyway.

One thing she did know was that Harry wouldn't appreciate it if she mentioned his name to the cops. And if he got mad, who knew what he might do. Mia needed to make sure Tianna was safe first.

"I'm going to have a quick word to Dalton and Reed," Logan whispered. Then he was gone, leaving her alone in the corridor to face the two cops. She tried to straighten her damp clothes and pushed her disheveled hair off her face. Painted what she hoped was a distressed look on her face— which wasn't hard to do—and went to meet the people in uniform.

"You one of the explosion victims?" The older policeman approached her down the corridor. He was squat and square-faced, the buttons of the light-blue police shirt straining a little in the middle. He was West Indian, his brown skin hardly showing any wrinkles, but Mia guessed by his graying temples he was in his fifties, at the very least. But he looked honest and likable, a bit like her father. Mia had seen him around the island, but never had the chance to meet him. Until now.

"Yes, I'm Mia Wilson," she responded, holding her chin up high.

"My name is Sergeant Noah Joseph." He held out his hand for her to shake. "And this is Officer Naomi Dartez."

"We're going to need to interview you all before you leave," Naomi said sharply, looking down her nose at Mia. Why was the woman looking at her as if she were a criminal, rather than a victim? She was also West Indian, but thin and muscular, Mia could see the ropey tendons on her neck as she spoke, her hair pulled back into a severe bun. And unlike Noah, who had a cheery, approachable manner, Naomi's mouth looked to be pulled down in permanent disdain. Mia took an immediate dislike to the female officer.

"No one is to leave this facility until we've spoken to each and every one of you."

What the hell? Mia took a step back from the female officer. Who the hell did she think she was talking to?

"Some of our group were injured." Mia directed her remark to Noah, deciding to ignore the woman. "At least two people are going to be transferred to St. Thomas by boat ambulance. So, you might just have to wait a while before you get all up in our faces." With these last words she looked pointedly back at Naomi, accentuating the point by putting her hands on her hips and giving her the death stare. How dare she come in here demanding they all talk to the cops immediately, treating her like *she* was somehow to blame for all this? Mia balled her fists on her hips to hold her rising anger in.

On a subconscious level, Mia knew her anger was a by-product of the stress and danger she'd just encountered. But who did this officer think she was? And why was she treating her like dirt? She was a fellow black woman; she should've been on her side.

Noah raised his hands in a placatory way. "Sorry, Officer Dartez didn't mean it like that."

He lowered his greying eyebrows at his partner, and while his comment earned him a haughty look, Naomi did finally mumble an apology. But the sour look on her face remained.

"You must be all very traumatized." Noah continued. "And scared by your ordeal. I'm sorry if Officer Dartez came on a little strong."

"Humph," Mia gave a grunt of displeasure. "The rest of them are all in there." She pointed to the private room.

"Who's the owner of the boat?" Naomi asked, barely keeping her voice civil. Wow, this woman really needed some lessons on compassion; she didn't seem like she had a single tolerant bone in her body.

Mia held in what she really wanted to say, eventually spitting out the words, "Logan Goldstein. He's in there with his two sisters and their boyfriends. He's the one you want to talk to." Mia wasn't sure why she'd pointed the finger at Logan so readily. The police would obviously find out soon enough he owned the catamaran, so why did it feel like she was betraying him by giving them his name?

But she suddenly needed the two police officers gone. The way Naomi was staring at her was giving her the heebie-jeebies. Did the woman know she was an exotic dancer? Did she have something against women earning a living using their bodies? Mia knew the idea was stupid, of course Officer Dartez didn't know what she did for a living. And even if she did, it should make no difference to the way she viewed her. As a victim of a crime. Not as the perpetrator.

Then Mia realized what was wrong. Why she could barely look these officers in the eye. Why she felt this sudden need to be alone, out from under the watchful glare of both police officers.

It was guilt. Pure and simple.

The flash of the man's face, just before Logan pushed him beneath the waves came to her in a shocking memory and she had to stifle a gasp.

Could they see it written on her face? Did they somehow know she was a killer, masquerading as a dancer? She was afraid she was going to give herself away. How did murderers do it? How did they keep their feelings, their deepest thoughts buried so deep no one could see the truth? She would make a terrible murderer. She *was* making a terrible murderer. Her hands were shaking, and she tucked them behind her back.

"In there," she said again, indicating with her head toward the closed door.

"Right." Sergeant Joseph gave her one more quick, quizzical glance before he said to Naomi, "I'll go and have a chat with the others. Can you arrange a suitable room somewhere, please? It might be more prudent to conduct the first interviews here, rather than back at the station. Especially if some of the victims are injured."

"Sure." Naomi didn't even look Mia's way as she ambled back down the corridor, like she owned the place.

"Take a seat, ma'am, I won't be long." Noah gave her a friendly smile and disappeared through the door, leaving Mia alone once more in the long corridor. She drew in a deep breath and let it out slowly. Then she collapsed into the nearest plastic chair before her knees gave way.

She wasn't able to do this. She'd thought she could keep this lie hidden. After all, she was good at keeping her feelings concealed. Not letting her true thoughts show. Her life as an exotic dancer meant she had to make it look like every single man she danced for was special, that they were powerful and virile, even while their fat, flabby bodies really repulsed her. She was strong, had grown up dealing with people from the streets, with unsavory types, along with the entitled rich men who thought they owned everything and everyone. Usually she could get whatever she wanted with a wink and smile.

But this was different. This was beyond her. She knew she'd buckle if she had to answer questions from that harpy of a woman cop. Her stomach was roiling at the mere thought of it all. Her breathing had become all sharp and uneven.

Mia glanced toward the end of the corridor, where Naomi had her back to her, leaning on the reception counter, talking earnestly with the nurse in charge. That way was blocked. And it was only a matter of time, perhaps only seconds, before Noah came back through that door.

Her gaze drifted to the other end of the corridor. A sign pointing to the bathrooms hovered over the last door on the left.

And right at the end, was door that said Emergency Exit.

It took her less than a second to decide.

She was up and out of her chair. In a dozen long strides, she was at the door. A quick glance over her shoulder told her Naomi was still with the nurse, and the corridor was otherwise empty. It was now or never. She had things she needed to do. Tianna's safety was weighing heavily on her mind. Where was she? Was she safe? Mia needed to find her and warn her; get her somewhere safe. Perhaps then she would come back and answer the cops' questions. But for now, it was up to Logan and the others to spin their stories.

She pushed the door handle, and slipped through, out into the bright sunshine.

# CHAPTER TWELVE

Logan fidgeted with a tiny bit of paper under the desk, folding and unfolding it over and over. It was the only outward sign of his agitation, but he hoped Sergeant Joseph couldn't see what he was doing. Logan also hoped this interview was just about over, because he was so fatigued, he might collapse in a heap on the floor at any second.

Keeping a tight rein over his features and emotions was doing his head in. It wasn't only mentally draining, it was physically exhausting. Add to that the drama of this morning's explosion, and Logan was surprised he wasn't a blubbering mess by now.

The other officer, Dartez, was waiting outside with everyone else. Probably keeping an eye on them, to make sure no one left before the police had a chance to talk to them. The nurse at reception had given the police the room they normally reserved for doctors when they were on call to hold their interviews. The desk was covered in doctor prescription pads and notebooks, a desktop computer sat in the corner.

"And you're sure you didn't see anyone near your boat before the fire?" This was the third time Sergeant Joseph had asked the question.

Logan kept his patience in check. "No. Like I told you, we

were all belowdecks for at least ten minutes before I smelled the smoke."

And for the third time that day, Sergeant Joseph gave him an unreadable stare. Did the guy believe him? Because that part, at least, was the truth. The bit about him having absolutely no idea how the boat caught on fire in the first place was a lie. Well, mostly a lie. Because he knew it hadn't been an accident, not a spark from a loose wire, like he told the cop. He knew the speed with which the fire had spread meant only one thing. That an accelerant of some kind had been spread around. And judging by the cop's unamused smile, he probably guessed the same thing. But it'd be hard for them to prove, with the boat resting in millions of tiny pieces at the bottom of the ocean.

"Hopefully we'll have some more answers for you once the divers have been down to see if they can recover anything," the Sergeant continued.

Logan broke out in a fine sweat. The last thing he wanted was police divers snooping around on the bottom of the ocean. He'd taken the man's body a good way out to sea before dumping it. But who knew what happened down there? Even with the heavy anchor weighing him down, there were ocean currents that could move a body a long way.

"That'd be great. I need to know what happened to my boat. The sooner the better." He tried to sound convincing; make like he was a man determined to find out what happened. Determined to buy himself a new boat so he could continue to live on St. John. And not like a man who was about to flee the island as soon as possible.

"We'll do the best we can," Sergeant Joseph said with a nod.

"I guess I'll need to find somewhere else to live for a while," he joked, pasting a smile on his face. The sergeant smiled back and then stood.

"Yes, you will." He patted Logan on the back, almost sympathetically, and Logan let out a slow breath. It seemed he'd made it through the interview. The cop was letting him go, and was even being friendly. Convivial. Not like he suspected Logan might know more about his boat blowing up than he was letting on.

At least Logan had had a chance to ask everyone else not to let on about the dead man floating at the bottom of the sea. Reed hadn't been happy with that, and Logan could see the man struggling with the ethics of not giving the police all the information. Logan could only hope he held his tongue, realized it was best for all of them concerned if the police were kept in the dark about that particular detail at the moment. Not being on the force himself, there was no way of knowing if Reed was ethically bound to tell the truth, even though he was in a foreign country. Would there be consequences for Reed if he was found out when he got home? Logan couldn't answer any of those questions. And he couldn't force him to keep his mouth shut, all he could do was hope and pray. Logan's fate was now in other people's hands.

"Right, well, that's everything for now. But don't leave the island, we'll have more questions for you."

"Yes, sure, Sergeant," he agreed. Whatever. He'd say just about anything to get out of here. He wanted to talk to Mia, see how she was holding up. She must be outside with the others, waiting her turn to be interviewed. Funny, he hadn't seen her in the corridor when they'd dragged him into the adjoining room for the first interview. Maybe she'd gone to the ladies, or outside, for a breath of fresh air.

He opened the door and was let back out into the foyer of the medical center.

Before Logan was even fully out of the door, the female officer was standing in front of him. "Where's your girlfriend?" The West Indian woman seemed to have a permanent sneer on her face.

"Sorry, what?" He swung his gaze around the long corridor. Dalton and Keira sat together on two plastic chairs a little farther down. And Sierra and Reed were probably already being shunted to the St. Thomas hospital; the police had agreed to question them later, once they'd been treated.

But Mia was nowhere in sight.

"She was gone when we came out," Keira called to him, a worried frown on her face.

"Did you check the ladies? Outside?"

"Yes." This woman was really starting to grate on Logan's nerves.

"It's okay, Naomi, I'm sure she hasn't gone far. We'll pick her up later for a chat."

"Yeah, well, I've already put out an island-wide APB, to make sure she doesn't try and leave the area."

"You did what?" Logan was flabbergasted. "We're the victims here. We haven't done anything wrong." Which wasn't technically true, but his wrath was getting the better of him.

"Haven't you?" The officer glared at him.

Jesus, this lady was on some kind of power trip. She was like the worst stereotypical bad cop from one of those terrible police procedural TV shows. And Sergeant Joseph was playing the stereotypical good cop.

"I'm going to look for her," he announced to Keira and Dalton. "I'm assuming I'm free to go now?" This question was addressed to the sergeant as he stared directly over Officer Dartez's head. The other man nodded in reply. "But like I said, don't—"

"Yeah, yeah, don't leave the island. I got it." Logan was practically snarling now. Probably not a good tone of voice to take with the local constabulary, especially when he needed them onside. But Mia was missing, and he didn't know what that meant. Was it as simple as she'd gone looking for her sister? Or was there something more? Did she plan on getting out while she could?

"Will you guys be okay?"

"Yes. Once we finish up here, we'll head back to our accommodation," Keira said. "Do you remember the address?"

"Tell me again," he requested. She'd told him once before where they were staying, but this time, he committed the address to memory.

Logan was about to say, *I'll phone you when I know more*, but then he remembered all of their phones had been ruined by their dunking in sea water. He couldn't even ring Mia to find out where she'd gone. If she'd even answer him, he thought darkly.

As if reading his mind, Dalton added, "I'll see if I can pick us up a couple of new phones later." That might not be as easy as Dalton thought, Cruz Bay was really only a small country town, with no shopping malls, or cinemas, mainly fresh food markets and tourist stalls. He might be able to borrow one, or buy a second-hand one on the black market, but Logan kept that thought to himself.

"We might have to go to St. Thomas for that," Logan said. "I'll see what I can find," he suggested, but he was already heading out the door, toward freedom. "Good luck," he called belatedly over his shoulder.

"You, too," Keira called back. But her attention was already on Dalton, who was being ushered into the interview room by Sergeant Joseph. Keira's face fell as she re-took her seat. Logan felt bad. He should stay and sit with his sister. They could both wait for Dalton to finish up. It was a lot to ask of them both, to lie for him. But there was no way he would be able to sit still while he worried about where Mia was and what she was doing.

Once he was outside, standing in the carpark, however, Logan stalled. Where to go next? He wasn't sure where to start. Mia told him she shared a house with a couple of other dancers, on the street up near Candi's BBQ. But she hadn't been specific about which one it was.

There was the gentleman's club where Mia worked. But he never even knew it existed until she told him. It was obviously kept a secret, even from the locals. But someone must know where it was. And now he knew to ask about it, perhaps Paz or one of his other mates might've heard of it.

Logan began walking towards the main street in town. It wasn't until he got his legs moving that he suddenly realized how stiff he was. He rolled his shoulders and felt a twinge in his neck and back. The nurse had given him a quick once-over, but he'd come out of the explosion relatively unscathed. There were a couple of grazes and a few bruises on his back, where he must've been hit by flying wood as the boat exploded. And some scratch marks on his arms and shoulders from Captain, who'd tried to use him as a life raft once they were in the water. At least his clothes were dry now, but they were uncomfortable and sticky from the saltwater. One of his shirt-sleeves was ripped, and there were a couple of scorch marks blackening the fabric. He must look a sight, more like a hobo than anything else.

All he had left was the clothes he had on his back. Literally. And the cat. At least Captain had survived. How would he cope living on land for a while? Logan was unsure where he might end up after all this was over, but if he could, he would come back for Captain. And if he could buy a new boat for the cat to live on, even better. At least his wallet had survived. The contents were wet and bedraggled, but if he was careful, the money would dry okay, and he crossed his fingers his cards would all still work.

He walked slowly up King Street, past the Jeep rental place and De Coal Pot, one of the island's trendier restaurants. Past a house painted bright pink, with a bright-yellow picket fence outside, and strands of bougainvillea draping over the walls. But the vivid colors of the island did little to cheer him up today. He stopped in the street next to The Longboard, a popular restaurant with locals and tourists alike. Where to next? He really needed to find Paz, and he could often be found hanging out at the Gekko Bar around the corner. Just as he was about to step off into the street, he heard his name being called.

"Logan. Is that you?"

Logan turned to see Tom and Dan seated at an outside table at Longboards, Tom hanging over the railing and beckoning to him.

"Jesus, man, we just heard about your boat. Are you okay?" Tom said, waving his arms for dramatic effect.

For a second Logan stopped to wonder, how the hell had they found out so quick? But then he supposed a boat exploding in the normally quiet and serene Cruz Bay would be the talk on everyone's lips.

He was about to answer, when he glanced at Tom's face, and the words died on his lips. Tom was a mess, his blond good looks marred and blackened. One eye was purple and blue, swollen almost shut, and a large cut split his lip. His face was a minefield of bruises. Logan couldn't see the rest of his torso, but he wondered if it looked the same as his face. Then he noticed the knuckles on both hands were bruised and raw. It looked like Tom had put up a fight. Logan winced at the thought. He'd completely forgotten about Tom in everything else that'd happened.

"God, mate. Look at you. I'm sorry." Logan clenched his fists at his own lack of ability to say the right words. "I heard, and I was going to come and see you, and…"

Tom waved away the rest of his apologies and said, "I'm beginning to take you seriously about not wanting your photo out there. If this is what happens."

"Tom, please tell me you're okay," Logan said, disbelieving Tom could brush it aside so easily. "Tell me what happened."

Tom gave a shrug. "Two guys appeared at my door. It was about ten minutes after you left. Perhaps that should've rung my alarm bells," Tom joked. "Or perhaps it was the fact they were wearing masks." Tom gave a broad smile at this, like it was some kind of big game, but it gave Logan chills. The guys had been protecting their identity. "But it wasn't till they started asking about you, that I began to put two and two together. I'm really sorry, man. I didn't mean to get you into any trouble."

What? Tom was apologizing to *him*? Surely, it should be the other way around. Logan glanced at Dan, but the older man sat there, listening to their conversation, not offering any judgments. Which was a little unusual. It put Logan even more on edge.

"Don't worry, man, I didn't tell them anything. My neighbor heard the noise and poked his head over the fence to see what was going on. I think his yelling spooked the guys."

"Thank God," Logan replied.

An uncomfortable silence descended, and Logan was trying to come up with an excuse so he could keep moving when Dan spoke for the first time. "Come join us. Grab a seat." Dan pulled a stool out from under the bench and patted it.

"I, ah…" Logan wavered. "I really need to be somewhere."

"I wasn't asking you, Logan. We need to talk. You owe Tom some answers." Dan was normally an easy man to work for; never demanding or nagging, he let his crew get by on their own initiative most of time. He was affable and genial, never raising his voice or using any kind of intimidation to get the work done. But the look on Dan's face right now had Logan in no doubt he wasn't going to be messed with. Not today. And he was probably right, Logan did owe them some answers. "Plus, we want to make sure you really are okay." Dan's voice softened slightly at this last comment.

Logan took the proffered stool. It looked like the two men had just finished a substantial lunch of Longboard's famous tacos. Logan could hardly believe it was still only lunch time, it felt like he'd already lived a lifetime, and this day was only half over.

"Do you want to order something?" Tom asked, and began to wave a waitress over.

"I'm good." Food was the last thing on Logan's mind. "But I could murder a beer."

Tom laughed and gave his order to the waitress.

Dan didn't join in the small talk and as soon as the waitress was gone, he cut straight to the chase. "So, Tom and I have been talking. I came over to the island to make sure he was all right when I heard what happened," he added for clarification. "And we've come to the conclusion there is probably some kind of connection between your boat exploding and the men who beat Tom up in a bid to try and find you. Are we correct?" Dan kept his voice low, so they weren't overheard, but Logan was still knocked back on his stool. He took a quick glance around the restaurant. The rest of the patrons went on with their own conversations and meals, oblivious to Dan and his dramatic topic.

Dan speared him with his intuitive gaze.

The thing that bothered Logan the most about this, was if they'd come to that conclusion so easily, then the police had probably done the same thing. No wonder they were treating him like he was the criminal. Funnily enough, they hadn't mentioned the episode with Tom in his interview at the clinic.

But the way the female officer was eyeing him and Mia made Logan think they knew more than they were letting on.

What was his best path here? Tell the truth? Or come up with some bullshit story and get away quick? He still needed to find Mia. Right at that moment, Logan's beer arrived, and he took a big swig as a way to buy himself more time.

"I'm not a hundred percent sure," Logan finally admitted. Perhaps it was time to let Tom and Dan in on some of the stuff he was going through. They might be able to help, as long as they promised to keep the information to themselves for now.

"Really?" Dan grunted.

"It's true, I'm not sure. I don't know exactly who did this, or why. But you're right that they probably are connected."

"So, is it because I shared your photo on Facebook?" Tom asked eagerly, his blue eyes lighting up with intrigue.

"Yes, I think so," Logan sighed. "Look, I don't have time to go into all the details, but there are two brothers from Mexico who've been after me for a while. They're not nice dudes, and now it looks like they might've found me."

"Then we need to get you off the island," Dan said quickly, his bright mind going through all the permutations before Tom could even open his mouth to reply. "I brought the research boat; we can smuggle you out on that…"

Logan held up a hand. "It's not as easy as that," he said ruefully. "It's not just me I have to worry about. My two sisters and their boyfriends arrived yesterday. We were all on board when the boat blew up. Sierra, my middle sister, and her man, Reed, were injured in the blast. They're on St. Thomas now, in the hospital. But Keira and Dalton are still on the island."

"Jesus," Tom whistled.

"All right," Dan said, pursing his lips. "We can still all fit on the research boat. Go get them and I'll take you all."

"Thanks, Dan. I really appreciate the fact you would be prepared to get mixed up in this. For me." Logan gave him a sincere smile. He'd never really considered it before, but Tom and Dan were both good friends. Not just work colleagues. "But that's not all. Remember Mia, from the turtle rescue?" He addressed this question to Tom.

"Sure do," he replied and tried to wink, but his poor bruised eye wouldn't cooperate, so he gave a smirk instead. "She's gorgeous, man."

"Well, she was on board as well. And she's kind of mixed up in this, too. I need to find her. But she's gone missing."

"Damn, Logan, you really know how to show a girl a good time!" Tom laughed, but Logan was finding it hard to find the humor in this.

"I know this is going to sound strange, but have either of you heard of a gentleman's club, here on the island?"

Dan shook his head, and Tom started to do the same, but then he suddenly stilled. "Wait. Do you mean like a dance club, with, you know, exotic dancers?" When Logan nodded, he said, "I did hear something from Matt, the guy who runs Steve's Bar. A couple of gorgeous girls came in one night while I was sitting at the bar. I asked him about them, and he said not to go near them. Said they worked for some guy who owned a dance club—can't remember his name—as dancers and that this guy was very *protective* of his property, as he put it. When I asked how I could get into this dance club, he said it was invitation only, but he'd heard it was in a warehouse out the back of The Marketplace, you know, up on Highway 104?"

"Was this guy's name Harry, by any chance?" Logan asked, but he already knew the answer.

"Yeah, that might've been it," Tom said, a look of pride crossing his face that he could be of help.

"I might go and check it out, thanks," Logan replied.

"Do you need help? Do you want us to come with you?" Tom's bruised face brightened at the prospect.

The last thing Logan needed was Tom to get into even more danger because of him.

"No thanks, mate, you've helped more than enough."

Dan seemed to know better than to offer his help to Logan. But he did say, "Call me if you need a lift out of here." He clapped a fatherly hand on his back. "Anything we can do, just let us know."

"Thank you." Logan was so humbled he could hardly speak.

The clatter and noise of the busy restaurant encroached in on Logan. He'd been so engrossed in the conversation he'd almost forgotten where he was. He knocked back the rest of his beer. Life was going on around him, everyone else oblivious to his troubles. People clinked their glasses together or sat back and patted full stomachs. Longboards wasn't luxurious, it had a rustic sort of beach theme going, but the food was great, and it was always busy. For a split second, Logan wished he could stay here with Tom and Dan. Order another beer and a famous poke bowl. And have a pleasant conversation with his two friends.

Instead, he hopped off his stool and slapped a soggy ten-dollar note on the table. "Thanks, guys. You have been more help than you realize. And again, I'm so sorry, Tom. I'd like to make it up to you, somehow. Soon."

"No probs, dude." Tom gave him a lopsided smile, then winced when it hurt his split lip.

"Stay safe," Dan warned.

Logan turned up the street and began to weave his way through the growing, mid-afternoon crowd.

# CHAPTER THIRTEEN

Mia stared up at the stars through the tiny window in the wall above. The window was too high to reach, even if she stood on Tianna's shoulders. But Mia still looked; yearned to climb up there. To freedom. She could see the stars Logan had shown her on the first night she'd spent on his boat. If only they could lead her out of here, the way they'd led Logan around the Caribbean. Pinning her hopes on the stars was stupid and futile. They were cold balls of gas burning millions of miles away. Nothing more. And they certainly weren't hearing her prayers tonight.

"What are you doing?" Tianna's voice drifted to her out of a dark corner of the room.

"Nothing," Mia sighed. She went over and sat next to her sister on the cold concrete.

"Trying to devise more crazy plans to get out of here?" Mia could hear the attempt at a teasing tone Tianna tried to inject into her voice, but she wasn't in the mood. She wanted to snap at her sister, tell her it was her fault they were in here in the first place. But she'd already said that, more than once. And it wouldn't change their predicament.

They were trapped.

In some basement room below Harry's gentleman's club.

The room was used for storage; there was a stack of metal boxes over by the other wall. All of them were locked and Mia wondered what the hell was in them. She had a few ideas, and none of them were legal. But apart from the boxes, the room was barren. No furniture, no chairs or tables. At least it was cool in here. Otherwise it would've been stifling, as there was no airflow, and the place stank of mold and long-forgotten dust.

The windows she could see up high were probably at street-level, as the floor of the basement was sunk below ground.

"How are you feeling?" Mia asked, her anger relinquishing its hold as compassion flowed back through her.

"I'm better. Not so groggy. I think I could probably sit up now."

"Okay, let's give it a try." Mia got her hands under Tianna's shoulder and gently levered her up, so her back was leaning against the wall. "Let me know if your head starts spinning again," she said, not letting go of Tianna's arm.

Her sister had been drugged. A powerful drug it must've been, too, because she'd only begun to wake up an hour or so ago. Nearly six hours after Mia had found her passed out in Harry's office this morning. It was taking a long time to wear off.

Mia should've known better. She should never have responded to Harry's message. Should've known it would be a trap. But what other choice did she have?

She'd been careful, at least to start with. After leaving the health clinic, she hadn't run straight home to see if Tianna was there. Even though that was her first instinct. Instead she'd gone and found the only public telephone booth on the island—her cell was beyond repair after its dunking in the ocean, and she'd had no time to replace it—and phoned Crystal. Just in case some of Harry's thugs were waiting for her. It was still only mid-morning by that stage, and if Crystal and Scarlett stuck to their routine, they'd be getting out of bed around now.

Crystal had picked up on the second ring. "Where you been, girl?" she asked. "You didn't come home last night. Again." Crystal's tone held all kinds of censure.

"Sorry, Crystal, I can't explain right now." Mia felt bad. She'd planned on sneaking off the island without telling her two friends. There was no way she was going to trust them with that kind of secret. They'd be mad when they found out. Mia had left some money for next week's rent on top of her dresser, which they would've found eventually. But the point wasn't really that she was leaving them without a paying roommate. The point was they would feel betrayed and angry, wondering where in the hell she'd gone. They'd worry about her. But Mia couldn't think about that now.

"Have you seen Tianna? Did she come home last night?" It was a vain hope; a stab in the dark. After their confrontation at the café yesterday, it was most unlikely Tianna would show her face, certainly not at home. But Mia had to check. Her next phone call was going to be to the boyfriend, Todd.

"No, we haven't seen hide nor hair of her skinny ass." Crystal's voice had taken on an edge; Mia wasn't sure what kind of edge, but it made her wary. Did Crystal know something?

"But?" Mia prompted.

"But we did get a message from Harry this morning. Early this morning." That got Mia's instincts on high alert. Harry didn't do early mornings and he knew Crystal and Scarlett didn't either.

"He said Tianna had been to see him. That she was very upset about something. And he would like to discuss her future with you. He said it was very important you come and talk to him as soon as possible."

Mia's blood ran cold.

"I'm not sure what that means. It's a little cryptic. Is Tianna all right?" Crystal asked.

"Yes, she's fine." Mia somehow stammered out the words, but her mind was far away. Hoping Tianna actually was fine. She wasn't sure what Harry's aim was, but she had a terrible feeling if she didn't go see him, Tianna might be in big trouble. Was he using her as bait? "Thanks, Crystal, I owe you one." Mia hung up the phone before Crystal could ask any more questions.

Should she tell Logan? She felt like she should. But how was she going to contact him? They'd both lost their phones, and there was no way she was going back to the medical clinic to try and see him in person. That witch of an officer was sure to detain her, at least until she'd interviewed her. And Mia needed to be free.

Mia slipped out of the phone booth and wandered over to the nearest park bench. There were lots of people in Franklin Powers Park, it was close by the ferry terminal, and most were loitering, waiting for the next ferry to arrive. She needed to think. Where would Harry be? Mia had hung up before Crystal had a chance to tell her where Harry expected to meet her. Crystal's words echoed in her head. Harry had said to come and talk to him, to discuss Tianna's future. The only other chats she'd had with Harry about Tianna had been in his office, inside the warehouse he used to camouflage the gentleman's club. But should she go there, unarmed and unprepared? Just walk in like she owned the place. What if one of Harry's thugs was waiting to ambush her as she walked through the door? Harry had definitely been acting a little off last night. Like she'd said to Logan, she couldn't put a finger on exactly why, but there was something not right.

Without conscious thought, Mia found herself standing, her feet moving over the paved pathway, toward the post office, then turning right up Prince Street and onto Highway 104. The warehouse was behind a large shopping center called The Marketplace, and it seemed Mia's feet were taking her there on their own.

She thought about trying to disguise herself, but then decided against it. Enough people knew she was on this island, and it was such a small island, going in disguise would probably attract more attention, not less. Her pink shirt and white shorts were definitely worse for wear, and her hair was a mess, but she probably blended right in with everyone who'd just come off the beach, so she decided to forget about it. The road was winding and there was no footpath, but it was the same everywhere on St. John. People walked on the road, there was no other choice. There were plenty of cars, scooters, and taxis all negotiating the highway, and Mia kept to the gravel edge as much as she could. It was hot, the humidity stifling. She should be used to this weather; she'd lived in the Caribbean all her life. But today she found it oppressive and all she wanted to do was go home and take a cool shower and gulp down a beer straight out of the fridge.

The heat and the stress of the morning were starting to take their toll. Mia's steps began to slow and a lump formed in her throat. What in hell was she doing? How had she ended up in this mess in the first place? Her life had been fine before she met Logan Goldstein. She made a good living out of being an exotic dancer, and while she had some worries about Tianna and her drug habit, she'd been managing it all. Hadn't she? Perhaps if she went to Harry, divulged everything that'd happened over the past few days, laid herself at his feet, relied on his mercy, he'd help her. She was one of his best dancers. It was why he agreed to the deal to free Tianna from his clutches. She was worth more to him as a dancer, than Tianna was as his sex slave.

The logical part of her brain knew she couldn't and

shouldn't trust Harry, not for a second. But at the moment, he seemed like the lesser of two evils. If it really was the two brothers who were hunting Logan that'd sent that man with the gun and blown up his boat—which it seemed more and more likely was the case—then Harry might help her. Or at least be sympathetic to her cause.

It was with these thoughts spiraling through her brain that she made the final approach up the hill toward The Marketplace. Out the front of the large, colonial-style building, cars and people were everywhere. Which was actually a good thing, as Mia would blend in with the crowd. She made her way past the Papaya Café, where a gaggle of elderly tourists took up most of the outdoor seating, sipping their lattes and talking at the top of their voices. It was surreal, that these people could go about their everyday lives, not even realizing Mia was on the run for her life.

A deep melancholy settled over Mia. Now was definitely not the time or the place to be contemplating the choices she'd made in her life. But nevertheless, she was feeling defeated and foolish, wishing she could be anywhere but here. Be anyone but herself. If she could go back in time, what would she change? She'd been so desperate to become a dancer, any kind of dancer, that she hadn't really listened to any of the other voices in her head. Back then all she'd felt was anger toward her father because he didn't have the money to send her to ballet school. He hadn't agreed with her choices, either. There had been another alternative, but at the time she hadn't wanted to see it. She'd been very good at science, loved nature and loved learning about ways to make this world a better place. Her high school teacher had spoken to her once about perhaps getting a scholarship to the University of the West Indies to study ecology; said her grades were good enough if she wanted to try for it. But Mia had brushed her off. The only thing that interested her back then was dancing.

What if she'd gone to university, instead? Where would she be right now? Perhaps doing what Tom did on the turtle research project for UVI? The idea had its merits. It was why she'd been drawn to volunteer at the turtle rescue in the first place. That little voice in her head that'd always whispered to her about her love for animals and the environment had finally gotten loud enough for her to listen. But it was all too little, too late now.

The pathway led her around the side of the shopping market and toward the back of the building. It was much quieter here, and Mia found herself suddenly on guard. She needed to pull herself together. Tianna was the important thing now. That, and getting off the island in one piece. She could think about her new life after.

Threading her way out behind the Dumpsters and piles of boxes used for storage by some of the shops, Mia wanted to cover her nose and mouth. This place was dank and smelled bad. Which was probably why Harry had chosen this dirty, forbidding warehouse nestled in the grime at the back of the shops. No one in their right mind came out here unless they absolutely had to. And no one would guess that down that small alley was a door that led to a luxurious and modern dance club, hidden in plain sight.

The mouth of the alleyway was dark and shadowed. Mia crouched behind one of the Dumpsters to watch. To decide her best course of action. There were other ways into the warehouse. The dancers often left by the back door, which was really an old fire exit, leading down into a small carpark surrounded by the ever-encroaching jungle. But the door only opened from the inside, so she'd have to wait for someone to come out before she could slip inside. She might be waiting all day for that to happen.

There were windows, running at street level at irregular

intervals around the building. But as far as Mia knew, most of them had metal bars over them. The only other way in would be to climb up on to the roof. Harry had built a private roof garden, where he liked to go by himself, on occasion. He rarely let anyone else up there. Tilting her head back, Mia looked up at the three-story building. Climbing up would be nearly impossible.

Which left the front door as her only option.

Besides, Harry was most likely waiting inside for her. He knew she'd get his message sooner or later.

Mia stood up and straightened her shoulders, readjusting her shorts and undoing two more buttons on her shirt, then untucking it from her shorts and knotting it at her waist. Harry liked her. She was going to play on that. It was the one weapon in her arsenal right now.

The alley was completely deserted when she peered around the corner. Was that a good thing, that there were none of his thugs stationed outside the door? Was it meant to lull her into a false sense of security? If it was, it was working.

This was it. She'd been through this doorway more times than she could count on her way to work. She just needed to pretend this time was no different. Mia strode up the disgusting alley, ignoring the stench of something rotting in the gutter, as well as the flutter of a piece of paper being blown lazily down the dirt path. Her hand reached for the doorknob and she sucked in a fortifying breath before yanking it open and walking through as if she owned the place. As if this was just a normal day, and she was here to have a normal chat with Harry.

The corridors were empty, which spooked her a little. But she made it to the door of Harry's office without incident. Readjusting her shirt, she made sure her bra was exposed and took a deep breath. If she was going to beat Harry at his own game, she needed to keep up an act of righteous indignance.

Bluff her way through. Without bothering to knock, she threw open the door and stalked in.

And stopped in her tracks when she saw Tianna slumped in a chair in the corner, Harry hovering over her.

"What have you done?" she said, an icy calm descending over her. She felt rather than saw one of Harry's thugs slide away from the wall behind her and shut the door with a solid thud. She was trapped.

Ignoring him, she took two steps across the room toward her sister. She needed to make sure she was still breathing. Harry stood up, barring her way, his rough hands biting into the flesh at the tops of her arms as he took hold of her.

"So nice of you to come when you're called, Mia."

"What have you done to her?" she ground out between gritted teeth. "If you've hurt her, or…" Mia couldn't say the words, because if her sister was dead, she wasn't sure what she would do. But the mere thought had her almost buckling at the knees.

"Just gave her something to help her sleep." Harry's fingers tightened, and Mia winced in pain. "But if I were you, I'd be more worried about what I'm going to do to you."

Mia let out a breath. Thank God Tianna was alive. Harry was a deceitful slime-ball, but she was pretty sure he wouldn't lie about that.

"What do you mean?" she snapped, her focus finally sliding to Harry's face. She jerked herself backward, out of Harry's grasp. She was tall for a woman, and Harry was short. The girls often liked to joke about his little-man syndrome. So, she was looking down at him now, which she knew would irritate him.

"You've been a naughty girl, Mia." His dark eyes fixed on her, his swarthy face lighting up with evil intent. "I know what you've been up to, and I'm not happy. Not happy at all." He leaned in toward her, his manicured beard tickling her cheek.

"I don't know what you're talking about." It was a weak attempt at a bluff, but Mia was struggling to get her brain working, to find the right angle that might get her, and her sister, out of here alive.

"Oh, don't you?" His smile didn't make it anywhere near his eyes. "Let's see if I can refresh your memory. First of all, there's the turtle guy, what's his name? Logan something? Now, you know how much I dislike you fraternizing with anyone outside my club." Harry stopped talking and stared at her, letting her absorb his words. But she wasn't really surprised, she'd guessed he'd find out about Logan sooner or later. She had a story already concocted to explain Logan and she opened her mouth to reply, when Harry said, "Or, how about the guy you killed down at the dock? Does that ring any bells?"

The blood drained from Mia's face and she felt slightly sick.

"How did you—?"

"Of course, I know, you stupid girl. I know everything that goes on on this island."

Mia's head was spinning. Did that mean the dead guy was actually working for Harry after all?

"Were you having me followed? Was that one of your guys?" she asked, not really expecting an answer. Of course, Harry knew what she'd done. It was a small island. How had she ever thought she'd have time to escape this place without him finding out first?

"I need to know what you did with the body. Although I have to say, I admire your audacity. I never thought you had it in you to take part in a murder and then cover it up. Did you dump him at sea? Is that what you did with him? You certainly are full of surprises." Dark eyebrows raised in contemplation as he stared at her. "But they can't have the cops finding the body, so I'll need to do something about it."

Harry glanced over the top of Mia's head and said, "Ain't that right, Serge?"

She thought she heard the man behind her mumble something like, "Bloody amateurs." Serge was one of Harry's regular guards, Mia recognized him as soon as she walked through the door. He was big and brawny, with brains the size of a pea, all traits Harry seemed to value in the men he hired.

All of a sudden, Harry's words struck home, and Mia realized all those vague things she'd thought about Harry and his business dealings were actually true. Her ideas of him using violence to get what he wanted, had been abstract at best. But now she had proof he and his thugs were very much into killing for their business. Harry was indeed a man to be feared. He was just as ruthless and barbaric as she always imagined.

And now she knew that the man with the gun had been working for Harry all along. Not the Ramirez brothers, at all. It had been *her* the man was after. Poor Logan had been caught up in her drama. Not the other way around, as she was starting to believe.

Logan had lost his beautiful boat because of her.

But as she thought about Logan's catamaran, questions began to form. Why would Harry want to blow up Logan's boat? If it was his way of sending a message, then he'd definitely made a hell of an impression. But he must've known there were other people aboard. If it'd been Logan alone, or just her and Logan, then maybe she could understand. But trying to kill six people didn't make a lot of sense. Not if Harry wanted to keep operating on this island. It'd be better if everything was dealt with quietly, on the down-low. It was a very strange way to handle it. Harry was hot-headed, had a temper like a striking viper when someone crossed him, but even he must've thought twice about blowing up a boat. Unless his information had been wrong, and he didn't know there were other people on board.

She couldn't help it; the question was out before she could stop it. "Why did you blow up the boat?"

Harry didn't answer, instead shooting an indecipherable look at Serge.

"What were you hoping to achieve? Where you really trying to kill us all?" she prompted. Was that a grimace she saw flash over his face? None of this was making a whole lot of sense. "I mean, I can understand why you might want me dead," she mused. "But Logan's family, as well? Did you know they were on the boat?"

"Enough," Harry roared. "In case you haven't noticed, you're in my office, under my control. You don't get to ask the questions, I do." His piggy little eyes bulged with rage, looked like they might even burst out of their sockets. "You've become a liability to me and my business. You've brought down all sorts of unwanted problems on top of me. I have other people I need to answer to now. We can't have you talking to the cops. Not about anything." Mia took a stumbling step backward at the cool, blank stare he gave her. As if she meant nothing to him. It scared her.

For a split second she thought about running. But then the burly man standing between her and the door came back to her. And Tianna. She couldn't leave Tianna.

"What are you going to do with us?" she mumbled.

"I need to know what you've said to the cops. I've got people hounding me for answers from all sides." He glowered at her from beneath bushy eyebrows. "We had an agreement, you and I, Mia. I'm sorely disappointed. I thought I could trust you. But it turns out you're just like the rest of them." Harry turned away, headed back to his desk and sat down with a grunt. If Mia hadn't known any better, she might've thought that was a trace of regret she saw echoed in the lines around his dark eyes. But the thought was gone in a second when his face transformed into a sneer. "Take them away, Serge. I don't want to look at either of them anymore. I'll talk to them later, when that one wakes up." He pointed a pudgy finger in Tianna's direction. "I've got more important things to think about." Harry ran a hand through his dark thatch of hair and Mia suddenly had the impression Harry was worried. About more than just her and Tianna. Like maybe all this had bigger ramifications for his company dealings. What had he said, he had other people he had to answer to now? Good. She hoped his dodgy business was brought crumbling to the ground and he rotted in hell.

"If nothing else, at least you'll make good bait," Harry had mumbled as Serge threw Tianna over his shoulder like she was nothing more than a sack of potatoes and shoved Mia to get her moving. "Remember the bracelet," Harry called to Serge, as they exited through the door.

Serge had dumped them unceremoniously in the basement. Then he'd done something completely incomprehensible to Mia, yanking at the bracelet on her wrist until it broke off in his hand, and left without even glancing back. Why the hell had he done that? Mia rubbed her sore wrist and glared at the door, but no answers came to her.

And now they were trapped down here. No one knew where they were. And she hadn't thought any more about Harry's parting words, until now. What had he meant by *bait*? Bait for what? Or for whom?

A horrible thought occurred to her. Was it Logan they were hoping to draw in? But what could Harry possibly want with Logan? Unless it was to finish the job they'd started by blowing up his boat. To make sure there were no witnesses left behind.

She found herself hoping Logan wouldn't come looking for

her, after all.

What was he doing right now? Would he even worry about her? He was probably too caught up with his own family dramas to give her a second's thought. She should've told him where she was going, she knew that now. But perhaps it was better this way. Logan might be able to leave the island and get away. Use his family as an excuse. Go over to the hospital on St. Thomas to visit his sister and Reed. Now she and Tianna weren't around to tie him down, he was free to flee to safety on his own. If he knew what was good for him, he would just keep going from St. Thomas. With his family around him, and the police keeping a close eye on him, he'd be protected.

Mia would miss him.

The thought brought her up sharp. Because in reality, there was no future for the two of them. It was pure fantasy, that they might've been able to get together, even before all this happened. What did she think was going to happen? Would she have moved out to his boat, to live with him? He could've kept on with his turtle rescue, and she could've kept on with her dancing, and they would've lived happily ever after? No. For one thing, Harry would never have allowed that.

Besides, she hardly knew Logan. And he hardly knew her. They were from completely different backgrounds. A white boy from a privileged Australian family, and a black girl from the poverty-stricken streets of Jamaica were never going to make it.

One thing she did know, he was a great kisser. The other morning on the boat still burned brightly in her memory bank. Before they'd been rudely interrupted by his family, he'd brought her body alive like no one had done in a very long time. Perhaps ever. It wasn't just his good looks that attracted her, although they didn't hurt. There were plenty of good-looking, rich men propositioning her almost every night, if that's what she was interested in. It was something that went way deeper, something she could see in his eyes. A connection, an allure. Magnetism, even. Whatever it was, it drew her to him like a moth to a flame.

He was kind, compassionate. She knew that from watching him with the turtle she'd found on the beach. He loved nature and the environment. So maybe they did have one thing in common. And he was funny, had the same sense of humor she did. Over their dinner at Sunny's, he'd had her in stitches with his jokes and easy manner.

"Are you okay?" Tianna's voice brought her back to reality with a thump.

"What? Oh, yes."

A heartbeat of silence hung in the air, then Tianna said, "Mia?" There was a wobble in her voice.

"Yes."

"I'm sorry."

"It's okay." Mia lay a comforting hand on her sister's leg.

"No, it's not. It's my fault we're down here. You warned me, and I didn't listen. I know I've acted like a selfish cow."

This was the first time Mia had heard words of true contrition come out of Tianna's mouth. She was so stunned that for a second, she couldn't speak.

Tianna filled the silence. "I've never really thanked you for what you did. You know, to get me away from Harry."

"Any sister would've done the same." Mia tried to brush off Tianna's words. Because it was true. Wasn't it? Who in their right mind could walk away from their own flesh and blood? She certainly couldn't.

"No, they wouldn't. I was too deep into my addiction to really care. Back then, I didn't want to admit it, but I would've done just about anything to get a fix. I *did* do just about anything, and I didn't give a shit," she amended. "I was blind to the fact Harry was taking advantage of me, that he owned me. And I couldn't appreciate all you did to help free me from his clutches."

Mia tipped her head on the side, considering Tianna's words. She was about to defend her sister, say that Tianna had been sick back then, she couldn't help it, that it wasn't really her fault, when Tianna interrupted her thoughts.

"But now I'm clean, I can finally see Harry for the pig that he is. All those false promises he made, how he used me. When I first met him, he made me feel special. You know, important; an exotic dancer, with the world at my feet. And, at first, I resented you. Thought all you wanted to do was steal my limelight. But I can see that was all a dream now. A stupid, shallow dream."

Tianna didn't know the half of it. She didn't know that Harry had been so close to selling Tianna off to the highest bidder, to be used as a personal prostitute. Mia had stepped in just in time. And she would do it all again, if it meant saving her baby sister.

"I'm going to be a better sister, I promise. I mean it, Mia."

"I know you do," Mia said, gathering Tianna into her arms. They hugged for many minutes, emotion clogging Mia's throat. But it was time to pull themselves together. It was nice to have Tianna finally see how damaging her actions had been. But they needed to survive this first, then they could have a much-needed talk about remorse and contrition, and how they could be better sisters to each other from now on.

Mia lifted her head. "I was thinking that perhaps we could drag a couple of these metal boxes over under this window." She pointed up to the tiny, square pane. "We might be able to get high enough to reach it."

"Aren't there bars on the window?" It was hard to see Tianna's face, the only light coming from the starlight shining through the tiny windows. But she could tell by the tone of her sister's voice, she was watching her with narrowed eyes.

"I'm not sure," Mia admitted, standing. She was right, the windows Mia had seen from the alley all had bars over them. But this window must be on the other side of the building, away from the alley and the front door, otherwise she wouldn't have been able to see the stars. Perhaps these weren't so secure. She couldn't see any bars from down here, but that didn't mean anything, they might be at too low of an angle to see for sure.

"How are you feeling now?" she asked Tianna. "Are you up to dragging a box or two with me."

"Sure. They might be heavy, though."

Mia felt her way over to the metal box in the dark. They were stacked three on top of each other, and there were three stacks. Using her fingers, she checked all around one of them, feeling the lid and the padlock—to make sure it really was locked—until she found a handle on each end. Gingerly, she tugged one of the handles. The box didn't budge. She pulled harder. It shifted about half an inch. When she pulled with all her might, the box creaked and she heard metal scrape on metal, but it still hardly moved at all.

They were damn heavy. For the second time that night, Mia wondered what on earth Harry kept in them.

"Come and give me a hand." She heard Tianna's footsteps on the dusty floor as she came over to join her. Together, they hauled and grunted and puffed, until one of the boxes landed on the ground with a resounding crash. They both stopped and looked in the direction of the door. Had Serge heard that? Was he going to come charging in to see what was going on? Perhaps tie them up, so they couldn't move?

"I don't think he heard," Tianna whispered, although why she was whispering, after all the noise they'd just made, Mia wasn't sure.

After a few more seconds with no sound of anyone on the other side of the door, Mia let her gaze fall back to the box, now lying on its side at their feet. It was no good, the boxes were too heavy, they weren't going to be able to move them. But as she bent down to look closer, using the starlight to see by, she saw one corner of the metal box had been damaged.

"Help me with this," she said, puffing with exertion as she tried to right the box again. With both of them pushing, the box finally landed back on its base with a clang. "The lid has lifted in the corner. The whole thing is twisted." Mia heaved with all her might and the lid suddenly popped open, sending her flying backward onto her butt. Scrambling up, Mia stood in time to see Tianna reach into the box and pull something out. It was large, and oddly shaped; it looked heavy as Tianna struggled with it.

"What is it?" she asked. Not guns, or drugs, which had been uppermost in her mind.

"I think it's a turtle shell," Tianna said, the confusion obvious in her voice.

Mia ran her hands over the rough surface, a shudder going through her at the feel of it under her fingers. It was, indeed, a turtle shell.

Mia didn't think Harry could sink any lower in her estimation. But this? This was the epitome of the worst kind of depravity. Turtle poachers were at the very bottom of the ladder on the rung of human mortality as far as Mia was concerned. And Harry *The Hook* was involved in the illegal trade. Selling their shells on the black market for millions of dollars. It seemed she and Tianna had unwittingly stumbled across a haul that was probably due to be shipped out to China very soon. Ironically, they'd possibly uncovered the big poaching ring the Coast Guards had been trying to capture for months.

Mia felt sick. Tears prickled at the back of her eyelids for all these poor, lost creatures. Such beautiful souls, who deserved to be allowed to live in freedom and safety. Fear for herself and Tianna was replaced by something much stronger. Hate and anger.

"We need to get out of here," she said. That was still her top priority, to get herself and Tianna to safety. But when they got out, she was going to make damn sure Harry was brought down for this.

# CHAPTER FOURTEEN

Logan struggled, trying to twist out of the man's hold. But every time he moved the guy tightened his grip, pulling Logan's arm higher up his back, until he was gasping in pain and had to bend over to ease the agony.

"Behave yourself, you little dipstick." The thickset guy gave a savage yank on Logan's arm and he cried out.

"All right, all right," Logan panted. He stopped struggling, but the man didn't ease his grip on his arm. Logan gritted his teeth against the pain. God, he was a stupid ass. How had he thought he was ever going to get into this warehouse unseen? At the time, it'd seemed fairly straightforward. He'd been full of bravado and desperate to find Mia.

It'd taken him a while to find the warehouse after Tom's vague directions. At first, Logan had been sure this couldn't be the correct place. It was so old and dirty, looked disused, as if it should be condemned. Not the kind of place for a fancy gentleman's club at all. But looks could be deceiving, and after a quick search of the surrounding streets he came back to the building. This had to be it.

But he wasn't even sure Mia was in here. Wouldn't it be more likely she'd gone home? Logan was unsure what to do next. He could just walk in and demand to see the owner. Ask if Mia was there. But then, if Harry *The Hook* was behind the gunman, then he'd just be handing himself over, putting himself at the crazy man's mercy.

Dithering for a few more minutes, he decided to take a quick walk around the building. If he found nothing, he'd go and see if he could discover where Mia lived instead. Perhaps track down her dancing buddies, they might know where she was.

Strolling down the alleyway, he tried his best to look like a lost tourist. But he kept his eyes peeled, taking in every detail of this building. About half-way down the alley, a solid wooden door appeared in the brick work, the only entrance he'd seen so far. But Logan didn't stop, kept walking, not wanting to draw attention.

That's when he saw it. A glint of silver in the mid-afternoon sun.

He leaned down to take a closer look. And his breath stalled in his chest. It was a bracelet. Silver with a single turquoise bead in the middle.

Mia's bracelet.

He'd recognize it anywhere.

He picked it up and kept walking, madly trying to remember if Mia had been wearing it this morning.

It was all a blur, his sisters arriving early, the boat exploding, the cops interviewing him. But in amongst all that, Logan remembered Mia had been wearing the bracelet that morning. When he'd kissed her, the cool silver had slid up her wrist, clinked softly against his cheek as she took his face in her hands.

Which meant Mia had been here. Was probably still here, somewhere. He felt it deep down in his belly; she was in that building. And he needed to find her.

So, he'd waited till it was fully dark until he began his furtive exploration of the area. He'd been around the building twice. The rear of the warehouse backed directly onto a patch of raw jungle, and he'd had to claw his way through some of the denser sections. The insects had nearly eaten him alive, and he'd come out hot, sweaty, and scratching at bug bites. There were a few low windows that showed some promise. The best one was close to a small carpark at the corner, where the jungle gave way to dirt. But Logan would struggle to fit through. As far as he could tell, there was really only one door into the place. And he wasn't about to go marching straight into the arms of the enemy. Not if he could help it.

All his searching had been in vain, however, because he'd been captured by some hulking criminal—just the fact he was dressed in an Armani suit didn't make him any more sophisticated—and was no closer to discovering where Mia was.

The man had snuck up on him from behind, which again was surprising going on how big and imposing the guy was. Logan hadn't even had a chance to defend himself, let alone fight back. He should've brought backup. Dalton would've come with him, if he'd asked. But without a phone or any way to contact him, it would've meant Logan had to go back and find him, and he wasn't exactly sure where they'd be by now. Perhaps back at the rental villa, or perhaps they'd gone over to St. Thomas to be with Sierra and Reed. Logan didn't have the time to go searching. Tom might've helped him, but the poor guy had been through enough on Logan's behalf already.

And so stupidly—Logan preferred to think of it as courageously—he'd gone in alone. But the more he thought about it, bent over like a pretzel, helplessly waiting for the hulking guy to decide what to do with him, Logan began to think that perhaps being captured might have its advantages. He'd just about run out of options on how to get inside this place. And hopefully that was exactly where this guy was going to take him. Although what might be waiting inside was any man's guess.

He could feel the Hulk doing something behind his back, but because he was still bent over nearly double, he couldn't twist his head to see what he was up to.

"I got him." Logan was startled when the guy spoke from behind. It took him a second to realize he must be talking into a phone. "Yeah, he didn't even know I was there. Stupid little punk. What do you want me to do with him?"

There was a pause and Logan held his breath.

"Right, will do." The man moved behind him, and Logan assumed he was tucking his phone back in his pocket. "Let's go." He lessened the pressure on Logan's arm, so he could straighten up, but he didn't let go altogether. "Move." He was pushed, and he stumbled a few paces before being pulled back onto his feet.

"Where are we going?" Logan thought he'd try his luck. But he was met with deadly silence. His captor led them around the side of the building, threaded his way through a couple of Dumpsters, and then back down the alleyway. Logan was surprised when the main door opened as they got to it, and a man dressed all in black greeted the Hulk. This new thug didn't make any move to follow them as they went farther down the corridor, and Logan assumed he must be some kind of doorman, or bouncer. Were they expecting customers tonight? Mia hadn't filled him in on the details, but it seemed reasonable a place like this would operate on a Sunday night.

Logan hoped he might catch a glimpse of the interior of the gentleman's club. He was intrigued, he'd never been to an exclusive club like this before; one where your income had to be in the millions before you were invited in. But the Hulk kept frog-marching him down darkened corridors, turning this way and that, until Logan was completely lost. Then he pushed him through a door, and they were climbing stairs. Up three levels, at such a pace that Logan was puffing by the time they reached the top.

The Hulk shoved him through the door at the top, and Logan drew in a gasp of surprise. He was surrounded by small trees and shrubs; even brightly hued flowers. They'd come out into some kind of garden. A well-manicured and charming garden, with small, hidden, lamps illuminating a winding pathway in front. In any other setting, this would've been a delightful place, where you could come to find peace, and wander amongst nature. But what the hell was this garden doing on the roof of a strip club?

Voices drifted to him through the dark night air. A male voice seemed to ask a question, then a female voice answered.

Mia?

Was Mia up here?

"Stop gawking and move." The Hulk shoved him, and Logan followed the paving stones that wound their way between two large, potted trees. He emerged into a cleared area—was that real grass beneath his feet—which flowed towards an outdoor pavilion lit up from below so it resembled a Greek temple. A large pond full of water lilies butted up to one side of the pavilion, sitting just below the platform. Behind the structure, a low wall ran the length of the building, allowing a view out over the nighttime jungle. Logan could see the lights of St. Thomas twinkling on the horizon. The sight was so stunning that Logan almost didn't see Mia and another, smaller man standing beneath the pavilion, arguing.

Logan's chest ignited at the sight. She was alive. And just as beautiful as ever.

As Logan and the Hulk approached, Mia stopped talking and turned to look at them. Surprise turned to shock when she saw him.

"Logan! What the hell…?" She'd already taken two steps in his direction when the swarthy, bearded man grabbed her by the arm. She tried to shake him off, but he yanked her back toward him. Anger spiked in Logan's chest. How dare that arsehole treat her like that?

Mia opened her mouth as if to say more, and the guy— Logan assumed this was the infamous Harry *The Hook*—said, "Shut up, I do the talking here."

Mia closed her mouth but continued to stare at him, like he was some kind of ghost come to haunt her. He'd half been hoping she'd be pleased to see him, but the look she gave him now said she wished he was anywhere but here.

"What you want me to do with him, boss?" The Hulk said.

"Bring him closer, I want to look this jackass, who's been causing me so much trouble, in the eye." Harry's thug pushed Logan closer, not releasing his grip on Logan's arm. The smaller man narrowed his piggy eyes at Logan and glared at him. A death stare, full of petty hatred and ominous threat. Even though this man was shorter than Logan—he was pretty sure he could take him in a one-on-one fight—the guy had an aura of authority; he was used to giving commands and having them obeyed. Harry *The Hook* might be small fry compared to the Ramirez brothers, but he was still a force to be reckoned with. He continued to keep Mia clasped tightly in one meaty hand.

"You people, you're all such idiots. You know my men were watching you sneak around all night on the closed-circuit TV?" Harry sneered, his dark beard moving with his mouth.

Damn, Logan hadn't thought about that. Actually, there were a lot of things Logan hadn't thought through properly. And he was beginning to wish he'd brought Dalton or Reed along. They might've been better prepared; better able to handle these goons. But he was here now, and he needed to make this work if he was going to survive. If he was going to rescue Mia.

"Who do you think you are? Bloody James Bond, or something?" Harry laughed long and loud at his own joke. "You're no match for me. We were expecting you. Waiting for you. Used that stupid bracelet as bait. And you swallowed it, like the gullible fool you are, hook, line and sinker. Now you're going to end up just as dead as your girlfriend here."

Logan's stomach clenched painfully. How stupid could he be? Harry had put that bracelet there specifically for him to find. But then he bristled at the idea that he was some kind of bumbling buffoon. That he'd come in here completely unprepared. Yes, he understood he was by no means secret-agent material. But he was tough and strong. And determined. He knew a few things. A few tricks he'd picked up along the way. Like the small knife he had secreted in the heel of his shoe. The one he'd bought at the little stall around the corner. The Hulk hadn't bothered to pat him down when he first captured him. Only made him empty his pockets. Where he'd gleefully confiscated the Swiss army knife, along with Logan's other knick-knacks he always kept in there, and Mia's bracelet. And that was his first mistake. To underestimate Logan. The Hulk hadn't produced a gun; the arrogance of the man, he probably thought he didn't need it to subdue Logan. But Logan didn't doubt he was carrying so he needed to be careful. Needed to take that into account as he weighed up their escape options.

Logan did stop to wonder what Harry meant by *they'd been expecting him*. Was it that obvious he was going to try and rescue Mia? Before he could consider that idea further, something moved in the periphery of his vision. A man and a woman stepped out of the shadows on the other side of the pavilion. It was obvious the man was another one of Harry's hired hands—he was built like a brick shithouse—wearing another tailored suit. He hoped both the thugs were silently sweltering in their suits in this tropical humidity. But there was no sign of sweat on this guy's square-jawed face. In fact, he looked ice-cool, and mean as hell.

The man held a petite woman's arm in his large paw of a hand.

Tianna. It had to be Tianna.

The likeness to Mia was immediate. Although perhaps less sensual, she was equally beautiful. Toned, brown limbs, and long, dark hair—curlier than Mia's—left loose to furl around her face. But there was a sulky pout to her mouth Logan didn't care for.

Before Tianna appeared, Logan had been weighing up scenarios in his head. Working out how he and Mia might defeat these two thugs. But the odds had just taken a nosedive. Now there were three guys he needed to get past before they could escape, as well as freeing two other people and getting them to safety.

"What are you doing, Serge? I'm not ready for her yet." Harry waved a hand, as if shooing the couple away. "Take her over there, while I finish my conversation with Mia. Actually, take them both over there." He pointed an imperious finger toward the back of the rotunda, near the low wall. "The others will be here soon. But I need more information, first."

Logan wasn't happy when the Hulk led him away, around the back of the pavilion. He could still see Mia, but now he was some distance from her. How was he supposed to communicate anything to her from here? The plan he'd been forming in his head had been sketchy at best, but it'd all be shot to smithereens if he couldn't see her face. He wouldn't know what she was thinking, or how she was going to react.

"Sit down over there." The Hulk indicated to the wall, which came to waist height on Logan and would make a perfect bench seat. "But be careful, you don't want to lean back too far." He gave a mirthless laugh. Logan glanced over the edge of the wall and understood why. The wall was the very edge of the building. Below him lay a three-story drop, which would almost surely kill him. Perhaps he wouldn't sit after all. Leaning a hip against the bricks instead, he watched as the other thug, Serge, led Tianna over and wordlessly pushed her toward him.

"Hi, I'm Tianna, if you hadn't already—"

"No talking," the Hulk growled, taking a menacing step in their direction.

Tianna held up a placating hand, and they all four stood in a silent tableau, each watching the other warily.

This other guy, Serge, would most likely be carrying a weapon as well. Which now doubled the danger. Did Harry have a gun on him? If Logan had to guess, he'd say no. Harry would leave the dirty work to his henchmen.

Logan risked another glance over the edge. It was a long drop. A plan began to form in his mind.

Suddenly, Mia's voice got louder. She was angry at something Harry had said. Harry yelled something back, and then he slapped her hard across the face. Mia went down to her knees. Both of the thugs guarding them swiveled their heads to see what was going on. Logan's first instinct was to race toward Mia, Serge and the Hulk be damned. He managed to control the urge and instead he whispered hurriedly to Tianna, "I'm going to try something. When I do, get down on the ground and see if you can trip Serge." He hoped she understood, because he had no time to explain what was about to happen. All he needed her to do was distract or disable Serge for a few seconds.

He reached down and retrieved the knife from his shoe. Then he rushed forward and struck at the Hulk's face, quick and fast, and just as quickly withdrew to his spot next to the wall. The man roared in pain and grabbed at his face. Logan could see blood oozing between his fingers from the slash across his cheek. He had no time to see what Tianna or Serge were doing, his total concentration was on the man in front of him.

Then the Hulk did what Logan hoped he would. He lunged ahead, coming straight at Logan, intent on smashing him into the ground; not drawing his gun, wanting to hurt Logan with his hands to get his revenge. Logan waited until the last second. He ducked down below the height of the wall just as the enraged bull of a man swung his fist towards his face. The Hulk overbalanced, toppled forward into the space Logan had left behind. Logan grabbed the man's legs and heaved upwards with all his might, further destabilizing him.

All of a sudden, the man was gone. Disappeared.

Logan stood up and looked over the edge. Down at the tangled splotch of a dark human shape on the dirt carpark below.

He'd done it!

A cry of fear from behind him brought him crashing back to reality. He spun around to see Serge and Tianna on the ground, grappling like two wrestlers. Obviously, Serge was winning, Tianna had no real hope against the larger man.

Serge sat up, reaching for the gun inside his jacket pocket, when Logan said, "I don't think so, buddy." He'd snuck up behind the man while he was holding Tianna down, and now had him in a headlock with one arm, while the other hand had the point of his knife buried in the folds of the man's thick neck. The knife was small, but it was big enough to cut through a carotid artery. And Serge knew it. He stilled immediately.

"Tianna, get his gun," Logan said quietly. She did what he asked without hesitation, reaching up from where she was lying beneath Serge, plucking it from his shoulder holster.

"Do you know how to use it?" Logan asked. She shook her head. "Just hold it like they do in the movies."

She did as she was told, grabbing the holster in two hands and pointing the barrel at Serge's chest.

"Now release the safety catch, it's the little button on the left side, you just push it down." She did as she was told. "Good, now you need to make the gun ready to fire. Pull back on the hammer at the back of the gun with your thumb. Good girl," he said as she fumbled, but finally did as he asked. "The gun is ready to shoot. All you have to do is squeeze the trigger. Do you think you can do that?"

Tianna nodded, certainty growing in her eyes.

"Good. Serge, have you got that? Tianna will shoot you if you try anything."

The man never moved a muscle, but Logan was sure he'd got the message.

"Very slowly, you're going to stand up and get off Tianna."

The big man did as he was told, Logan still holding the knife tight to his neck.

"Okay, now you get up," Logan urged. "Keep the gun on him," he reminded her. "Now give the gun to me."

For a second, Logan thought she might not do it, she stared so hard at Serge, with such hatred. But then she handed the weapon over and Logan took it with a sigh of relief, releasing Serge's neck, pointing the gun at him instead.

The whole thing had only taken a few seconds. Enough time for Harry to work out something had gone wrong.

And speak of the devil, Harry appeared with Mia held tightly against his side. "What the fuck is going on?" He demanded.

# CHAPTER FIFTEEN

Mia was clamped so tight to Harry's side, it felt like they were doing the lockstep. He had one arm fastened around her waist, the other held her upper arm in a vice-grip. But Mia's attention was so focused on Logan and Tianna, it was almost as if Harry wasn't there. He'd grabbed her as soon as they heard the awful animal yell from one of his thugs, at first pulling her in front of him, using her like a human shield. Fucking coward. It soon became obvious Harry wasn't in immediate danger, but there was a fight or scuffle going on over with Logan and Tianna.

The lighting at the back of the pavilion was dim, but from what she could see, two figures were struggling on the ground. It was impossible to tell who it was from this distance.

So, Harry had taken hold of her, his face like black thunder, and marched her down the steps and around the side of the rotunda. "Fucking imbeciles. Do I have to do everything around here? They can't even complete a simple task like guarding two unarmed civilians."

As they got closer, Mia still couldn't tell who was struggling on the ground, but suddenly a third figure came up behind the one on top and grabbed them around the neck.

What was going on? And why could she only see three people. Who was missing from the picture?

Harry seemed to come to the same conclusion, because he stopped well short of the trio on the ground. She felt some of that arrogant bravado drain out of him.

He kept his voice loud and demanding, however, when he said, "What the fuck is going on?" As he spoke, the trio disentangled themselves, and Mia could finally see who was who. Tianna got up from the ground and backed away toward the wall, leaving Logan—yes it was definitely Logan—and one of Harry's thugs facing each other. Logan was in a half-crouch, like he was ready to pounce at any second. The thug was Serge, the man who'd thrown her and Tianna into the basement. Which made her wonder where the other hired hitman had gone. The one she'd recognized as the man who held her by the throat yesterday under the turpentine tree.

She didn't have time to wonder for very long, because Logan moved slightly, and Mia caught sight of the gun in his hand. A gun! Where had Logan got a gun?

"Put your hands in the air, where I can see them," Logan demanded. Mia hardly recognized his voice, it was so deep and authoritative. Serge slowly did as he was told, his brows drawn down in a deep glower.

Before she knew what'd happened, Harry had moved, quick as lightning, trapping her in front of him, again using her as a human shield. Whispering into her ear, he said, "You're coming with me, bitch. No quick moves. If you care about your sister, you'll do as you're told." His arm was pressed so hard against her windpipe she could hardly breathe, let alone shout a warning.

Mia's head was spinning, and her legs moved instinctively back, one step at a time.

"Stop where you are," Logan said, as he noticed Harry dragging her backward.

"Why? What are you gonna do?" Harry goaded him. "You gonna shoot me? Because if you point that gun away from Serge for even a second, he's going to come down on you like a ton of bricks."

A sob rose up Mia's throat but couldn't get past the arm cutting off her air supply. Harry was right. Even though Logan had the gun. And even though it seemed like Serge was alone up here on the roof now, they were at a stalemate.

"And if you do try and shoot me, you'll want to make sure you're a crack shot with that thing. Otherwise you'll end up killing your girlfriend here. Are you prepared to take that risk, Logan?"

Logan chanced a quick glance at her, a split second was all he dared to take his eyes away from the gorilla in front of him. But that was all she needed to know that Harry was right. All his posturing and bravado was for show. He was completely out of his depth, just as unsure what to do next as she was. Yes, he'd shot the man down at the dock, but that'd been at point-blank range. He had no idea if he had the accuracy or the resolve to shoot to kill for a second time.

"If you do fire, the sound will bring the rest of my men up here before you can say Jack Rabbit," Harry added. "So, you'd better be damn sure you're a good enough shot to kill all of them, too."

He was right, they weren't going to make it out of here. Because as soon as Harry made it to the exit, he'd call in reinforcements and it'd all be over in seconds.

A spark of anger at Logan for messing this up ignited in her chest. How dare he put them all at risk like this? But then another, louder voice, answered, telling her that at least Logan tried. At least he wasn't going to let himself be led away like a lamb to a slaughter. At least he was doing something, even if that something had backfired.

Mia looked over at Tianna, who was huddled by the wall,

completely terrified. What would happen to Tianna after they killed Mia? Would it be a quick, single shot to the head? Or would Harry keep her as his sex slave instead? Keep her imprisoned, at his beck and call, give her to the highest bidder?

It was this final thought that spurred Mia into action. Anger at Harry, hot and fierce flowed through her like a river of lava. She wasn't going to let that happen.

It suddenly occurred to her to ask herself why was she letting Harry drag her off like this? He had no weapon. She'd finally had enough of doing Harry's bidding. It was time to fight back. He wasn't taller than her, but he was obviously stronger.

*Think, Mia, think.*

Then it came to her.

She let herself go, dropped like a rag doll onto his chest. Made herself as heavy as she could. She wasn't small and petite like Tianna. Slim and toned, yes, but that muscle and her height made her weighty. Enough to cause Harry to overbalance.

The pressure of his arm increased on her neck, but because he was caught completely unaware by her move, he staggered under the drag of her unexpected burden. Stumbled back, one step, two steps. Then Mia pushed herself to her feet again in a sudden swift move, propelling herself sideways, away from his grip around her neck.

She was free.

But Harry was right there. Moving in to grab her again. So, she did the only thing she knew was certain to disable a man. She kicked out as hard as she could and felt the satisfying soft thud as she connected with his balls.

Harry bent over double with a yowl of pain.

What, did he think she was going to fight fair?

Harry screamed obscenities at her, and then began to

straighten. Her kick hadn't completely incapacitated him. She crouched down, ready to have another go at him. When, out of nowhere, Tianna appeared from behind him, slamming a rock down on his head. Too late, Mia heard Serge yell out a warning to his boss. Harry crumpled to the ground like a boneless fish.

"Take that, you bastard," Tianna screamed, standing over Harry's now prostrate body.

For a second, all Mia could do was stare at her little sister. Then her face split into a broad grin.

"Thank you," she said.

"It's the least he deserved." Tianna gave a defiant flick of her hair. "And after all, I couldn't let him hurt my sister any more." She grinned back at Mia, a glint of triumph and something else—was it dignity—in her eyes. A surge of pride for her sister ballooned in her chest.

Mia glanced quickly at Logan to establish he still held Serge at gunpoint. The man was clearly agitated, not happy with the turn of events. She bent down to feel for a pulse, not really caring whether the disgusting pig was alive or dead, but she needed to know either way. He still had a pulse.

"Keep an eye on him," Mia said to Tianna. "Use that rock again if you have to." Her sister nodded and picked up the rock, standing ready over his prostrate body.

"I'm going to find something to tie him up," Mia said, casting around the garden, looking for something rope-like.

A few minutes later, Mia came back with her makeshift rope; a couple of strands of fairy lights she'd stripped off the roof of the pavilion. Together, she and Tianna first tied up Serge, who grunted and snarled like a riled-up tiger, while Logan kept the gun trained on him. And then Harry, who had started to come around. Mia ignored his feeble attempts to plead with her and then to struggle against the tight bonds around his wrists. He was beyond her contempt.

Once they were both restrained, Mia walked slowly over to where Logan stood, gun still dangling in his hand, a look of incomprehension on his face. But when she touched his arm, he seemed to come back into himself and reached for her, encircling her in his arms, pulling her into his chest. His embrace was everything she needed right at that moment. For most of today she'd believed she might never see him again. And that thought had filled her with a deep sorrow. An ache for what might've been sat low and heavy in her stomach. But now he was here, alive and warm in her arms. All the things she'd wanted to say him got caught in her throat, forming a lump that had her eyes prickling with tears.

"Thank God you're okay," he murmured into her hair as he held her close. "I was so scared I was going to find you…" He swallowed loudly but didn't have to finish his sentence. Mia knew what he was implying.

Mia felt a light touch on her back and turned to find Tianna standing there, a forlorn look on her face. "Come here," she said, dragging her sister into a three-way embrace. It wasn't until that moment Mia finally allowed everything that'd happened to hit her. Her knees went suddenly weak, and if it wasn't for Logan and Tianna's support, she might've fallen. She could hardly believe they'd just beaten Harry at his own game. And survived to tell the tale.

"You all right? Do you need to sit down?" Logan's concerned voice broke into her hazy thoughts.

"No, I'm good. We need to get out of here, though. Harry has other guards in the building." She indicated to the exit with her chin.

"I know, I saw one of them guarding the door as we came in." Logan began to ease away from their embrace. Tianna took a step back, sniffing and rubbing her eyes. She was probably suffering from shock, just like Mia, was at a loss on how to handle this new reality, where they'd just fought for their lives. And won. Then Logan stared down at the gun still in his hand, as if he'd forgotten it was there. After a second's hesitation, he reached around and tucked into the back of his shorts. In a moment of near hysteria, it made Mia want to laugh at the absurdity of Logan acting like one of the many characters she'd seen in all the cop TV shows she'd ever watched.

Regaining her composure, she asked, "Where's the other guard?"

Logan pointed wordlessly at the wall. What did he mean? She went over and looked down. There was a dark patch on the gravel of the car park. A low moan reached her ears. Jesus, could someone survive that kind of fall? If he had, then he was in no condition to chase them. Mia felt little compassion for the man who had held her by the neck and threatened her. It meant all three men who'd been on the roof with them were now effectively out of action.

"Come on," Logan growled, clearly agitated. "We need to get out of here ASAP." Logan had Tianna by the arm, as if supporting her or leading her to safety, Mia wasn't sure which.

"Give me a second," she said, crouching down next to Harry, prostrate on the ground. He looked so funny, all hogtied and helpless, Mia wanted to laugh at the incongruity of it all. Three minutes ago, he'd held all the power.

And now the power was in her hands.

She got down on her hands and knees and leant in, making sure Harry could hear her. "Listen up, and listen good to what I'm about to say." Harry turned his face up toward her, with a snarl so vicious she almost drew back. But she wasn't going to be put off by him, not now. "The second I get out of here, I'm going straight to the USVI Coastguard. And I'm going to tell them about all those illegal turtle shells you've got stored down in the basement." Harry's snarl dropped from his face, his eyes going wide with shock, then disbelief. It was the perfect way to get to Harry. The local police might be corruptible, Harry might well be able to buy some of them off with his millions. But the USVI Coastguard were different; honest and trustworthy, they wouldn't rest until they had an arrest.

"I've got one of those shells stashed away, to show them. So even if you clean out your basement, I'll still have the evidence." This bit was a lie, but she hoped Harry was too shocked to realize her bluff. "My advice to you, Harry *The Hook*," she spat those words in his face, "is to get the fuck off this island and never bother me or my sister again."

Harry made a blustering noise, his dark beard bristling with indignance. But as Mia stared at him, he could see the truth written in her face. Then he began to struggle against his bonds as the ramifications of what she'd said became clear.

"Let me go, you fucking bitch."

Mia had no doubt Harry would rant and yell and spit fire, proclaim that he was going to kill her and Tianna. But she also knew if he was smart, and if he wanted to keep his business going, he'd leave the USVIs as soon as possible, and take his gentlemen's club with him.

"We can go now," she said, straightening up. She joined Logan and Tianna as they made their way back across the beautiful roof-top garden. She drew in a sharp breath and crossed her fingers. Her escape route relied on Harry's other guards staying in their designated spots in the building. There was always a guard at the front door at this time of night, waiting to admit customers. Another always stood unobtrusively just inside the door of the clubroom, watching the girls as they came in for the night. Watching to make sure the customers behaved themselves.

"Follow me, I know a back way out of here," she

whispered, hoping like hell they didn't have someone guarding the back exit. A part of her also wondered what Harry had meant when he'd said *the others would be here soon.* Who else was he expecting? But more to the point, if others were coming soon, then they needed to hightail it out of here before they were discovered.

# CHAPTER SIXTEEN

Logan nearly tripped over a rock in the dark. "I can't see where I'm going," he complained quietly. Mia was taking them via a back route, through dark alleyways and abandoned blocks of land, already being reclaimed by the jungle.

"Sorry, here, hold my hand, I'll lead you." Mia's hand sneaked into his, small and warm. All of a sudden, he almost didn't mind stumbling blindly around in the middle of the night. In reality, he shouldn't be thinking about how her hand felt enclosed in his. He should be more worried about whether they were being followed by any of Harry's goons. But her presence beside him, and her hand in his, made him aware of the softness of her skin, the way her bare arm brushed up against his as they walked.

"We're almost there," Mia added.

"Thank God. I thought you'd gotten us lost." Tianna's voice came from behind. He could feel some sort of tension going on between Mia and Tianna, but it wasn't the kind he'd been expecting. It was a positive feeling, not a negative one. Logan had thought Mia might be mad at Tianna for not listening to her, for being captured and used as bait. Instead she seemed proud of her sister. There was an aura of hope and optimism around them now. As if something had fundamentally shifted in their relationship.

After they made it out of the warehouse, by slipping out of the rear exit unseen, they'd stopped to catch their breath and regroup underneath the cover of a street-stall awning. Logan felt the awkward weight of the gun still tucked into his waistband. The urge to pluck it out and throw as far as he could into the nearby bushes was great. But it was probably something they should hold on to for the next little while, at least.

"Aren't Harry's men going to be coming after us in droves, once they find him all trussed up like a chicken?" Logan had asked, thinking they should be heading straight for the docks to find a way off the island.

"No, I don't think so," Mia had answered thoughtfully. "I told Harry about what I found in his basement. There must've been hundreds of turtle shells down there. He's the poacher the Coast Guards have been looking for. He must be the mastermind in this big poaching racket we've all been so worried about."

Logan had been shocked beyond words. This was amazing news, if it was true. He couldn't wait to tell Tom and Dan. His friends would be ecstatic when they heard, it would be a weight lifted from all their shoulders.

"As soon as I get somewhere there's a working phone, I'm going to call the Coast Guard hotline and give them the big anonymous tip. You know they'll be here by tomorrow morning, ripping his warehouse apart."

Yep, he did know; they took this kind of thing very seriously. Anyone prosecuted for poaching could easily end up in jail. But sadly, while the maximum penalty could be up to ten years, most poachers got off way too lightly. It'd be great if Harry was sent to jail for ten years, but somehow Logan thought he was too wily to be caught like that.

"So, I'm guessing Harry will be too busy clearing the hell out of St. John to be worried about following us right now," Mia added.

"Really?" Logan wasn't certain.

"I'm not so sure, either," Tianna piped up. "Harry's just plain mean; he might send his guys after us just to spite us." She put her hands on her hips to accentuate her statement.

"You may be right. And perhaps, once he gets to safety, he may do just that. Send one of his thugs to get us as payback. But I think now, he'll only be considering one thing, and that is self-preservation. You need to trust me on this one." Mia had touched Logan's face then. It set off tiny little sparks inside his chest. How could he not trust her, after what they'd just been through?

"You're saying you think we're safe?" he asked.

"Yes, I am. Harry told me he knew about the guy with the gun, he even knew we'd gotten rid of the body. Said he was going to clean up the mess we left, so the cops didn't find him." Logan stared at her so long, she went on to add, "So, that means the guy with the gun was sent by Harry. Don't you see?"

Logan wasn't sure what to say.

Mia huffed. "If you need more proof it was Harry, then I can tell you that the guy you tackled, the one you pushed off the roof, he was the same guy who warned me to stay away from you. The one who grabbed me by the throat. Remember?"

Logan nodded. He remembered clearly Mia's tale of the man who'd accosted her on her scooter. He searched her face for the truth. She seemed so adamant, and it was probably true, she wasn't likely to forget that guy's face in a hurry.

"Don't you see? It means your theory about the Ramirez brothers sending someone after you was wrong all along."

"Oh." It took a few seconds for his mind to get around

what she was saying. He'd been so sure it was the Ramirez brothers. Everything pointed to it being them. Could it really have been Harry all along? "What about my boat?" he asked. "Why would Harry want to blow up my boat?"

A light frown furrowed her brow. "That part, I'm not so sure about. He wouldn't give me a direct answer. But he certainly didn't deny doing it. Which means perhaps he made a mistake, didn't realize we had your sisters on board, and then wouldn't admit it. I do think he was mad enough to try and kill me. And you, as well. Although it does seem a little of a grandiose gesture, even for Harry." Her beautiful nose wrinkled in thought, as if she wasn't fully convinced, either. It made him wonder.

"Hmm." He gave a noncommittal reply. There were still lots of loose ends. Like the two guys who beat up Tom. But they could easily have been Harry's lackeys, Logan mused. It seemed like Harry had admitted to sending the guy with the gun. Logan decided to go along with Mia. For now. But he still planned on getting off this island as soon as possible.

"I think we should go back to my house," Mia announced.

But Logan had balked at this plan. Instead, they'd agreed to go to the Airbnb. Logan argued it was safer. Harry was less likely to know about that place, and Dalton would be extra protection if they needed it. Logan wasn't all that happy about getting Keira and Dalton involved again, but he was fast running out of options. They couldn't wander around the dusty back streets of Cruz Bay all night.

Mia broke through a scrubby patch of vegetation and stepped out onto a narrow road, Logan right behind her. "This is it," Mia whispered. "If the address you gave me is correct, their villa should be at the top of this hill."

Logan had no idea what the time was; his phone was destroyed and he didn't wear a watch, but he was guessing it was around eleven. As he knocked quietly on the door, he hoped someone was still awake. The door flew open almost immediately, and Keira stood there, hands on hips, Dalton hovering close behind.

"Where the hell have you been? We've been worried sick about you."

"Sorry, sis," he said, pulling her in for a quick, placating hug. "We're here now. I'll tell you all about our little adventure, but if you could spare some food and something to drink first, that'd be great." He tried for one of his cheeky grins, but fatigue foiled him. "This is Tianna, by the way," he said, as both women followed him into the brightly lit villa. "Mia's sister."

Keira introduced herself, as Logan made his way farther into the house. It was impressive. Luxurious, but not pretentious. Decorated in a modern beach theme, with white tiles on the floor and eggshell-blue walls. Logan dropped down into the nearest tan-colored sofa, sinking into its welcoming softness with a sigh. Mia sank down next to him, stretching out her long, cocoa legs beside his and leaning back, also with a sigh of relief. He wanted to reach for her hand, keep it enfolded in his. But he settled for just having her close, her shoulder almost touching his, as they lounged against the back of the sofa.

"Jesus, what have you three been up to?" Keira had followed them into the large, open-plan living area, Tianna trailing behind her.

Logan looked down and for the first time, noticed his own, tattered condition. Bare legs and arms were covered in scratches and bug bites, from where they'd all stumbled through the jungle. His shirt was almost ripped completely off at the shoulder. He wasn't sure how that'd happened, perhaps when he'd ditched the Hulk over the edge of the building. Scuff marks and splotches of dirt had turned his tan shorts almost black. Some of the marks were from being blown off his boat. But most of them were from his escapades at the warehouse.

"It's a long story," he said wearily.

*  *  *

Mia lay back on the queen-size bed and watched as Logan said goodnight to his sister in the doorway. The bed was large, comfy and smelled faintly of lemon. Crisp, white sheets were folded back with exacting perfection, and there was a small, wrapped chocolate seashell on each pillow. It was the most perfectly sumptuous thing she'd slept in…well, probably forever. Mia guessed this room might even rival those at the famous Caneel Bay Resort. Even though she'd never seen the place with her own eyes, she'd certainly heard about it. Sadly, the double devastation of hurricanes two years ago had caused so many problems for the resort, they were still unsure if it would ever open again.

Logan turned off the overhead light and made his way to the bed by the light of the moon streaming in through the open curtains. He stood at the edge of the bed, looking down at her. "Sorry about this. It's the only spare room they've got. And at least it's not the couch. Although I'm sure Tianna will be comfy out there." He smiled a little sheepishly. "I think my sisters may have got the idea you and I are…well, you know, together."

Were they together? Mia took him in as she considered his words. He was a mess. Exhausted. Deep lines bracketed his mouth that she was sure they hadn't been there yesterday. His beautiful blue eyes were shadowed and sunken. Even after a quick shower, his brown hair, normally perfectly groomed, stuck up at all angles. She must look much the same, she thought with a grimace. A hot mess. The T-shirt he'd borrowed from Dalton was too big, and made him look almost child-like in the dim light. Even after he'd been blown into the water by the explosion and then had to fight for his life against Harry's thugs, he still looked so gorgeous her stomach fizzed at the sight of him. Reaching out, she took his hand and dragged him onto the bed beside her. She didn't know the answer to the *together* question. What she did know was that tonight, she wanted him with her.

"I'm too tired to care," she said, snuggling into his side. "And I'd much rather you sleep up here, beside me, keeping me safe."

It was now nearly two o'clock in the morning. It'd taken a long time to tell their story to Dalton and Keira. Dalton especially kept asking in-depth questions, trying to get his head around everything that'd happened. To say Dalton wasn't happy with all that'd transpired was an understatement. Especially after Logan produced the gun he'd taken away from one of Harry's thugs and handed it gingerly over to Dalton for safekeeping. Dalton paced the length of the tiled living room the whole time she and Logan relayed their story, reminding her of a caged leopard. He was certainly intense, probably too much so for her liking. She preferred Logan, his humor and his laid-back, laissez faire style. But she could see what Kiera saw in Dalton. He was also athletic and dependable, but with that hint of a rough diamond that most women loved to think they could tame. Dalton had tried to persuade them to go and talk to the police straight away and told them in no uncertain terms they had to hand that gun in as soon as possible. Logan disagreed, saying the police had been less than useless so far and might even try and throw him in jail.

In the end, they came to a compromise, consenting to go down to the police station first thing tomorrow morning. Logan also wanted to go over to St. Thomas afterwards, to make sure Sierra and Reed were doing well.

Mia made her call to the Coast Guard. They had a twenty-four-hour hotline and Mia gave them the exact particulars of what she'd seen and heard. The gruff man on the end of the phone took everything down and asked very detailed questions. He said they would make it a top priority to investigate her claims.

Then she made another phone call to Crystal and Scarlett, who, in Crystal's words, *had only just got home after some kind of upheaval at the club, where Harry had sent them all packing like he had a firecracker up his butt.* Mia warned them that something big was going down, and to stay away from the warehouse altogether. Crystal wasn't pleased to hear that she might need to start looking for a new job, but Mia didn't have the time or patience to argue or explain. In the end, she'd hung up. And now she was feeling guiltily about jilting her friends.

Snuggling in closer to Logan she decided she would call Crystal again tomorrow, talk to her when she wasn't so strung out and stressed. It'd been a hard day, after all. With her head pillowed on Logan's shoulder, she let the fatigue finally seep into her body.

"I don't think there is one bit of me that doesn't hurt," she admitted, murmuring into his neck.

"Me either." His deep voice rumbled through his chest, tickling her ear. It was a comforting sound. It took her back to the past few nights spent just like this, on his boat. And that morning, when he'd kissed her. And she kissed him back. Something warm and hungry stirred in her belly. She lifted her hand and laid it gently on his stomach. The ridges of his abs were firm beneath her palm. Drawing light circles, she traced the lines of his muscles over the fabric of his T-shirt. She had a sudden urge to feel his skin, run her hands over his heated flesh. So, she lifted the hem of his shirt and wriggled her hand beneath it. He'd said nothing so far, remained completely still, letting her explore at her whim. But suddenly, there was a slight quiver beneath her fingertips, the only giveaway that he wasn't immune to her touch.

After all she'd been through—they'd been through—today, she thought any kind of love-play would be the farthest thing from her mind. But her body had other ideas. The warm kernel of want in her belly quickly expanded, flowing down her legs, settling in her groin.

Logan's fingers began to play with her hair, tugging the strands between his thumb and forefinger, his hand, that'd been curled around her shoulders, came up to entangle in the long waves, which was still wet from her shower. It felt nice as he stroked her head, awakening the nerve-endings on her scalp. His other hand drifted up and he ran his fingers gently down the length of her arm, raising goose bumps wherever he touched.

They lay in this warm embrace, gently caressing, for many minutes. It was nice, soothing, comforting. But it was also, slowly but surely, setting her body on fire. She wanted to feel more of his rock-hard body. Wanted to run her hands up and down his chest, explore the ridges of his pecs, the line of his oblique muscles. When she'd first lay down on the bed, sleep had been the only thing on her mind. But now…

Now she wanted Logan.

She made a decision. Who knew where they would be tomorrow? Or the day after that? Mia wanted to make love to Logan. Tonight.

Sitting up in one, quick motion, she lifted her leg and straddled him. Logan drew in a quick intake of breath at her sudden movement. Now she could see his face fully. The light of the moon was enough for her to make out its contours, see how his dark gaze fastened on her.

"Take off your shirt," she commanded.

There was no reply, but she watched his biceps bulge as he tugged at the hem, lifting his torso off the bed to pull the clothing over his head. Mia had seen him shirtless before and had enjoyed the view back then. But tonight, his body seemed to be made of marble, cut from the same cloth as a Greek God. And last time she hadn't had the luxury of time to explore that body. This time she was going to make the most of it. She spent a good many minutes investigating every nook and cranny of Logan's chest and abdomen, finally deciding that he was indeed just like her very own Apollo. Stopping at the deep scratches on his shoulder, where Captain had clung to him for dear life, her touch turned tender. She didn't want to hurt him, but his palms, hot and earnest, branding into her back, urged her on. When her fingers wandered down to the waistband of his shorts, then dipped underneath, he at last let out a low groan.

"Mia, you're killing me."

She began to undo the top button of his shorts, all the while watching his face. Those dark eyes glowed with hunger, his mouth serious now, lips straight and firm as he watched her with an intensity that burned right through her.

An idea suddenly occurred to her. "Have you got protection?"

Logan's eyes widened with surprise, as if he hadn't thought it would really go that far. "I put one in my wallet yesterday," he replied, not quite meeting her eyes. And she knew he meant he'd done it after he'd met her, that he'd been hoping to get lucky. But it was exactly what she wanted to hear, so she didn't dwell on it. His brow furrowed. "Do you think it'll have survived inside its wrapper after the ocean swim we had this morning?"

It was a risk Mia was prepared to take. She nodded her head.

"My wallet's in my back pocket," he said.

It was past time he took his shorts off anyway. She undid the zip quickly and then helped him out of his pants and underwear. Forgetting for a second that she was looking for his wallet in the pocket, she stopped to stare. If he wasn't the perfect male specimen, then she wasn't sure what was. Lean, well-sculpted, Mia decided that her first thought, back when she'd seen him on the beach with the turtle, had been correct; he could grace the catwalks in any city in the world and fit right in. Mia wasn't a fool, she knew that Logan understood he was good-looking, and played on it to get what he wanted sometimes. But most of the time he was completely unaffected, it was so refreshing. Like now, he was looking at her with a moody hunger, but there was also self-doubt hovering behind those hooded eyes. As if he couldn't quite believe this was happening to him; that he was the object of her desire.

Shaking her head, she brought herself back to reality, found the wallet and handed it to Logan. Now it was her turn to get naked. It'd been a while since she'd slept with a man. At least a year. Having Harry watching her every move had put a real damper on prospective boyfriends. But Mia wasn't intimidated or afraid. She sat on the bed next to Logan, and he propped himself up on one elbow so he could watch her. Shaking her hair back over her shoulders, she gave Logan a sultry glance, wriggling her hips as she took the top button of her blouse between two fingers. Ever so slowly she undid it. Then the next one. And the next. Enjoying how his gaze centered on her every move. At last she bared her stomach, exposing her simple, white bra. Pity she hadn't thought to put on one of her little lacy numbers last night before she met him at the dock. But then she'd thought they'd be sailing out on the ebb tide, away from this godforsaken island. Not getting hot and heavy together.

Logan reached out a hand and she tutted at him. He gave her a baleful look, but dropped his hand back on the coverlet and continued to watch.

Slipping her blouse over her shoulders, she knelt up on the

bed and began to shimmy her white shorts slowly down over her hips. They joined the blouse in the growing pile of clothing on the floor. Still kneeling on the bed, Mia leaned toward Logan, at the same time reaching behind her back and unsnapping the fastener on her bra. Slipping the straps over first one, then the other shoulder, she let the garment drop to the bed.

Logan's eyes were transfixed.

"Jesus," he whispered softly. "I always knew you were beautiful. But…" He stopped and licked his lips. "You are… amazing." He placed his hand on her forearm, holding it there, and she saw the contrast his white skin made against her cocoa. It was almost shocking in the moonlight. "I love that we are so different. But yet the same. I want you."

Mia felt a flutter of delight. Somewhere, deep inside, a small voice had been worried that Logan would find her lacking in some way. But he liked what he saw. She grinned like a child in a candy shop.

"Come here," she said, releasing the last of her inhibition and moving toward Logan. He buried his head between her breasts, and she let out a sigh of pure pleasure as a bolt of desire pulsed through her. This was going to be good.

# CHAPTER SEVENTEEN

Logan stood at the end of the driveway, watching Mia walk toward him, hips swaying rhythmically. He wondered if she did it on purpose, walking like a sultry seductress. Or was it innate? He decided it was just part of what made Mia, Mia. She had a natural, unfettered beauty, that shone out of her very soul.

And after last night, he was beginning to think he was falling in love with that soul.

It was now after ten in the morning. Logan had wanted to sleep all day, but Dalton knocked on their door an hour ago, rudely rousing them out of their deep slumber, saying they needed to go and see the police. After only having had a few hours' sleep, Logan had grumbled like a bear with a sore head, but Mia agreed with Dalton. They needed to get this over and done with. Out of the way, so they could be in the clear, once and for all, with nothing hanging over their heads anymore. And he wouldn't have traded those lost hours of sleep for anything.

Logan suggested that instead of getting up, they could go back to their nocturnal activities. Mia was warm and luscious, stretched out naked beneath the sheet, all tangled together with his arms and legs.

She was such a passionate, giving lover.

Sofia had been fiery and ardent, too. But her lovemaking had an air of desperation, as if she thought she had to be perfect, the consummate lover. Sometimes her need to get it exact every time left no room for spontaneity. With Sofia, she always had to be in control. She spent hours in the bathroom beforehand, making herself *pretty for him,* as she used to say.

But Mia was so different. She made love with abandon, seeming to enjoy the mess and disarray Sofia had scoffed at. Because sex could be messy, and sweaty and exhausting—in a good way. And it'd been all those things with Mia, but she embraced it as she enfolded him in her arms and looked deep into his eyes. He'd got lost in her eyes last night, couldn't get enough of watching her. Watching the different emotions, so evident on her face.

Mia finally arrived by his side and he couldn't help himself, he leant in and kissed her, deep and intense. He wanted her to know how much last night had meant to him. How much he wanted to do it again, just as soon as possible. He was wearing a borrowed shirt of Dalton's, but still had on his own shorts from yesterday. They'd have to do until he could get to town and buy some more clothes. Mia, too, was wearing a blue, borrowed blouse donated by Keira and a pair of tan capri pants, that were a little on the big side. Not nearly as fetching as her outfit from yesterday, but at least she looked clean and neat once more. All traces of yesterday's escapades wiped away.

After they made love the first time last night, Logan had told her about her bracelet. That he'd found it in the alleyway and picked it up, then the Hulk had taken it from him. But now they both knew it'd been the bait to draw Logan in. He promised her he'd buy her a new one, but she said not to worry. That bracelet had meant something special, and nothing else could really replace it.

Even the small movement of leaning in to kiss Mia made his back protest in pain. The bruising and scratches from the boat explosion had made him stiff and sore. Last night he'd been able to ignore all that, but in the stark light of day, he was feeling each and every injury.

"Are they coming?" he asked, after finally drawing back and casting a quick glance up at the house above them on the hill.

"Yes, Keira has gone back to find Tianna. I don't know what that girl is doing now." Mia gave a loud sigh. "Dalton is starting the car. See?" She pointed up the driveway as the garage door began to trundle up. Logan had gotten tired of waiting for them all to get ready, and told them to pick him up at the bottom of the long driveway.

The big Jeep Dalton had rented to drive around the island rumbled to life, its engine deep and throaty. Both Mia and Logan turned to look up the driveway, waiting for him to back out. Keira emerged on the front porch, fussing with her handbag.

Perhaps it was the sound of the engine, mixed with the reverberation of the garage door still creaking open and Keira shouting out to Dalton from the front door, something about a set of keys that were missing. Or perhaps he'd become complacent, with Mia by his side and a night of good loving making him drowsy and replete. Whatever the reason, Logan missed the sound of another car approaching slowly up the winding road. It wasn't until a door clicked open behind him that Logan turned around in surprise, Mia turning with him.

By then it was too late.

A man dressed all in black grabbed him with lightning speed. Logan yelled, struggled with all his might, but the man had surprise and sheer bulk on his side. Before he knew what was happening, Logan was bundled, headfirst into a large black SUV. Mia landed unceremoniously on top of him, then slid to the floor, and before either of them could scramble to sit upright, Logan heard a door slam shut and a deep voice said, "Don't fucking move a muscle."

Logan froze, as cold metal pressed against his temple. Mia squealed in alarm but was quickly silent as she took in the deadly intent of the man with the gun. At least she was jammed between him and the car door, away from the hooligan with the weapon. The car's front door slammed, and the SUV took off, tires squealing on the pavement. A tiny part of his mind registered that the driver must've pounced on Mia, while he was being manhandled by this other brute.

Logan didn't dare turn his head, not with the gun pressed to his brow. But he didn't need to. He recognized this man, would know his ugly, scarred face anywhere. And the car. It was the same one he'd seen heading to Tom's place. This time, the guy was wearing his gun holster for all to see, having discarded the sports coat.

"You just sit nice and calm," the scar-faced, ugly man said. "There's some people who want to talk to you. And they want you in one piece, so don't make me have to get rough." Ugly Guy stared at him for a few seconds, before adding, "Hell hath no fury like a woman scorned, huh? But I don't really blame her. What kind of man leaves a woman at the altar?" He made a spitting sound of contempt. Logan still didn't dare turn his head, but the hostility emanating from the thug beside him was palpable.

Logan's stomach plummeted. Mia had been wrong all along. And he'd been right, after all.

* * *

Mia's mind couldn't comprehend what was going on. Or rather, she didn't want to believe what was going on. She was tied to a chair. Tied to a fucking chair, for Christ's sake. Who did that to people? Who tied an innocent person to a chair and then let them wait for hours in an empty, stiflingly hot room?

Crazy people. That's who.

Either that, or she was being pranked.

Perhaps she was really on that show, the one with James Franco and his buddies. Maybe the Hollywood hunk was going to come barging through that door any second now and go, *surprise!*

Except Mia knew it wasn't a prank. This was real. She shuffled around on her chair, trying to get comfortable. But it was impossible when your hands were tied behind you. Her back ached and pins and needles shot up and down her shoulders and arms like a thousand tiny, angry knives. They'd been blindfolded in the car, so Mia had no idea where they were. Even though the island was small, there were still plenty of places to hide. The car trip had taken less than ten minutes, which meant they were still in the Cruz Bay area. After the thugs had pulled them roughly out of the car, she'd clung to Logan's arm as they were led, still blindfolded, down a maze of corridors and through doors, until they ended up in this dead-end room. It had windows, but they'd been boarded up from the outside, and the only light came from a bulb swinging lazily overhead.

"I need a drink of water," she croaked, her throat was parched and her tongue dry and swollen. How long had they been in this sweltering room? It felt like days, but was likely only a couple of hours.

The man standing guard in the corner of the room ignored her. He was ugly as sin, with a large scar marring his battered face.

"Water," she beseeched. "Can't you at least give us some wa—?"

Before she could even finish the question, the man took two menacing steps toward them. "Do you want another?" He raised his hand in her direction, and she shrank back as far as she could in the high-backed wooden chair. She shook her head. No, she definitely didn't want another backhander from him. The first one had nearly knocked her unconscious and left her seeing stars, because she dared to ask the man a simple question; why were they here? Even though she'd guessed the answer by now. Logan had roared abuse when the man hit her, and struggled so hard he'd tipped his chair over, ending up on the ground. The guard had picked him up, and then punched him in the face, as well. They'd both remained quiet after that. Dried blood now caked Logan's face, where his nose and lip had started to bleed.

She couldn't help it, a sob escaped from between her dry lips.

Logan twitched beside her and when she looked up, he had his mouth open, as if about to speak. A glance at the guard had him closing his mouth again. But his gaze, so full of concern, entreated her to be quiet. Then his eyes filled with tears and she knew he was blaming himself for their predicament. But he shouldn't, not really. She'd led him to believe they were safe. That Harry was the mastermind behind everything that'd happened to them. How could she have got it so wrong? She'd been replaying her conversation with Harry over and over in her mind for the past few hours. And now, she could see she'd perhaps made assumptions. Wrong assumptions. Harry hadn't actually confirmed it was his man they'd killed at the docks. He'd only wanted to make sure the body was disposed of properly, to make sure the cops didn't come looking at him if he was found. Harry was cleaning up after somebody else. And he'd never really answered her question about Logan's boat, either. But by that stage, she'd been biased, already believing he'd done it. It was a little odd that Harry hadn't outright denied his involvement, and Mia puzzled over this one for a while. Perhaps he didn't mind taking credit for someone else's dirty work? It only made him look more intimidating to his rivals. It'd look better on his resume, if others in the business thought twice about messing with him.

They should've gone straight to the cops last night, like Dalton wanted. Then they wouldn't be in this mess right now.

At least Tianna was safe. Or, she hoped she was safe. Dalton and Keira would protect her. She hoped they'd called the police when they'd seen the abduction. Problem was, after the way they'd been treated at the hospital, she didn't place much faith in the cops. She and Logan were pretty much on their own.

There was a sound, and Mia looked up from her contemplation of the dirty concrete floor.

A woman in a tight, red dress and high heels strolled through the door. It was the last thing Mia was expecting, and she almost did a double-take. The woman was pretty, curvaceous, with long dark hair falling in waves over her shoulders.

Logan gave a sharp intake of breath as he looked up and it all suddenly became crystal clear.

This had to be Sofia. His ex-fiancée.

Two men followed the woman in the red dress through the door. Again, Mia was guessing, but she didn't have to be any kind of detective to see the similarities between the three of them. This must be Diego and Leonardo, the two Ramirez brothers. Scarface slipped quietly outside when one of the brothers waved a hand at him.

Logan gave a low moan, and Mia glanced over to see his face had gone as white as a sheet, as if all his nightmares had suddenly come true. And she didn't blame him, because if half the things he'd told her about these people were true, they were in a shitload of trouble.

"Nice to see you again, Logan," the woman purred, her heels clicking on the concrete as she walked toward him.

Sofia didn't even glance in Mia's direction. As if she didn't exist at all.

"Sofia," he replied, voice tight and strained. "What are you doing here?" He gave the two brothers, who were lounging against the far wall as if waiting for the entertainment to start, a quick glance.

"I've come to see you." The woman had reached Logan's chair and now bent over to stare into his face. "But I'm not liking what I see. What's this on your face?" She brushed a hand over his rough stubble, and Logan drew back from her touch. "You've let yourself go."

Mia could see the open confusion on Logan's face. He was as unsure what was going on as she was. From everything he'd told her, he was expecting Leo and Diego to be hunting him down. To kill him for what he'd put their sister through. That's what all their threats had implied. But he'd never mentioned anything about Sofia being involved. What did she want? Was she looking for closure? To have a civilized little chat with Logan about what went wrong?

Logan voiced these very questions, when he said, "I thought your brothers here—" he tilted his chin in their direction, "—were after me. I was scared they wanted to kill me. To avenge you. When I…" Logan seemed to choke on the words, unable to get them out.

"When you betrayed me like a gutless coward," she finished with a grim smile on her red lips. "You thought Diego and Leo were doing this for me?" She gave a soft burbling laugh. "You silly man." One red fingernail drew a line across Logan's shoulders as she walked around behind him. "Well, I guess in one way, you were right. They were doing it to avenge me. They would do anything to defend their sister's honor. Their family's honor. But they were doing it on my orders. I was the one who wanted vengeance, not them." She stopped her slow circle around the chair, putting her hands on her hips.

Sofia's English was good, but her accent was strong, and Mia struggled to understand her softly spoken words at times. She sounded exactly like one of those sultry, South American actresses in the one of those B-grade, bodice-ripping, wild-western movies. It was easy to understand what Logan had seen in her. She was sexy as hell, and beautiful, fiery and willful. But in other ways, Mia wondered what Logan had been thinking. Had he really been prepared to marry this woman? She seemed to be the exact opposite of all he stood for. He loved an uncomplicated life, loved nature, and wanted to protect it. While she seemed…high maintenance. Was all about her designer clothes and beauty regimen. But then, hadn't she thought the exact same thing about her and Logan recently? That they were so very different. She'd wondered at the time if that was a good thing or a bad one.

Looking at Sofia, she still didn't have an answer.

Logan narrowed his eyes at the petite Mexican woman standing in front of him. "Look, Sofia. I'm sorry about the way I left. And I'm sorry I hurt you. I really am. But I couldn't condone what your family was doing. Surely, you have to see that? So, please call your brothers off, and we can have a civilized discussion about this."

But Mia realized Logan was wrong; he wasn't seeing the danger here. This wasn't something he was going to apologize his way out of. Sofia was the one he should be scared of. He needed to stop speaking, before he made everything worse. Before he got her really angry, because God knew what this woman was capable of. She didn't want to hear his platitudes, but she did need to be talked down off this scary ledge she was standing on. Maybe Mia could appeal to her, give her a more logical viewpoint.

"Logan," she whispered. Then when he glanced over at

her, she shook her head vehemently.

She looked Sofia directly in the eye. "What Logan did to you was a horrible thing," she said. "But what you're doing here is completely illegal and immoral, and—"

"A-ha, it finally speaks," Sofia cut her off, fastening her predatory gaze on Mia's face, looking at her for the first time. "I was wondering how long it'd take you to butt in. I'm going to enjoy watching Diego and Leo have their fun with you. You seem like a feisty woman. Exactly their type."

Mia withdrew in horror. What had she just said?

"But first of all, I might start with this." She leaned over and grabbed a length of Mia's hair, yanking her head down as she pulled hard.

Mia screamed in pain.

"Give me your knife," Sofia demanded of one of the brothers.

Mia screamed again, this time in panic, as one of the brothers—the bearded one—peeled away from the wall, pulling a knife out of an ankle holster and handing it to Sofia.

"What the fuck are you doing?" Logan yelled.

The knife flashed before Mia's eyes and she flinched, waiting for the pain to hit. Instead the pressure suddenly eased on her scalp, and Mia opened her eyes to see Sofia standing triumphant, a lock of Mia's long, dark hair in her hand. Before she knew it, Sofia had another hank in her hand and was sawing at it, until that, too, fell on the ground with the first one. There was nothing Mia could do to stop her, as Sofia cut more and more hair off, except sit in that damn chair while she was slowly disfigured.

In a distant part of her mind, she could hear Logan still yelling, his face going red as he roared at Sofia to stop. But Logan was equally as helpless as she was to halt this.

Eventually, Logan's yelling must've become too much for Sofia, because she motioned to one of the brothers, the one who'd handed her the knife, and he came over and punched Logan in the gut so hard she heard the air leave his lungs in a whoosh, and he doubled over, gasping for breath.

But it seemed Sofia was riled up by her small victory, and she began yelling too. "You still don't get it, do you, *honey*?" She waved the knife dangerously close to Logan's face, as he remained doubled over on the chair. "I told Diego to blow your fucking boat up. I wanted to see you suffer, like I have suffered. At the very least, I thought if you lost your precious boat it would be a way to wound you. But better yet, I was hoping you would die a slow, agonizing death from your burns. We are *not* going to talk about what you did. I'm here to watch you die. You and your *girlfriend*," she spat this word out with great distaste, "are going to die, and then I'm going to go home and live the rest of my life a happy woman."

Jesus, she really was completely crazy. For the second time that day, Mia wondered what in hell Logan had seen in this woman. By the look on his face, he was clearly wondering the exact same thing.

# CHAPTER EIGHTEEN

"Oh no, I broke a nail," Sofia sighed, looking down at her left hand. Logan was aghast. After what she'd said and done mere seconds ago, that was all she was worried about? "I need a smoke. And perhaps a drink, too," she said mildly. "All this excitement has been too much for me."

"You go take a break, Sofia. We'll look after them for you," Leo answered, moving swiftly to open the door for his sister. The smug shit.

"Don't do anything while I'm gone," she warned. "I want to see everything. And besides, I haven't determined quite how Logan is going to die yet. Smoking might help me decide."

Logan was so shocked by her parting words, his mind shied away from the consequences. Instead, he remembered smoking was one of the habits he'd detested about Sofia. He'd asked her to give it up, for him, if not for herself, many a time. To no avail. But today, ironically, it might give them a few moments' reprieve. Logan could hardly believe this was the same woman he'd been in love with. She looked the same. Still classy and meticulously dressed. He'd once thought it as sexy as hell. But where had this callous, barbarous streak come from? Had it always been there, and he just didn't want to see it? Was she more like her father than he first thought? And her brothers?

It'd been a huge shock to see Sofia again. She was the last person he expected to walk through that door. It'd taken him a few moments to regain his power of speech. For a second, he'd been transported back to Mexico, to the first time he'd set eyes on her, back in the San Cristobal marketplace. She'd looked so free and happy and alive. He'd been drawn to her like a bee to honey. But now he knew better. Her type of honey hid a dark and dangerous poison.

As soon as Sofia exited the door, Diego came toward him.

"Well, hello, old buddy. Glad we could finally catch up." Diego slapped Logan playfully a couple of times on the back, like one old mate greeting another. Which couldn't be farther from the case. Logan hid the wince of pain. The slap had hardly been friendly, it'd been much harder than it looked, and Logan's bruised back protested.

"Knock it off, Diego," he said warily.

"What? Don't you like your girlfriend's new haircut? I kind of dig it, myself." Diego was really enjoying himself now. Rubbing it in for all he was worth.

Logan glanced at Mia, and this time he couldn't hide the grimace. All her beautiful hair lay in drifts around the legs of her chair, her short hair sticking out in ragged tufts all over her head. But she sat up ramrod straight, shoulders back, and looked him directly in the eye. And that's when he realized, nothing could dim her beauty. It shone out of her like there was a tiny, glowing sun inside her. He'd been about to apologize for what Sofia had done. Apologize for getting her mixed up in this in the first place. Had been about to give in and weep. For her, and for him, and for the hopelessness of it all. But one look from her changed everything. It was as if she were talking to him, though no words left her lips, and he knew what she wanted from him. She was a strong woman, who wouldn't go down without a fight. And now he knew, neither would he. He'd fight for her until his very last breath.

He would fight for her because he was in love with her.

The revelation didn't shock him nearly as much as it should. Because part of him had known all along he was falling for her.

The notion filled him with renewed strength. If they were to get out of here, he needed to start thinking. Start acting. He tried not to let his newfound determination show on his face, looking away from Mia and at the floor instead. But not before he gave her a quick wink, hoping she understood his sign. If only he hadn't given that gun to Dalton last night. But it was no good regretting it now, he probably wouldn't have had a chance to use it anyway, not before Scarface found it and took it away.

Letting his mouth sag in what he hoped looked like defeat, he asked, "Can you at least tell us where we are? What you plan on doing with us?"

Diego looked at Leo and shrugged. "Guess there's no harm telling them now." A dark smile curled his lips at the corners. "This place belongs to your buddy, *The Hook,* I believe they call him."

"What?" Logan couldn't put the two notions together. Harry and the Ramirez brothers? What did they have to do with each other?

"Yeah, Harry had to leave the island suddenly. Jumped on some big private boat of his and got the hell out of here. But he was more than happy to hear about our plans for you and your little lady here. We must remember to send him some proof when we're through." Diego stroked his beard, as if in deep thought. "He seemed quite uptight. Said he wouldn't rest until he knew this woman here was dead. You must've done something awful bad to annoy him." Diego grinned. Mia looked up sharply at his words, the blood draining from her face.

"Yeah, that was a sweet yacht Hagman owned. I think we need to get ourselves one of those," Leo mused, joining the conversation. Logan couldn't believe the man was more interested in Harry's boat than on the words his brother had just uttered. He must be inhuman. Logan and Mia were just another job. Nothing more, nothing less.

"Your guy, Harry, he wasn't going to help us at first," Diego continued. "But after a few…shall we say, inducements, he came around to our way of thinking. Was most helpful, if I do say so myself. He did most of the dirty work for us. While we sat back and enjoyed this wonderful island of yours. And I must say, it is a paradise, isn't it? I can see why you chose this place."

Logan stopped listening as Diego went on to explain about the wonderful villa they'd stayed in for the past few days; how blue the water was, and how white the sandy beaches. So, Harry had been in league with the Ramirezes all along. Logan could already imagine what kind of inducements Diego was talking about. Blackmail. And with everything Harry was into, it probably hadn't been hard to blackmail him. Perhaps they'd even known about his illegal, turtle poaching side business. If only he and Mia had left on his boat that very first night, they might've been able to escape all this.

"Too bad about the bounty guy you killed. He did a great job of finding you." Diego's comment broke through Logan's musing.

"Yeah, I'd definitely would've used him again," Leo added. "Better than any tracker hound we ever used before."

"But I guess after he saw the post on Facebook and tipped us off, led us to the island, he wasn't much use anymore. So maybe this punk did us a favor."

"You're probably right there."

The two brothers were talking like they were having a private conversation, as if Logan and Mia weren't even in the room.

He dropped his head and turned it slightly, so he could look at Mia out of the corner of his eye, wanting to make sure she was all right. A small movement caught his gaze. She didn't glance in his direction, kept her stare fixed on the brothers arguing good-naturedly in front of them, but he could just make out her hands working slowly and methodically behind the chair.

She was trying to get free.

And he could see it now, one of the ropes was looser than the rest. A little bit of slack, that was all she needed. Those small, fine-boned hands might be extra beneficial today.

It took a second for Logan to realize the Ramirez brothers had stopped talking. He kept his head low, not looking either of them in the eye, as if he'd been cowed by all their talk of killing, not wanting to give away Mia's endeavors.

"Where the hell has Sofia got to?" Leo growled, obviously tired of waiting for his sister.

"She'll be back when she's good and ready, you know that," Diego replied. A sudden malicious light came into his eyes as his gaze fell on Mia. "We could always find ways to keep ourselves entertained while we're waiting." His highly polished black shoes made an ominous tapping sound as he walked over to her chair. He leaned down so his nose was hovering mere millimeters from the side of Mia's neck. "I mean, Sofia didn't say nothing about helping ourselves to the goodies while she was away. We could get things warmed up for when she comes back." He sniffed deeply, as if drawing Mia's scent into his lungs. "Mmm, she does smell delicious." He plucked at a tuft of her short hair. "And I don't actually mind this hairdo, it brings out her lovely eyes, don't you think?"

Mia stiffened, sitting unmoving in her chair, not daring to look at the bearded oaf.

"Leave her alone." Logan said the words carefully and slowly. Neither of these assholes was going to touch her.

"Or what?" Diego taunted. "What you gonna do, big boy?" He drew the small knife out of the ankle holster and passed it slowly in front of Mia's face. She let out a small whimper.

Logan tensed his muscles, tried to kick out with his feet at Diego, who was just out of range.

"Don't make me laugh," Diego said cruelly, edging around Mia's chair until he was in front of her, still bent over, so he could look her in the eye. He ran the blade lightly down her left cheek, and Logan roared his protest. Rage burned bright and hot in his chest. They were *not* going to hurt Mia. He needed to get out of this chair. Madly, he wrenched his hands around in the ropes, but all he achieved was a searing pain in both wrists. The bonds were too tight.

Mia hadn't moved, like a bird caught by a snake's glittering gaze, as if paralyzed.

Diego's other hand came up and grasped Mia's breast, squeezing it tightly through the blouse. "Nice. Just the right size," he drawled. "Not too big, not too small. But I guess you already knew that, didn't you?" His last question was directed at Logan.

Something inside him snapped. It was too much to bear, watching Diego goad him at Mia's expense. Her face had gone pale and pasty, a look of horror in her eyes.

Logan bucked and writhed on his chair, desperate to get loose as it clattered over the concrete.

"Take care of him," Diego snarled. "He's ruining my mojo here with the pretty lady."

Leo came toward Logan a gleam of anticipation in his eyes. Logan tried to swivel, tried to duck out of the way of the punch he knew was coming. But it was no good, he was tied to a chair with nowhere to go. Leo wasn't tall, built more like an ox, with a thick neck and brawny shoulders. Logan also knew he'd spent time as an amateur in the boxing ring, back in Mexico. Leo drew back, bent slightly at the knees, and let go. His fist collided with Logan's stomach so hard it felt like a sledgehammer hitting him. The force of the impact actually lifted the chair off the ground and sent him hurtling backwards, where he landed on the ground with a sickening crack.

He couldn't breathe. Logan tried to suck in air, but nothing would come. Stars danced before his eyes, the world going dark and hazy, like he was looking at everything through a tunnel. The old injuries on his back were nothing compared to this new pain.

"That should keep him quiet for a while," Leo said, standing over him, legs akimbo. Logan lay on the ground, gasping like a fish. Jesus, he hurt. His stomach felt like it was on fire. And his left arm, the one that'd taken the brunt of the fall, was screaming in agony. Logan tried to roll over slightly, to ease the pressure on his shoulder. And something gave way behind him. The ropes were loose around his wrist. A part of the chair must've splintered or broken under the impact. None of this showed on his face, however, as he lay on the ground. He gave a low groan for good measure and Leo turned to walk back to his spot by the wall.

His eyes found Mia as he stared mutely at her. Had he just fucked this all up for both of them?

She moved suddenly. Head-butted Diego straight in the face, screaming at him. Then just as suddenly, one hand came up and grabbed him between the legs, squeezing and twisting with all her might. Taken by surprise by the double-whammy attack, Diego fell to the ground like a sack of potatoes with a howl of rage. Logan's heart leaped into his throat. She'd got her hand free after all.

The knife in Diego's hand skittered across the concrete floor, coming to a stop a foot in front of Logan's face.

He stared at it, and then at Diego, still writhing and howling on the floor, blood streaming from his nose.

Leo stopped mid-stride, glancing between Logan and the knife. Then he turned slowly, stalking back, meaning to pick up the knife. He wasn't in any hurry. Because he was under the impression that Logan wasn't a threat, still strung up like a suckling pig.

But he was wrong.

With a superhuman effort, Logan wrenched his uninjured hand out of the ropes, rolling onto his back as he did so, the chair between him and the floor. Leo saw what was happening and lunged, but Logan kicked out with his foot, half-tripping the stocky man. It wasn't much, but it gave him just enough time to snag the knife and hold it, point upward, as Leo stumbled again and then fell, straight on top of Logan.

Logan thrust upward.

The knife bit deep into the other man's flesh as he fell.

It was on odd feeling, Logan thought distractedly. The knife must've been sharp, because it sliced through Leo like he was cutting butter. But then, it seemed to hit something hard and lodged there. Leo was now lying on top of Logan, his immense weight crushing him against the chair back, causing his shoulder to scream in agony.

With a mighty heave, Logan used the hilt to lever Leo, rolling the man away so he landed on his side next to Logan on the dusty floor. Logan glanced at his hand; it still held the knife, dripping with Leo's blood. Strangely, Leo hadn't made a sound, but now he sat up, a look of confusion on his face, looking down at his chest. Bright-red blood gushed out over his immaculate, black, suit lapels.

"Miguel, get the fuck in here. Now." Diego tried to scream, but it came out more as a whimper.

If the guard had heard, they had mere seconds left before they were outnumbered and overpowered. Killed.

All eyes swiveled to the door. But no one came charging though it.

"Miguel," Diego cried again, louder this time.

Leo collapsed onto his back on the floor only a few feet away from Logan, an animalistic sound escaping his throat.

Logan didn't know what to do. He was still lying on the floor. Even though he had the knife, he couldn't get off the ground to use it, as his other, injured arm was still strapped to the chair. Mia too, was still bound to her chair, although now she was madly tearing at the ropes binding her other hand. But she wouldn't get them off in time. Diego was already trying to stand, one hand still cupping his genitals, his other levering him onto his knees.

"I'm going to fucking kill you both," Diego wheezed. "Miguel, get in here now, or you're fucking fired."

Diego slowly struggled to his feet.

Did he have a gun on him? It was a question Logan hadn't asked himself before now. Which was careless and stupid. Because it could mean the difference between life and a very quick death for them both. The brothers had never worn weapons in Mexico. Even after Logan had been let in on the family secret and they'd relaxed their guard around him, Logan never remembered either of them carrying. Diego always had that knife on him. That was nothing new. And Leo? He didn't think he carried anything. Perhaps they relied on their hired thugs to do their dirty work for them. Both guards were definitely armed.

Logan took a punt. He rolled fully onto his back and ignoring the searing pain in his shoulder, steadied his arm and lined up his target. He'd never thrown a knife before in his life. But if he didn't do something, they were both dead. Taking a lungful of air, he held his breath, narrowed his eyes and threw.

The blade whistled through the air and landed with a surprising wet thud in Diego's ribcage.

Diego gave a high-pitched scream and stumbled, one hand still cupping his groin.

He overbalanced straight onto Mia, almost landing in her lap. He struggled to right himself, but it was too late.

Mia's other hand suddenly came free, but Logan couldn't make out what was going on from his vantage point on the ground. His shoulder throbbed, the agony almost unbearable. He tried rolling farther onto his back, to ease the pain.

"Mia," he yelled. "Mia." It looked like they were wrestling for control. Diego's hand was suddenly at her throat, and she choked out a scream.

Then Diego's eyes went wide. Logan couldn't see; Mia's body was blocking his view.

Diego stood up, allowing Logan a sudden, clear view. The knife stuck out of the Mexican's neck, just below his well-manicured beard. Mia stared at him, arms up and ready, as if expecting him to come at her again.

But he didn't. He fell to his knees in front of her.

Then the door burst open.

Expecting the guard, Miguel, to come charging through, Logan braced himself for another onslaught. Logan's heart was beating so fast he was sure he was having a heart attack, but when he saw who stepped through the door, he knew their nightmare had finally ended.

It was Dalton, with a young island policeman hot on his tail.

Dalton's quick eyes took in the scene in front of him as he pointed his gun at Diego. Then he gradually lowered it. The policeman was slower on the uptake, swinging his gun around wildly, looking for a target. Perhaps he'd never encountered a real-life situation like this before, Logan thought vaguely.

"Everybody down. Nobody move," the cop shouted in an authoritative voice.

Logan almost laughed at the absurdity of it.

Instead he said, "Help us up, will you." Logan had now almost freed his other hand, but his legs were still bound tightly to the chair.

The policeman had finally settled on a target and was now pointing his gun at Diego, but there was no need. Although the man was still alive, he'd collapsed with a gurgle onto the floor and was now writhing like a stranded eel.

"Keep an eye on him," Dalton advised the cop, then bent down to help Mia finish untying herself from the chair.

"You okay?" he asked softly, staring intently into Mia's eyes.

"I'm not injured, if that's what you mean," she replied.

"That'll do for now." Dalton moved over to Logan and began untying him.

"Is Keira here?" Logan asked, peering around Dalton's shoulder, even as he helped him up off the floor. Some part of him hoped that Dalton had made his sister stay safely away. But he knew Kiera better than that, and he guessed Dalton would've lost that particular argument.

"Yes, she's outside, having a little chat with your ex-fiancée." Dalton couldn't quite hide his deep frown and Logan knew Kiera had definitely won that altercation.

The police officer was talking quickly into his transmitter radio, calling for paramedics and more back-up, still with his gun pointed at Diego, who'd stopped moving.

Mia was standing in one corner, as far away from Diego and Leo as she could get. Clutching his arm against his body —he wondered if his shoulder was dislocated—Logan went over to her.

"Hey, gorgeous," he whispered in her ear, pulling her into

his body with his good arm. "Are you okay?"

She was shaking like a leaf.

"No, I'm not okay. None of this is okay," she sobbed, burying her face into his chest. Large sobs racked her body, and Logan held her and let her cry.

Part of him knew it was shock. They were both suffering from deep, appalling shock. Normal people didn't have to contend with this kind of thing. Tears also ran down his cheeks, but some of those tears were from relief. They were alive. They had lived through something terrible and violent. They had survived.

And there was a spark of hope in his heart. Hope that he and Mia could find a way forward from here. To a stronger place, where they could be together. Because he knew he didn't want to lose her.

Logan stroked her hair as if she were a small child, and let her wail out her grief and rage, let her use him as her rock, so she could weather this storm and come out the other side.

# CHAPTER NINETEEN

Mia sat on the plastic chair, watching the hubbub go on around her at the police station with detachment. Logan was seated next to her, his hand resting on her knee. The warmth of his palm felt like it was the only thing anchoring her to reality.

Police officers swarmed through the small building, more than were normally here on the island. Two detectives had flown in from mainland USA—Chicago, Mia thought she heard one officer say. This thing was much bigger than St. John usually dealt with. Two men confirmed dead, one rushed to emergency surgery on St. Thomas, and a suspected body disposed of in the ocean. Three more in custody; including the woman, Sofia.

Mia couldn't get her head around the fact that she'd played a part in those men's deaths. Yes, they had probably been going to kill her and Logan if she hadn't done something. And at the time, she'd been acting on a kind of survival instinct. Using her wits and a violence she never knew existed to remain alive.

Keira was sitting on Mia's other side, her eyes sliding continuously to the door of the interview room, where Dalton had been answering questions for the past hour. Keira and

Mia had both already been debriefed, in a makeshift office at the back of the station—it seemed there was only one official interview room. And now Logan was waiting his turn.

"I need a coffee," Keira said, standing up abruptly. "I'll get you both one as well." Without waiting for an answer, she stalked off down the corridor to find someone to make her a coffee.

Mia was glad Kiera was here. She'd been as much of a steadying influence as Logan in the aftermath of it all. Keira had held her hand and explained in as much detail as she could what was going to happen to them now. But that was only after she'd answered Logan's million-and-one questions when they first arrived at the police station.

"How did you find us?" he'd asked in a hissed whisper, looking up at Officer Naomi Dartez, who was standing at the end of the corridor glaring at them. Guarding them, to make sure no one escaped before the police had all the answers.

"I managed to get the license plate of the SUV as it drove off up the hill," she said, with a pleased smile. "I was looking for the keys to the front door when I heard the scuffle. But by the time I got down the driveway, it was too late to stop the car. Thankfully, Tianna was still safe inside at that stage. You should've heard Dalton. He was most pissed off. Kept saying we should've gone to the police last night, like he told you." Keira grimaced at the memory.

"Yeah, yeah. I owe him an apology," Logan agreed. "But then what?"

"Dalton called Reed's mate, Police Captain Porter, and told them there'd been a kidnapping. The cops said they were busy with a death at a warehouse and he would send someone around when they could. Dalton absolutely lost it. Said it was incompetent policing and that if they weren't going to do it, then we bloody well were. I don't think the Captain really believed us," Keira said in a lowered voice.

"After all, who gets kidnapped on a tiny Virgin Island like this one? I'm not sure they've ever seen anything like this before."

"You're probably right," Mia agreed. "And I'm still not sure half of them believe our story." She stared pointedly at Officer Dartez, and Keira gave a conspiratorial nod.

"Anyway, Dalton couldn't sit and do nothing, so we dropped Tianna at the police station, to see if she could convince them we were for real. Not that she wanted to go. She was very determined she was coming with us. Kept saying she was going to rescue her sister. But we knew she'd be safer there, so Dalton managed to convince her it was in your best interest if the police were out looking for you."

Something Mia was eternally grateful for. She silently thanked Keira and Dalton for looking after Tianna when she wasn't around. The police had sent Tianna home a little while ago, after she became belligerent and started to yell that Mia was innocent and they should let them all go. Even Mia hadn't been able to calm her down. Poor Tianna, she was just worried about Mia, scared they were going to throw her in jail. She'd go and talk to her as soon as she was able, let her know everything was all right.

Keira continued. "Then we decided to drive around the town, see if we could get lucky and spot the car ourselves. Which was a long shot, I know," she added at Logan's glance of disbelief. "We stopped a couple of times to ask the locals at a street stall or in a bar, if they'd seen a car matching that description. I wasn't hopeful," she said with a rueful glance. "I honestly thought you guys were gone for good." There was a catch in Keira's voice and Logan patted her reassuringly.

"But out of the blue, we asked this old guy, who was sitting in a chair by the side of the road. We're still not sure what he was doing there, just watching the world go by as far as we could figure. He said he might've seen something like that car, but he needed something to jolt his memory. It wasn't until Dalton brought out of a wad of bills, his eyes lit up and he confirmed he'd seen the car and pointed to a driveway leading up to a large villa on top of a hill."

"Harry's place," Logan muttered.

"Yes, and what a place it was," Keira muttered back. "That man must've had a lot of spare cash."

"Pity all we saw was some gloomy basement he obviously kept for solving problems like us," Mia replied. She wasn't surprised she hadn't known anything about Harry's huge mansion in the jungle. Why would he tell the likes of her about his business dealings? She was merely a dancer, one of his pawns, to be used and then discarded when she became too much of a complication.

"We parked the Jeep, to see if we could find a way in without being seen. I wanted Dalton to wait for the police and he wanted me to stay in the car. Eventually we came to an…agreement." Keira gave a smile that Mia recognized. It meant she'd won the argument, which didn't surprise her in the least. They'd called the police, and Keira also hadn't stayed safely in the car. Logan had been right when he'd described his sisters as spirited and stubborn. Mia thought she'd add feisty to that description. They didn't seem to be scared of anything. And Mia had no doubt at all, that if Sierra hadn't been confined to a hospital bed, she would've been there as well, making damn sure they found her brother alive and well.

"I think we already told you Dalton has a bounty hunter's license, back in Hawaii?" Keira glanced at Mia for confirmation. "Which turned out to be a good thing, because it means he's allowed to carry a weapon. Unfortunately, he didn't bring it with him on this trip. We didn't think we'd need it," she added, shooting a dark look at Logan. "Fortunately, Dalton still had the gun Logan stole from

Harry's man. I don't particularly agree with Dalton's use of deadly force myself." Keira drew her perfectly sculpted, dark eyebrows down in a frown. "But I guess this time it came in handy."

Logan butted in. "Damn right it did. If you guys hadn't stopped that ugly dude from charging back in, we would've been goners."

Keira gave him a level stare, and Mia was suddenly reminded of Sierra. She almost laughed when Logan grimaced. She was beginning to see he reverted to his childhood habits when he was around his sisters. He hated being told off, even if it was non-verbally.

"As I was saying," she continued. "We crept up the driveway, found a spot to hide behind a large hibiscus bush. There was a big dude standing in the shadows of the main entrance. Dalton said he had a gun in a shoulder holster, but I couldn't see it, so I just had to believe him. We were going to wait for the police to come, because we still weren't sure if we had the right place. That's when I saw Sofia come out of the door. She was smoking a cigarette. I recognized her from photos you sent us, even though I never got to meet her in person." She pursed her lips in Logan's direction and he scowled at her pointed dig at how bad he'd been at keeping in touch with his family.

"When I told Dalton, he decided we needed to move. It was now or never; we couldn't wait for the police to turn up any longer."

"Weren't you scared?" Mia was amazed at how calm Keira seemed to be about the whole thing.

"Yes," she replied honestly. "But also no. You remember my story, how the Yakuza were after me because of my swindling, dirty ex-husband?"

Mia nodded.

"I figured nothing could ever be as bad as that. And we

had the element of surprise on our side. Plus, I trust Dalton. With all my heart."

Mia felt sudden tears prick at the back of her eyelids from Keira's simple statement. Because she knew it to be the truth. She'd seen it with her own eyes, how seamlessly these two fitted together. Their faith in each other was absolute.

"It was almost too easy. We crept a little closer, while the guard and Sofia chatted. And then Dalton stepped out of the bushes with his gun pointed directly at them. Dalton may not be a cop, but he's arrested hundreds of bail jumpers in his time. He knows what he's doing. The guard didn't even have a chance to draw his gun. At least the guard knew when he was beaten. That woman, however..." Keira sucked in a fortifying breath. "She was a bit more of a handful. She swore and cussed like I've never heard before. Tried to make a run for it, wearing those stupid high heels. Dalton had to fire a warning shot over her head to make her stop." Keira shook her head at the memory.

"After that, he called me and handed me the guard's gun. I've been doing some shooting practice at the range, Dalton said it never hurts to be able to handle a weapon." Keira puffed out her chest a little, lifting her chin, and Mia agreed with her. After the events of the past few days, she was going to look in to shooting lessons herself. She never wanted to feel that much at a disadvantage ever again.

"Just as we finished trussing them both up like a pig in a poke, we heard a commotion at the bottom of the driveway. It was the cops finally arriving. They asked all kinds of questions, weren't happy we seemed to know more than they did; that we were doing their job for them, really." Keira smirked and lifted an eyebrow. "Anyway, Dalton got tired of their questions real quick, and said he was going in to find you guys. One of the cops, a young guy, followed Dalton when it was obvious he wasn't going to do as he was told."

"And thank God he did. If he hadn't snuck up on that other guard, stopped him in his tracks, we might not be in such good shape," Logan replied.

"Yes, thank God," Mia echoed Logan's words. Her mind shot back to those few seconds, back in the basement, as she waited for that door to open and Miguel to come charging in. To take away their only hope of getting out alive. She stifled a sob. It was still so real and raw. She hoped the details, the images, would fade over time. Of Diego with the knife sticking out of his neck—God had she really done that to him? Of the other brother, Leo, his lifeblood pumping out onto the concrete. They learned later that the knife had hit the Mexican man's heart. By the time the paramedics arrived he'd lost so much blood, there was little they could do for him.

"You okay?" Logan's concerned voice broke through her thoughts.

"I don't know," she whispered. Leo was dead. That was sad. He had a family back in Mexico, children who would never see their father again, and a wife who wouldn't ever hold her husband. And Diego was fighting for his life in hospital. At least she didn't have his death on her hands. Because she was the one who'd driven the knife into his neck. She wasn't sure if she would be able to live with that. No matter what those men had done, their families didn't deserve that. Mia knew it was crazy, but she prayed Diego made it through.

Then there was the other guard Logan had pushed off the roof. The police told them he had died as well. Two men dead from this whole debacle.

Logan pulled her into a one-armed hug. His other arm was in a makeshift sling. A doctor had put his dislocated shoulder back in, but warned him it would be sore for days.

"We'll be okay, sweetheart," he said fiercely.

Mia let his body heat sink into her, thaw her from the outside in. Even in this tropical humidity, she couldn't seem to get warm. Logan was her only constant, at the moment. His first concern had always been about her. He'd come looking for her when Harry had her trapped, when he shouldn't have. All he'd had to do was leave the island with Keira and Dalton and he would've been safe. But he stayed. For her.

Even while everything had been unfolding with Sofia. The way he'd looked at her after that bitch had cut all her hair off. Like he'd seen right into her soul, as if he'd come to some decision. His eyes had glowed. Blue and brilliant. Full of adoration and…dare she say it? Love.

Was Logan falling in love with her?

Was she falling in love with him?

She pulled back a little, so she could look him in the face. Studied his nose, the curve of his lips, square jaw, the way his hair curled over his forehead.

Maybe. Maybe she was.

*  *  *

Logan ducked his head to avoid Sierra's gaze. She was glowering at him from her spot on the second couch, arms crossed in front of her chest. Reed sat protectively by her side, and he was also glowering at Logan. They made a great pair, Logan thought abstractly. They could glower at each other with equal fervor, with never a clear winner being declared.

Keira came into the room, carrying a tray laden with glasses of beer, breaking the tension. Mia trailed behind her, a plate of pizza they'd picked up on their way home in her hands. Logan smiled at Mia as she lay the plate on the small table and sat down next to him. He shuffled closer, so their legs were touching. Keira put the tray down and handed out everyone's beers. Dalton came in last, carrying his own beer and took a seat next to Keira, on the same large couch as

Sierra and Reed.

It was now late in the evening, and they'd all gathered back at the Airbnb. Sierra and Reed had arrived back from St. Thomas that afternoon, while the rest of them were still being interviewed by the police.

"You should've stayed in the hospital," Logan said, cutting through the awkward silence, going for the caring and compassionate brotherly tone. "There was no need for you to check out early. You should be looking after yourself." But it came out sounding more like a sulky teenager, and he knew it. How could it be, that a grown man of thirty-one could still be made to feel like a guilty child by his bossy sister? He cleared his throat and sat up taller. Mia stirred beside him and he put a comforting hand on her knee. This must be awkward for her, not only because of the trauma of the past few days, but also to be caught up in his family drama.

"Really?" Sierra pursed her lips at him. "My little brother ends up kidnapped, then nearly killed by a raving lunatic and her two brothers, and you think I could idly sit by and not want to make sure you were okay?"

"Well…" Logan was lost for a response. Because he would've done exactly the same thing, if the tables had been turned. But he still felt bad that Sierra and Reed had discharged themselves a day early, as soon as they heard the news. It was his fault they'd been in the hospital in the first place. He opened his mouth, to try and find the right words to express his guilt and regret, but shut it again. There were no words that'd ever make this right.

Reed filled the void for him, perhaps understanding a little of his anguish. "Sierra is fine. The doctors have said she and the baby are just fine." Keira had already told Logan this, but having Reed confirm it, having Sierra here in front of him, in the flesh, seemed to validate the truth for him. Sierra and Reed would be alright. Their baby was unharmed. They both had some second-degree burns on their backs—Dalton's burns were worse, some of them third-degree—but they were small and localized. The internal injuries the doctors had been worried about had been discounted. And an ultrasound confirmed the tiny baby growing in Sierra's belly was thriving. Still, Logan felt this chest squeeze tight. Things could've turned out so differently.

"Oh, stop catastrophizing," Sierra said loudly. Logan blinked and stared at her. "You haven't changed much," she added. "You always did love the melodrama of things."

"That's not true—" He began to argue, voice rising.

Keira cut him off. "Let's not reduce this to a family squabble just yet, please." She thrust the plate of pizza toward him, a warning frown drawing down her dark brows.

"Sure. Sorry," he apologized, snagging a piece and biting into the melted cheese. Partly to stop himself saying anything more, but also because he was starving. They hadn't eaten all day. Well, you couldn't really call the soggy sandwiches the police had served up late in the afternoon proper food. After tasting one, Logan definitely hadn't gone back for more.

"At least we're all safe. And back together. We can sort the rest out later," Dalton said into the sudden silence, and Keira shot him a grateful glance.

"Yes, that may be true," Sierra said in a gentler voice. "But there are so many questions that need answers. Like, why did you decide to go to the warehouse looking for Mia on your own? And then, once that debacle was over, why didn't you go straight to the police? If you had, then Sofia might never have got her claws in you. Thank God for Dalton's quick thinking. Otherwise…well I hate to think what the outcome might've been." Logan could see Sierra's hand was shaking, as she carefully put her glass back on the coffee table. "You know police divers pulled a body from the bay this afternoon. Who knows how long it's going to take to clear your name,

Logan? We might be stuck here indefinitely, at least until the police have finished with us and their investigation," she added.

"Oh, well, perhaps we can all have that island holiday we all talked about." Reed had finally stopped glowering at Logan and flashed him a conspiratorial grin. At least the man didn't hold a grudge. And Logan didn't really blame him for any vestiges of ill-feeling he had towards Logan. Reed's main priority was keeping Sierra safe, and Logan didn't blame him one little bit. He felt exactly the same about Mia. Shifting his hand, he leaned back and draped his good arm around her shoulders. Immediately she moved closer, molding to his side. He liked the way she felt next to him. Like she was drawing support from him. But also lending her own strength. They were equals in this partnership.

"We'd be more than happy to show you around, when you're up to it," Mia said, speaking for the first time. "We can show you special places. Take you to Maho Bay; it's in the top ten of all beaches in the world. When you're up to it, of course," she added again, looking over at Sierra and Reed.

"I'll even take you snorkeling, see if we can find a turtle or two to swim with," Logan added, liking the way Mia was trying to lighten the mood. Besides, it wouldn't help to dwell on what was going to happen next. He hoped with all his heart that the police would find it was an act of self-defense, his shooting the guy at the dock. All he could do was stay upbeat and positive. He was alive, and so was Mia. And that was all that mattered.

Sierra's frown finally lifted. "That does sound nice," she admitted. "But Reed and I will have to stick to land-based activities for now," she added.

They spent the next hour or so rehashing everything that'd happened that day, filling Sierra and Reed in on the details.

Finally, Mia gave a huge yawn next to Logan. He glanced

up at the clock on the wall, surprised to see it was almost eleven at night.

"I need to hit the hay," he said.

"Agreed," said Reed. He got up slowly from the couch, wincing a little as he straightened. Then he reached down and gently helped Sierra to her feet. "It's been a big day," he said, but although he was talking to everyone, Logan felt like there was a special meaning in his words meant only for Sierra. She locked gazes with him, and for a second, they seemed to forget there were other people in the room.

"If you don't mind, I'd like to go home tonight. To see Tianna, and assure her I'm safe. And to fill my flatmates in on all that's happened," Mia said into the silence.

"Good idea," Logan said. "I'm coming with you." As much as he knew his sisters cared about him and they only wanted him to be safe and well, he needed to get away from their claustrophobic smothering for a while. To be alone with Mia. The thought had his heart rate rising.

They said goodnight, promised they'd come back early the next morning, and left them all waving from the front door. The walk wasn't long, and they held hands in the dark, not saying much at all. For once, Logan was all talked out, and it was nice to walk in comfortable silence, with Mia's hand warm and soft in his. The balmy, Caribbean night air enfolded them, a slight breeze blowing in off the ocean. A perfect evening in paradise. And now, for the first time since their date at Sunny's, they could walk without fear. It was liberating, and Logan's heart lifted the farther down the road they walked.

At Mia's little house, she introduced him to her two flatmates and dance partners, Crystal and Scarlett, who exclaimed long and loud about her poor, butchered hair, and worried over Logan's arm in the sling. Tianna came running down the stairs at the sound of Mia's voice and embraced her sister in a long hug. The other women stood back, looks of surprise crossing their features, like they'd never seen Tianna so devoted to her sister before.

Crystal and Scarlett were shocked to hear Mia had been at the epicenter of the trouble at Harry's last night, but not overly surprised to hear he had fled the island. They were pragmatic about finding a new dance gig, saying they may as well move back to St. Thomas, Crystal even saying it might be the kick in the pants she needed to finally go home to her family. Scarlett recounted in detail, what they'd heard through the grapevine, about the Coast Guard raiding the gentleman's club. The gossip was all over town, of how boxes and boxes of illegal turtle carapaces and other merchandise were hauled out of the warehouse. And how Harry *The Hook* was nowhere to be found. Silently, Logan thought Harry would resurface somewhere else, perhaps under another name, but still doing the same old shit. Men like him always survived, knew how to disappear, then reappear later on.

While Crystal and Scarlett had a lot more to tell them, Mia yawned and stretched and said, "I need to go to bed now."

"Why don't you stay down here with us tonight?" Crystal suggested to Tianna, as they all got up from around the cramped kitchen table. "You can sleep on our couch."

"What? Why?" Tianna asked. "I'd much rather—" She stopped abruptly as she caught Crystal's eye, and it suddenly dawned on her what the other woman was getting at. Giving Logan and Mia space and time to spend alone together. "Oh, yes, I'd love to stay down here," she said. "By the way, I tidied up upstairs for you," Tianna added with a sheepish smile.

Mia raised a bemused eyebrow, but she said nothing, instead taking Logan by the hand and leading him upstairs.

"Night, everyone," she called out.

They entered her little upstairs studio, and he closed the

door quietly behind them. Mia flicked on a light switch, and he vaguely took in a small room, with a couch, small table and TV all crammed in, and a double bed curtained off by a row of hanging sarongs in one corner.

Alone at last.

He couldn't wait any longer. Taking her gently in his good arm, he buried his face into her neck. Keira had lent her some more clothes, because the ones from this morning were covered in Diego's blood. This time, she was wearing a flowing skirt and white T-shirt, both a little big on Mia, but they brought out the colors of her skin. They stood there, in each other's arms, for many, uncounted minutes. He savored the feel of her, the smell of her. It was such sweet relief to be able to hold her. To know she was safe. They were both safe.

There were so many questions needing answers. Where was he going to live, now that his beautiful boat was gone? Would he still have a job with Dan Brown and Tom when he called them tomorrow? How was Mia going to survive, now that her dancing gig was gone? But most of all, he wanted to know if he and Mia had a future together. Because he knew he wanted one.

As if reading his mind, Mia pulled away slightly and said, "Can we think about everything tomorrow? I just want to curl up in bed next to you and sleep for the next year or so. Would that be okay?"

Holding Mia close to him, feeling her breasts pushed into his chest, had awakened other thoughts in his head. And his body. It was reacting to having her near as it always did, growing hot and heavy with desire. But he knew she was right. They both needed sleep. He could put his body's clamoring on the backburner. For now.

She took his hand and towed him toward the bed. He watched as Mia pulled back the orange-and-scarlet coverlet—she liked to decorate with bright colors, it seemed—and then his gaze was drawn to her lithe body, as she dragged the T-shirt over her head in one quick movement and dropped the skirt almost as quickly, leaving her with only bra and panties on. She had an exquisite body, that was for sure. And she wasn't afraid of showing it, for which he was doubly grateful.

She slipped between the sheets and he stripped down to his boxers, removing his sling at the same time, and hopped in bed with her. Entwining their arms and legs, he gathered her up and they let out a simultaneous sigh as they both relaxed into the pillows.

"I don't want to live through another day like that again, ever," she whispered.

"Me either," he agreed.

"Tell me a story," she said, her breathing already slowing down. "To get my mind off everything that happened today."

He told her the story of how he and Captain got lost one night on their way between Haiti and St. John because his GPS system had malfunctioned. He'd taken out the old sextant and some charts and spent hours looking at the stars to make sure he was on course. At the same time, he stroked her hair, twirling the short tufts between his fingers, mourning the loss of her luxuriant locks. But even before he was halfway through, she was asleep. He lay awake for a few minutes more, enjoying the slow rise and fall of her chest against his. A steady peace filled his soul. A feeling that this was where he was meant to be; that they were meant to be together.

He finally admitted to himself that he'd fallen for her, this exotic dancer with a heart of gold.

"I'm in love with you," he whispered into the air. Then he closed his eyes and followed her into the land of dreams.

They both slept like the dead, only waking when the sun crept in through the curtains to announce the morning. Neither of them seemed to have moved during the night, as they were entwined in exactly the same position Logan remembered going to sleep in.

He was the first to stir, a shaft of sunlight hitting him in the face, so he could no longer pretend he was asleep. His body was already awake, clamoring for Mia's touch. And this time he wouldn't deny its cravings.

Mia lay encircled in his arms, her cheek nestled against his good shoulder, her breathing slow and steady. He looked down at her. They'd managed to kick the sheets off during the night, exposing most of her warm, brown body. As soft as a feather, he ran his fingers along the length of her arm, which was thrown over his torso, hugging him tight. He knew she was still asleep, her breathing never changed, but goose bumps rose up on her skin wherever his finger went; her body reacting to his touch. The same reaction she'd had the first time he'd done this back on his boat.

Letting his finger trail lower, over her hip and across her belly, he reveled in her curves, the dips and hollows. She was sleek, reminding him a cat, long limbs curled up and sinuous.

Then her eyelids fluttered open and she rolled her head back to look up at him.

"Hi, gorgeous," he muttered, bringing his hand up so his finger could trace the outline of her lips. Soft and pouting, still vulnerable from sleep, they drew him in.

"Hi," she said, as he dropped a velvety kiss on her mouth, the merest brush of his lips against hers. He was already hard, just from looking at her, but when their lips met, a red-hot heat shot through his groin and he groaned with need. Urgent desire flashed through his veins. Her tongue flicked out to meet his, and her eyes lost their sleepy haze. He'd meant to wake her gently, tug her out of slumber, by teasing her body until she wanted him as much as he wanted her. But now his hunger had awakened, and all he could think of was being inside her. With tremendous effort of will, he lifted his head to stare down into her eyes.

"How are you this morning? Are you—"

He'd wanted to do the chivalrous thing, make sure she wasn't still suffering from the distress of yesterday's drama. But she cut him off mid-sentence by smiling at him, an erotic grin full of eager craving. That look made him want to slide on top of her, pin her to the bed and drive into her. Which it seemed was exactly what she intended, because the next thing he knew, she was lying on top of him, kissing him hard. He took that to mean she was feeling much better today. It took her two seconds to remove her bra, then she stroked her bare breasts over his chest, and he felt her nipples harden at the contact. She ground her hips into his, pushing against his erection. Her mouth came back down on his, those lips normally so soft and pliable now hard and demanding.

The other night, back at his sisters' Airbnb, they had made love more than once, and it'd been wild and passionate. But at the same time, he knew he'd held something back. Had remained civilized.

This morning felt different. He wanted her fast, hard, and hot. They'd both survived a tsunami of violence and turmoil, had thought they might die. And now, he wanted to prove to himself how very much alive he was. It seemed she wanted the same thing.

Mia fumbled with a drawer in a tiny table beside the bed, producing a packet of condoms. He thanked God she was prepared, and had one out of its packet and had sheathed himself in seconds.

He flipped her over so now he was on top, ignoring the twinge in his shoulder, and for a second, he hovered over her, hoping to regain a shred of self-control, but her hands clawed at his back, her legs wrapped around his hips, and he couldn't help it, he drove inside. Again, and again, until she let out a guttural scream of pleasure.

Later, they lay on their backs, staring up at the ceiling, enjoying the feeling of ease and fulfillment. It was natural, their being together. He propped up on an elbow and began to absentmindedly stroke her arm, his eyes taking their fill of her naked body.

She turned her head and speared him with her gaze.

"I'm in love with you, too," she said simply.

What?

What had she just said?

He stopped stroking, stared down at her. There was no question in her dark eyes, just absolute certainty.

"You thought I was asleep, but I heard you last night. When you said you loved me."

He was stunned to speechlessness. But this was a good thing.

A great thing.

"You don't think it's too fast?" People would tell him that love didn't hit you like a thunderbolt from the sky. Sierra would probably lecture him on how true love took time and patience to get right. But when something felt this right, then nothing should get in the way. And now he thought about it, both of his sisters had fallen hard and fast for their soulmates. So perhaps it ran in the family. And perhaps they'd understand.

"Nope. The last few days have taught me to take nothing for granted. To savor every moment, and to grab what I want with both hands. And I want you, Logan Goldstein. With all my heart."

His chest felt like it was about to explode. A million balloons expanded inside him, almost lifting him off the bed. They would make this work. If she loved him as much as he loved her, they would make this work.

Logan dropped his head and kissed her beautiful lips.

# CHAPTER TWENTY

*Five months later*

Logan concentrated on the feeling of Mia's hand in his, their fingers interlaced. His back was cocooned by the still-warm sand as he stared up at the night sky above. This was all he ever needed. Him and Mia together. Forever.

"I can see what Sierra and Reed like about this place. It's beautiful in its own way. But give me Maho Bay any day. The warm air, the bluest of blue water, and swimming with the turtles," she said quietly.

They'd arrived on Kangaroo Island two days ago. Sierra and Reed's wedding was tomorrow, but he and Mia had escaped the madhouse of pre-wedding jitters to come and lie on the gorgeous beach below Sierra's house for a few precious moments together.

He laughed. "Don't tell anyone, but I think I agree with you." Australia was still his home; would always be his home. But there was a lot to be said for the tropical equator and the tiny island of St. John. Mia being the biggest drawcard, of course. But there was also his job with Dan Brown and Tom, researching the turtles. It was important work, something he was intensely passionate about.

Thankfully, Dan had offered him a two-year contract. Brushing away his concerns about the danger he'd inadvertently put Tom, and perhaps everyone else in, saying *all's well that ends well*. Dan had also talked Logan into starting an undergraduate degree in ecology at UVI. He was doing it part-time, to fit in around his job, but already he was loving the learning, loving unlocking the mysteries of the world.

"I can't wait to get home, either," he added.

"Won't you miss your sisters? And your mum? Now that you've reconnected, it's a shame to leave again so soon."

"I'll certainly stay in touch this time. I've learned my lesson. And I'd like to catch up with them in person at least once a year from now on. But we lead different lives. Mum has Sierra and Reed, and soon the new baby to keep her busy." Logan still couldn't put into words how pleased he was for Sierra. For her to be starting again after such a tragedy in her life. When she lost her daughter, Grace, in the accident, no one ever thought she would go on to re-marry and have a new family. But miracles were possible. "I think mum is a little worried about her," Logan confided. "But Sierra's not even forty yet. Lots of women are having babies into their forties. Besides, she's a strong, determined woman, I don't think anything would dare go wrong now."

"You're right," Mia agreed. "Sierra is one of the most determined women I've ever met. She and Reed will do fine. As will Keira and Dalton." They were both silent for a second as they considered his two sisters. "I wonder when they'll announce their engagement?"

Logan laughed. "Do you think we'll be heading to another beach wedding in Hawaii soon?" he asked.

"I've always wanted to go to Hawaii." she squeezed his hand. "Maybe we could have a beach wedding one day, too. Make it three from three," she murmured.

He turned his head in sharp amazement. It was the first time she'd mentioned getting married. His heart did a small dance in his chest. He hadn't asked her to marry him. Yet. But they both knew it was an unspoken contract. They were meant to be together forever. One day soon, he would get down on one knee and propose.

"I'd like that," he said simply.

They lay in relaxed silence for a few moments, until Mia breathed the words, "The stars are so different here."

He rolled his head to the side so he could look at her profile as they both lay on the beach, staring into the night sky.

"I mean, I think I can see Venus. Is that right?" she asked. When he nodded his head, she continued. "But where is Antares? Can we still see all the same stars?"

"Yes, and no," he laughed, surprised. He was pleased she really had been listening to him as he rattled off the names of planets and constellations. "We can still see some of the stars that lie nearer the equator, but they are low on the horizon for us now." He pointed, and her gaze followed his finger.

"I still recall that very first time we were on your catamaran. Do you remember?" A dreamy tone entered her voice.

"I could hardly forget," he murmured in reply. That was the night their lives changed forever. But he wouldn't trade it for anything, because it'd given him Mia. That night he'd shot a man. Logan had replayed that scene over and over in his head, wondering if he could've done something differently. Telling himself it was the law of nature, kill or be killed. And he'd had to act. If not to save himself, then to save Mia.

But the nightmares still haunted him.

At least, the law had finally seen his side of things. It'd taken long, drawn-out months for the police to come to a decision, and for most of that time, it'd felt like he and Mia were locked in limbo, a no-man's-land. But eventually, the verdict they'd all been waiting for was handed down. Logan was a free man.

Diego had survived the knife Mia had plunged into his throat, and was now recovering in a Florida jail, where he'd been transferred from St. Thomas to serve the next twenty years for kidnapping and attempted murder. Sofia was also serving a jail sentence at the Lowell Correctional Institution for women in Florida. It was hard to unearth many details, but it seemed Sofia's father had also gone into hiding since the incident, and Logan hoped his people-smuggling days were well and truly over.

"I hope Tianna remembers to feed Captain," Mia mused.

"Don't worry, she loves that cat more than she lets on." Logan smiled to himself. "He's probably going to be fat and completely spoiled by the time we get back." It was true, Tianna made comments about how much she hated the cat, he was dirty and old and bedraggled, she said. But more than once, Logan had come home to find the cat curled up on her lap as she watched TV, or Tianna secretly sneaking food to him under the table while they ate.

Captain had settled quite nicely into the apartment. Had taken well to being a landlubber, considering he'd spent all of his life aboard a boat. Almost as if he didn't even miss the sailing life at all. Which was one less weight off Logan's mind.

He and Mia had taken over Crystal and Scarlett's rental of the downstairs section of the house, after the two women decided to move to St. Thomas to find work.

Tianna now had the upstairs section to herself. Which seemed to be working. Most of the time. She and Mia still fought, usually when Mia tried to tell Tianna what to do. But Tianna had become a lot less self-absorbed, and was still eternally grateful to Mia for all she'd done for her. They'd become a small, tight-knit family and it was working out well.

"Maybe we should take Captain out with us next time we sail *Skipper*."

Logan liked to listen to the sound of Mia's voice as it drifted up to join the stars. He got so lost in the resonance, he almost forgot to answer.

"Nah, I think he's fine at home. Besides the new boat might not be to his liking. *Skipper* is a lot smaller than what he's used to."

"Maybe," Mia agreed.

After Logan lost *Leopard*, his catamaran, he was so sure he was going to replace it as soon as was humanly possible. He'd loved that boat nearly as much as he now loved Mia. But there'd been more obstacles than he first imagined, money being the major one. The catamaran hadn't been insured, because Logan couldn't afford it. He'd had a lot more on his mind when he first bought the boat; fleeing Mexico his main objective. His life had transformed since then. And after only a very short time living with Mia, he'd changed his mind. The catamaran had been a lifestyle for him, living as a bachelor while hiding from the world. He no longer needed to sequester himself on a boat. He and Mia were free to come and go as they pleased. He didn't need to own a boat to be happy.

But Mia knew him better than that. Out of the blue one day, she announced she wanted to buy a boat, one in which they could take short sails and visit the beaches. There was one for sale down in the marina, and she thought they should go and look at it that very day. It was a small J22, a twenty-two-footer Jboat, single hull, named *The Skipper*. Big enough for day cruises out of the bay, it had a double berth up front, and just enough room for a bench seat and small table and galley in the main cabin. Mia said it was perfect; he could teach her to sail and they could explore the islands on their days off. A few times already, they'd sailed around to Trunk Bay and anchored off the beach. Spent the day snorkeling in the azure waters with the fish, spotting turtles as they glided through the water.

"Maybe we can take *Skipper* out as soon as we get home," Mia said, a tad wistfully. "I miss it already."

"Sounds good," Logan replied. Then another thought occurred to him. "Will we have time to go sailing? By the sounds of your dance schedule, you might not have a lot of spare hours left in your day."

"Yes, it's true. I don't want to let the kids down. But we'll squeeze it in somewhere. Maybe we could take them all sailing with us," she said.

Logan was horrified at the thought of all those little girls piling onto *The Skipper*.

"I don't thin—"

"I was kidding," she joked lightly. "But I can't wait to start the program with them again."

Logan was proud of Mia. After Harry disappeared, she was left without a job; not that she would ever have worked for that scumbag again. But a few weeks after they moved in together, Mia had skipped into the small kitchen and jumped on Logan, wrapping her legs around his waist and locking lips with him in an excited kiss. She could still hardly believe it herself, but a boutique dance studio over on St. Thomas had offered her a job as a teacher. She taught a couple of different age groups in contemporary dance, which meant she worked almost full-time. Mia found it hard to understand her luck, but Logan knew better. "You're an amazing dancer," he'd told her. "Just because you don't have any formal qualifications doesn't mean you're inferior. And finally, someone has recognized that. Grab this chance with both hands and go for it," he urged.

So, she had, saying, "You know, I always wanted to start up my own dance troupe, my own dance club. To be the master of my own destiny. At first, I wasn't sure if this is what I wanted, it felt like a step down. But after I thought about it, I'm still the master of my own destiny, and this way I'm helping other little girls fulfill their own dreams, as well. And maybe I'll open my own dance studio in a year or two. What do you think?"

"I love the idea," he agreed.

Mia had told him about the tin of money she'd left on his boat. Her whole entire life savings had gone up in the explosion. But they'd both started a new fund, not a tin box hidden in a kitchen cupboard this time, but a joint savings account. Hopefully, one day, there'd be enough money in there for Mia to fulfill her dreams and start up that studio of hers.

Logan rolled over so he could rest on his elbow, staring down at Mia. She wore a short, cut-off top that showed her taut stomach, and a light, floaty skirt that drifted around her thighs; one of his favorites. The starlight reflected in her eyes, and she giggled as he traced a hand across her bare midriff. He leaned in and kissed her luscious lips.

"I want to make love to you," he said. And he was serious. She looked more beautiful tonight than ever. Since the night Sofia had cut off her hair, Mia had decided to keep it short. The hairdresser had turned the messy, ragged cuts Sofia had inflicted into a cute pixie style, shorter on the sides, with a long sweep of fringe over her eyes. It suited her, and was just one more way Mia had thumbed her nose at the pain Sofia had tried to wreak. By embracing the cut, rather than trying to hide it, she showed Sofia her intent to wound and maim had not worked.

Logan wanted to get close to Mia, make slow, sweet love to her until she cried out in ecstasy.

"What if someone comes?" she giggled again.

He loved the sound of her laugh. Tenderly, he brushed her fringe away from her forehead. Dark eyes fixed on his face, she lifted her head to meet his lips.

"I love you," she said.

"And I love you right back," he replied. "I can't wait to spend the rest of my life with you."

She laughed and rolled them over in the sand, so she was now on top. "To the stars and back," she said, and drowned him with her kisses.

*   *   *

Mia buried her toes deeper into the soft sand. She glanced over at Dalton, who stood by Reed's side, fidgeting with his cufflinks, looking uncomfortable in his gleaming, black suit. Mia hid her smile. Reed's gaze was fixed on the winding wooden steps leading down to the beach. Waiting. His face showed no emotion, but Mia could imagine the jumble of thoughts that might be tumbling through his head right now.

The celebrant stood in the middle of the semi-circle, her long grey hair left loose and a serene smile on her face. It was all right for her, Mia thought, she did this kind of thing every day. Mia had only ever been to two other weddings, and waiting for Sierra to appear was killing her.

"You okay?" Keira whispered beside her.

"Yes," Mia whispered back, a huge grin on her face. "Just excited." Keira nodded her agreement. She looked absolutely gorgeous in the dusky-pink, strapless dress that fell to her feet. It showed off her impressive curves to absolute perfection. Keira readjusted the posy of wildflowers to her other hand to push a strand of hair back into place. The breeze had just started to pick up in the last few minutes, and a puff of air ruffled Mia's dress—identical to the one Keira was wearing—drawing the silky material around her thighs. Even without Logan's appreciative glances, she knew the dress suited her, too. The color a perfect foil for her cocoa skin and her dark hair, which Mia had decided to keep short. Logan said the pixie cut suited her beautiful face. Mia saw Keira glance at Dalton, the other woman's eyes overflowing with love and the words she couldn't say. She looked away quickly, the emotion in her expression affecting her more than it should. The last thing she needed was to cry and smudge all her mascara.

Her gaze roved over the coastline, instead. This was the beach below Sierra's house, and Mia couldn't imagine a better place to get married. Black rocks reared up at odd angles, a sharp contrast to the soft, beige sand. Nearby, the trickle of water over ridges of sand could be heard, where a freshwater creek flowed into the ocean. Hills surrounded the beach, cocooning it in their valleys, the slopes covered in short, scrubby growth that at first had seemed half-dead to Mia after the lush, tropical green of her jungle island. The ocean was behaving herself today, sending petite waves to break upon the shoreline. The sunshine was warm on her back, but the water was still cold. Colder at least than the balmy oceans of the Caribbean she was used to. Logan warned her, even though November was late spring in Australia, the weather could still be unpredictable and even downright cold here on Kangaroo Island. But Reed and Sierra couldn't have asked for a more ideal day for their wedding.

It was a small gathering, approximately twenty people in total. Exactly how Sierra and Reed wanted it. Mia checked out all the invited guests as she waited for Sierra to appear.

Mia had met Sierra's neighbors, Sam and Debbie Lewis, when she and Logan first arrived to stay at Snellings Beach three days ago. A lovely, older couple who adored Sierra and treated her like a daughter, they owned all the rental properties in the area, including the one she and Logan were in.

Mia had been introduced to two of Sierra's closest friends on the island, Kylie and Rhianna, at the impromptu hen's night two days ago. She'd also met, Jen, an African American lady whom Sierra had laughingly presented as her editor on the same night. Jen was now standing barefoot and glorious in a flowing, red dress that stood out among the others, along with her husband, who had on a more subdued black suit. The group all gathered together off to the side, with Rhianna's husband and another man, who'd been laughingly called, *Kylie's boy-toy*. Then there was Sergeant Don Coldwater, Reed's boss, and Eric and Olivia, his fellow island officers, all looking imposing in their dark blue uniforms.

Of course, Logan's mum was there, standing in the front row, her eyes glistening with unshed tears. Mia had been nervous about meeting his mum, but soon learned she had nothing to fear from Aileen Goldstein. The very first time Mia met her, at the Adelaide airport when she and Logan flew in, Aileen had drawn her into a tight embrace, exclaiming how beautiful she was, chatting about how she couldn't wait for Mia to see KI—it'd taken a while for Mia to understand that KI meant Kangaroo Island—and putting her completely at ease. Mia could see who Sierra and Keira got their dark looks from, but they must've got their height from their father, because Aileen only came halfway to Mia's shoulder. However, she made up for her lack of stature with her sunny, caring nature.

Shelly and Nikau Kapua, Reed's parents, stood alongside Aileen, Shelly quietly handing a white handkerchief to Aileen when she noticed the emotion shining in the other woman's eyes. They both looked so proud of their son. Sierra had told her a little about Reed's story, coming from the wrong side of the tracks, nearly being dragged down into the underbelly of the gangs in New Zealand. If it hadn't been for his father stepping in and moving the family to get both his sons away from the bad element, Reed may have turned out to be a very different person. So, Mia could understand the satisfaction and dignity hovering in both his parent's faces. Seb, Reed's younger brother, who was ridiculously handsome, even by Logan's standards, had his arm draped around his latest girlfriend. The difference between Seb and Logan was that Seb used his looks to his advantage and had become a well-known male model, living in Sydney, traveling the world. But even he looked a little awed by today, his normally cavalier, slightly self-important attitude muted now as he stared at his older brother, the solemnity of the moment getting to him.

There were a few others who Mia had been introduced quickly to this morning, but she couldn't remember their names, including a young, blonde guy and his group of park rangers, who all worked on the island. Mia was happy to see such a mixture of cultures and races around her. Everyone was completely accepting, not even seeming to see the color of her skin.

Suddenly, the quiet murmur of the crowd ceased, and everyone turned toward the steps. Sierra appeared on Logan's arm. In the absence of their father, Logan was giving Sierra away.

Mia had seen Sierra's dress before; she and Keira helped her dress earlier today. But now she could see Sierra in her glory as she descended the last few steps. It was a simple, sleeveless, ivory satin wedding dress. With a jewel neckline and a mermaid train that spooled around her feet. A low-cut back with see-through satin showed off a row of tiny buttons up the back. Her dark hair was stunning against the ivory. The dress did nothing to hide Sierra's growing bump. Pregnancy suited Sierra. Mia had always thought the term *pregnancy glow* was stupid and clichéd. But now she was beginning to understand. The dress and the setting were so simple, yet so perfect, it made Mia's throat close up at the sight.

Logan looked up and winked quickly, before returning his attention to the momentous business of escorting his sister down the stairs.

She could hardly believe this gorgeous man was hers.

Mia suddenly knew, with a clarity that shocked her, that she was going to marry this man one day. She was going to spend the rest of her life with him. Even have his children. She'd put the idea of a family on the back burner for so many years now; her lifestyle hadn't been favorable before. But now, she had the right man. He would be a great father, she'd watched him with the kids at the turtle rescue, teaching them the best way to handle the baby turtles that'd just hatched. He loved her, he showed her that every day. And she loved him.

Sierra took the last step down onto the sand, her long hair flowing softly over her shoulders as she made her way toward Reed. Her normally serious eyes were alight with love and laughter. Mia smiled and brushed a pesky tear away from her cheek.

Logan led his sister to stand next to Reed and the ceremony began. When the celebrant asked *who gives this woman to be married to this man?* Mia heard a hitch in Logan's voice as he replied *I do*. Then he took his place next to Dalton, his mouth set in a serious line and she could've sworn he surreptitiously swiped at a tear when he thought no one was looking.

His gaze found hers and his mouth turned up in a secret smile, meant only for her. That sexy, cheeky smile she loved. She wanted to go up and take his hand. Feel that buzz of warmth and sanctuary she always got when she was near him. She wanted to lay her palms along those wonderful cheekbones, feel the clean-shaven skin beneath her fingertips, kiss him long and slow and intense. But there would be time for that later. Plenty of time. She switched her focus back to Reed and Sierra, watching as they said their vows to each other.

This was one perfect day, a gem that would remain in Mia's memory forever.

If you liked Bound by the Stars then you might like the other books in the series.

**Bound by Truth**

**Bound by Silence**

*The books in this series can be read as stand-alone novels, but are enhanced if you read them together.*

# Also by Suzanne Cass
## NEW

**Stormcloud Station Series**
**(A Stargazer Spinoff Series)**
**Small Town Romantic Suspense**
## Clear Skies
## Starlit Skies
## Crystal Skies

**Stargazer Ranch Romance Series**
**Small Town Romantic Suspense**
**Combustion: Prequel Novella**
**Wildfire**
**Firelight**
**Snowbound: A Christmas Novella**
**Snowfall**
**Cloudburst**

**Island Bound Series**
**Mystery Romance (on an Island)**
*Books can be read as stand-alone*
**Bound by Truth**
**Bound by Silence**
**Bound by the Stars**

**Colors of the Earth Series**
**Small Town Romantic Suspense**
*Books can be read as stand-alone*
**Shadows in the Dust**
**Shadows in Deep Blue**
**Shadows of Red Earth**

**Romantic Suspense**
*Single Title*
**Island Redemption**

**Glass Clouds**
**Chasing Bullets**

**Love in the Mountains Novella Series**
**Small Town Short Romance**
*Novellas can be read as stand-alone*
**Rain on a Tin Roof**
**Lost and Found**
**Rescue his Heart**

**Please Leave a Review**
The greatest gift you could ever give an author is to leave a review. You will be helping other people to discover this book and making a difference to me as an Independently Published Author. If you liked this book and want other people to read it to, please leave a review.

## Connect with the Author

I really hope you enjoyed reading Bound by the Stars. For more action romance info, upcoming release dates, and access to free books join the exclusive Suzanne Cass reader club. As an added bonus, you'll get a copy of my FREE STORY.

### Solar Flare

http://www.suzannecass.com/contact/

Or you can stay in touch via my website
**www.suzannecass.com**

Facebook: www.facebook.com/suzannecassauthor/
Instagram: www.instagram.com/suzanne.cass/
Pintrest: www.pinterest.com.au/suzanne_cass/
Twitter: twitter.com/SusieCass1

## About the Author

Suzanne Cass is an Australian author who writes rural romance and romantic suspense abounding with passion and danger.

Her debut novel, Island Redemption, won the Romance Writers of Australia Emerald Award in 2016. Suzanne was also a finalist in the 2019 Romance Writers of Australia RUBY award.

She had always had a fascination with the tough resilience of people who live in our amazing red-dirt outback country. When not writing about the characters that inhabit her head, Suzanne can be found roaming the Perth beaches with her border collie, or encouraging from the sidelines as her two sons play sport.

Visit her website www.suzannecass.com or subscribe to her newsletter via: www.suzannecass.com/contact

# Acknowledgements

This is the third and final book in the Island Bound series and follows the youngest Goldstein sibling, Logan, and his journey towards finding love and freedom. The sisters, Sierra and Keira also continue their stories in this last installment. It was the hardest of the three books to write, because although I've always wanted to visit the Caribbean, I've never been there, so my research was time consuming and detailed, but definitely worth it. (Now I *really* want to go there one day.) There kernel of the idea for this book came from a post I saw on Facebook, talking about conservation of turtles in the Caribbean. From there I built my character Logan, whose research may help to save these beautiful creatures.

There isn't an actual turtle hatchery on St. John. There are hatcheries in other parts of the Caribbean and I liked the idea so much I used my creative license to put one on St. John. But the Friends of Virgin Islands National Parks do have a sea turtle monitoring program, and volunteers do go out to hunt for nests and help dig them up and protect the baby turtles, helping them to the ocean. And the rest of St. John is pretty much true to life, it's a sleepy little town, with a laid-back attitude, set amongst the most beautiful, vivid scenery you will ever see.

Of course, this book wouldn't have been what it is today, without the help and guidance of my author tribe. Jillian, Rose and Rachel are three other authors who have given me unending support and loving counsel on how to make my books better. Thank you from the bottom of my heart.

There is a team of people who I also couldn't do without, beta readers (big thanks to Rebecca) and my ARC team, who are essential to an Indie Author like me. Big thanks to my editor, Tanya Saari.

To my husband, Gary and to my two beautiful boys (who are soon to be gorgeous men) Thank you for your unconditional love.

I am so very grateful to all the readers who have bought and enjoyed my books and who will continue to do so. Writing for you is what keeps me focussed and motivated.